Advance Praise for
Higher Ground

"Once again, Sherye beautifully blends her characters' lives in a story filled with heart and faith. In this book, we see characters shaped by their mentors, learning to forgive deep hurts and ultimately accepting that God has a greater plan for each of us. Through forgiveness, they're able to move forward and live in the fullness of God's will. This story also inspires us to love others the way Christ loves us—deeply, selflessly, and without condition. *Higher Ground* is a charming and moving tale of love, forgiveness, and redemption."

— **Debbie Upchurch, 50+ Minister at First Ridgeland**
   Ridgeland, Mississippi

"As someone who spends a lot of time studying Christian history, I really enjoyed how *Higher Ground* shows the same truths we see throughout the church's story, such as faith in hard times, the believer community stepping in when families fall apart, and God's grace making a way forward. Sherye Green has written a novel that feels honest, hopeful, and rooted in the kind of faith that has carried believers for generations."

— **Nick Walters, Founder, Center for Christian History**

"*Higher Ground* is a sweet story that beautifully illustrates what it means for Christ-followers to 'pray without ceasing' as you walk through life—through the ups, the downs, and the all-arounds. God is good! And as you come to more deeply know each of her characters, Sherye reveals the depth of God's providential goodness in both inspirational and highly encouraging ways that will personally bless your life!"

— **Hess Hester**
   Retired Lead Pastor of Southern Hills Baptist Church
   Tulsa, Oklahoma

"Sherye Green has penned a beautiful tale of healing and hope in this final installation of *The Timothy House Chronicles*. Her unrushed style and gentle prose make reading *Higher Ground* like savoring a cup of tea on a crisp fall day. With tender details that drop us into the hearts of her characters, Green gives readers a front-row seat to what it looks like to forgive and trust, while also stepping out in faith. We're treated to a delightful journey as she weaves together a host of lovable characters, continuing story threads from the first two books of the series. Love is found. Betrayal is healed. And joy is celebrated. Don't miss the conclusion of this heartwarming series."

— **Sondra Kraak, author of eight historical romances**

"*Higher Ground* is a compelling story of compassion, forgiveness, and redemption. Readers will appreciate how author Sherye Green develops each character in a way that is believable and relatable. The storyline elicits a range of emotions with a healthy balance of drama, suspense, grace, and hope. For anyone needing to be reminded of the power of the gospel to heal and restore, this novel is for you!"

— **Bill McGee, Educational Consultant**

Higher Ground

The Timothy House Chronicles: Book Three

Sherye S. Green

an imprint of Sunbury Press, Inc.
Mechanicsburg, PA USA

an imprint of Sunbury Press, Inc.
Mechanicsburg, PA USA

For information about special discounts for bulk purchases, please contact Sunbury Press Orders Dept. at (855) 338-8359 or orders@sunburypress.com.

To request one of our authors for speaking engagements or book signings, please contact Sunbury Press Publicity Dept. at publicity@sunburypress.com.

Scripture quotations taken from the (NASB®) New American Standard Bible®, Copyright © 1960, 1971, 1977, 1995, 2020 by The Lockman Foundation. Used by permission. All rights reserved. www.Lockman.org.

Scripture quotations taken from The Holy Bible, New International Version®, NIV®. Copyright © 1973, 1978, 1984, 2011 by Biblica, Inc. Used with permission of Zondervan. All rights reserved worldwide. www.zondervan.com

Scripture quotations marked NLV are taken from the New Life Version, Copyright © 1969 and 2003. Used by permission of Barbour Publishing, Inc., Uhrichsville, OH 44683. All rights reserved.

FIRST SCRIPTORIA PRESS EDITION: December 2026

Set in Adobe Garamond Pro | Interior design by Crystal Devine | Cover by Lawrence Knorr | Edited by Sarah Peachey.

Publisher's Cataloging-in-Publication Data
Names: Green, Sherye S., author.
Title: Higher ground / Sherye S. Green.
Description: First trade paperback edition. | Mechanicsburg, PA : Scriptoria Press, 2026.
Summary: *Higher Ground* brings Abbie Richardson and Keith Haliday full circle after suffering betrayal, searing pain, and heartrending loss as a new era dawns at Timothy House. No matter how abandoned one may feel or how dark the valley, God's plans always lead to higher ground.
Identifiers: ISBN : 979-8-88819-316-7 (softcover).
Subjects: FICTION / Christian / General | FICTION / Christian / Contemporary | FICTION / Religion.

Designed in the USA
0 1 1 2 3 5 8 13 21 34 55

For the Love of Books!

This book is lovingly dedicated
to
my dear friend,
Martha Stockstill,
whose sure footsteps and godly example
have always led me to higher ground.

"… lead me to the rock that is higher than I."

—Psalm 61:2 NIV

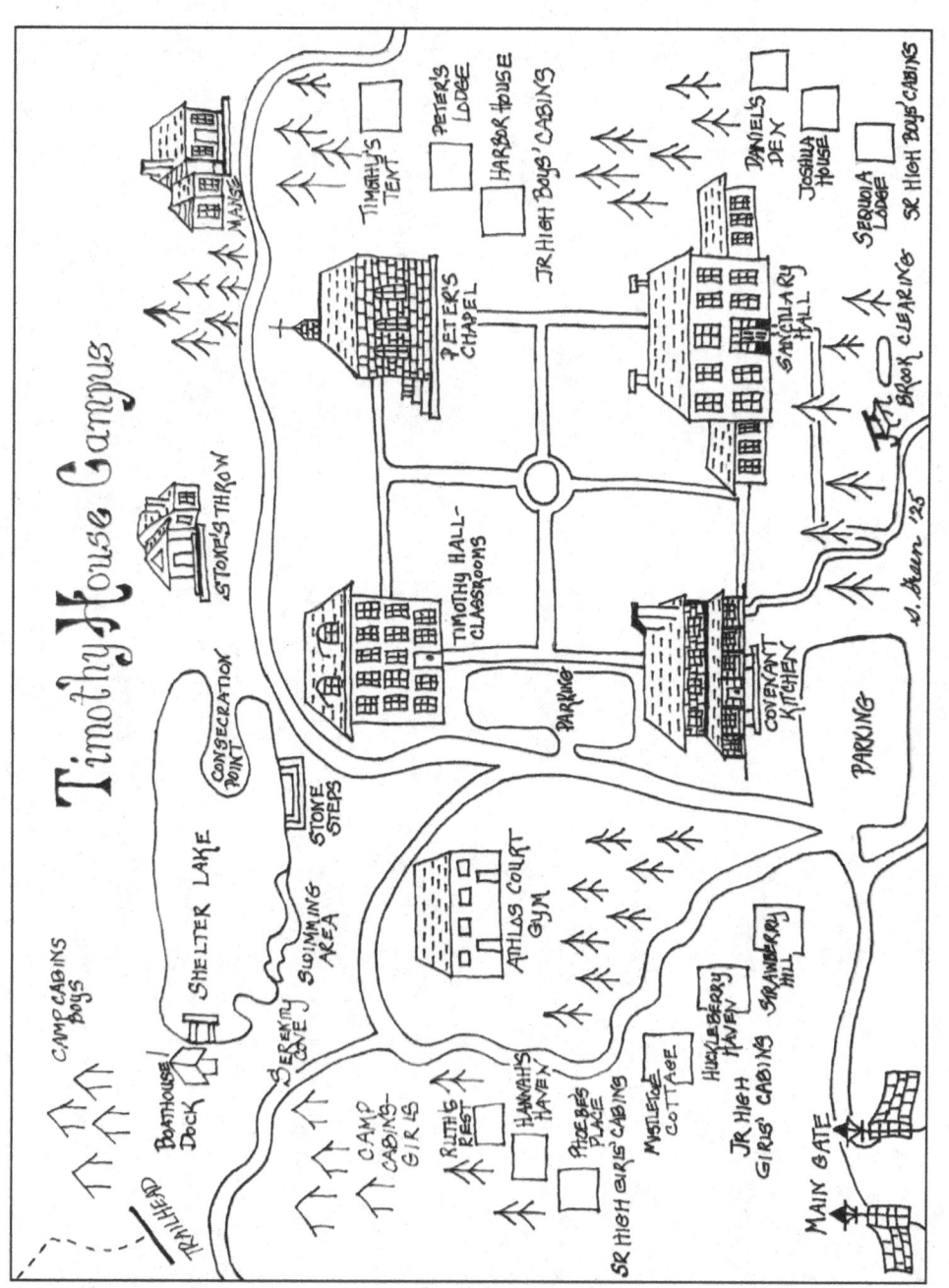

Timothy House Campus

CHAPTER

1

The door to Trent Lockhart's office suddenly flew open.

"We got 'em," said Tony DiMarco as he stood on the threshold of the chief's office. The man's face was flushed, his eyes blazing with excitement. In his haste, he hadn't even bothered to knock.

Startled by the noise, Trent Lockhart looked up from the stack of paperwork on his desk.

"Oh, I'm sorry, Chief," the young detective said, stepping back as he recognized his blunder. "I didn't realize you were busy."

"Come on in, Tony," Trent told him, welcoming the interruption. "I'm always glad to hear from you."

The detective re-entered the police chief's office. Turning back toward the doorway, he said, "Mind if I close the door?"

"Not at all," replied Trent. "I'm all ears."

For forty minutes, Tony told Trent how officers had arrived at the Henderson home around six-thirty a.m. Both husband and wife appeared to have recently woken up and seemed caught off guard. The detective explained that the couple had initially been belligerent and disrespectful, but once the officers served the search warrant, Hope and Kevin became quite docile. While one officer kept an eye on the Hendersons in the living room, three others searched the premises.

As he told the story several times, Tony returned to one critical component of the case—how brave Chloe, the Hendersons' foster child, had been when talking to investigators and how instrumental her testimony was in securing a damaging piece of evidence. Though the investigation had taken several months since Chloe's removal from the Henderson home in July, the dogged detective had pursued the case with laser focus.

As Trent listened to the investigator speak passionately about this case, he thought, *Little Chloe is someone many of us know to be brave.*

A file folder, hidden atop an old, dilapidated bookcase, had been found right where the child claimed it was. In it was a diary of sorts, the ramblings of Hope Henderson and her plans to scam the Department of Child Services. She had detailed names of foster children, dates of their placement with the couple, and even details about what Hope and Kevin had done to the poor children. Chloe's name was among those mentioned. The papers, written in the wife's hand, corroborated every allegation Chloe had made.

"The Hendersons were booked into the jail early this afternoon," said Tony. "I'm heading to Judge Turner's office first thing in the morning to ask for a possible indictment from the grand jury."

"Sounds like you've got a pretty solid case," said Trent, respect for his junior associate evident in his voice.

"We sure hope so," concluded Tony. Rising from the chair in front of Chief Lockhart's desk, the detective extended his hand toward his boss.

Following the man's lead, Trent stood and shook his hand firmly. "Great work, DiMarco," he said. "Now, get out of here and get yourself a nice meal tonight. You've earned it." Tales of the single detective's empty refrigerator were legendary around the department.

"Thank you, sir," said Tony brightly, "I will."

"Oh, and one more thing," continued Trent. "Let me know as soon as you hear from Judge Turner on the grand jury motion."

"Will do, Chief," said the detective, who seemed practically giddy with the thought of the successful raid. "See you in the morning."

"Sounds good." Trent watched the young detective disappear down the hallway. A sense of pride washed over him, not unlike that a father feels for his son.

Sinking back into the comfort of his armchair, Trent took a deep breath. After holding it for a few long moments, he exhaled slowly, hoping some of the tension he usually carried in his upper back and shoulders would escape along with his breath. Though he could hear the faint sounds of police department personnel through the door, Trent's private office was peaceful and quiet. Glancing at the clock on the wall, he knew he needed to head home to his wife, Mary, and their children. She would understand if he arrived late. The police chief chuckled as he thought over the earlier events of this momentous day. *It's been a long time since Robbinsonville had this much excitement.*

Ever since this past July, Trent and his department had been putting together an investigation after his good friend, Don Fielding, the director of Timothy House, brought allegations of possible child endangerment to his attention. Chloe Minton, a ten-year-old female attending the school's Camp 4Ever summer program, told a counselor that her foster parents were mean to her. That comment led to a further discussion with the child, who shared that the Hendersons sometimes locked her in a closet for hours and even whipped her with a coat hanger, which cut her leg. The wound required stitches from a local hospital's emergency room.

When Don's call had come that fateful day in late July, Trent immediately reached out to Hayley Collins, one of the best investigators with the Tennessee Department of Child Services (DCS). Hayley arrived at Trent's office later that afternoon and took the statement from Abbie Richardson, the counselor at Camp 4Ever, who had heard the child make the allegation. Don's wife, Doris, was also present during the second visit with Chloe.

Within a day of authorities receiving the allegations, Hayley had interviewed the child and believed her testimony to be credible and the evidence substantial to warrant an investigation. Chloe had then gone immediately into the home of Tim and Taylor Nunley, husband and wife teachers at Timothy House, who knew the child and, because of infertility struggles of their own, had recently filled out paperwork that now allowed them to serve as temporary foster parents for the girl.

A few days later, before Hope and Kevin Henderson could leave for the Timothy House campus to pick her up, they received an unexpected visit from DCS personnel. Two uniformed officers of the Robbinsonville Police Department accompanied the DCS officials to notify the couple that an investigation might soon follow into Chloe's allegations against them.

Tony DiMarco was one of the up-and-coming detectives with the Robbinsonville Police Department. Only weeks before, Tony had closed the books on one of the largest drug busts in state history with the arrest of C.J. Dykes and his accomplices. When he specifically asked Trent for the Henderson case, the police chief couldn't say no. Tony's tireless efforts and commitment to excellence in all aspects of the investigation led to the Hendersons' arrest this crisp October morning and to officers securing information and materials critical to the case.

Trent thought, *Hiring Tony DiMarco was one of the best moves I've made in a long while*, before turning off his office lights and heading out of the station.

This morning's arrest marked a real turning point in making the Robbinsonville community safer for all its residents, especially those who were innocent and vulnerable because of their young age. Trent hoped the Washington County grand jury would see the facts of the case against the Hendersons as clearly as he and his police department did.

Only time would tell.

CHAPTER
2

After unbuckling his seat belt, Keith sat for a few minutes, looking through his windshield outside Gravlee's, as a steady stream of customers entered the diner. Keith was here to meet Don Fielding on a fact-finding mission involving Teencie Curtis. Both men had come to know and respect the hard-working waitress. Don had been in Robbinsonville for almost thirty-four years, so he had known the lady much longer. Keith had only been in the town for eighteen months, but had also found in her a warm, compassionate soul, one genuinely interested in her customers. Teencie took pride in her work and strove to provide the best service possible.

These two men knew part of Teencie's story, some of it told by her and the rest filled in by information gleaned from the local grapevine. She was a single mother whose only daughter, Erica, had been born with intellectual disabilities. When the girl was two, the child's father had walked out on Teencie and their daughter, and neither had heard from him again. Teencie, relying on the kindness of neighbors and a local childcare facility with a good-hearted director, cobbled together a series of jobs over the next few years to provide for the two of them until Erica reached school age.

Teencie sent the child to the local public elementary school, which had a special needs program for kindergarten through sixth-grade children. Erica attended kindergarten, first, and second grade there. However, during that third year, the school discovered that Erica's needs were too special for their well-trained staff. Teencie endured a challenging

end-of-the-year conference in which the principal informed her that the
school could not accept Erica for the upcoming year.

The waitress was devastated at first. She stayed home with her daughter for months, trying to homeschool as best she could. Money was tight,
and the mother and daughter lived off the meager savings Teencie had
socked away in earlier years. The fellowship of her church family, Wright's
Creek Community Church, helped keep Teencie from going off the deep
end—emotionally, financially, and spiritually. Rod Eichman, the church's
middle-aged pastor, using special funds from a church account established to assist those in need, provided financial assistance to Teencie.
He was also a source of wise counsel and a strong shoulder upon which
Teencie cried many times. Rod and his wife, Karen, welcomed Teencie
and Erica into their church and their family's life. Karen, especially, was a
great encourager. Teencie had found genuine, Christlike compassion and
love in the Eichmans, a couple whose walk matched their talk.

Erica was stronger than she seemed, despite being small for her age.
Trying to reason with and discipline her daughter soon became a real
challenge for Teencie. Temper tantrums and long bouts of screaming,
mostly filled with unintelligible sounds uttered by the child, became the
norm. Teencie wondered some days if Erica even understood what her
mother was saying to her.

Following these "storms," as Teencie came to call them, and long
after Erica had drifted off to sleep, Teencie would sit at her kitchen table,
crying out to the Lord until, from exhaustion and despair, she fell asleep
with her head on the table. Somewhere in the middle of the night, Teencie would drag herself to bed, only to wake up an hour or so later to
repeat the nightmarish routine.

Late in the spring of what should have been Erica's third-grade year,
the girl's physical outbursts became too much for the young mother to
handle. Teencie suspected that something more than a mental impair-
ment was at play. In a fit of rage, the girl struck her mother full in the
face with a clenched fist. The wallop brought tears to Teencie's eyes and
punched a hole in her soul. Although the child had hit or kicked her
mother before, this was Erica's worst outburst. Teencie soon discovered
a large, red welt across one cheek and a bruised right eye. To calm her
daughter, Teencie half-dragged, half-carried the girl to her room, closing

the door behind her. Not knowing what else to do, the hysterical mother called Karen Eichman. The pastor's wife could hardly understand Teencie due to her uncontrolled sobbing. She had reached the end of her rope.

About two hours later, Karen arrived at Teencie's home accompanied by a social worker with a regional facility for severely handicapped children. The professional helped Teencie bathe and put Erica to bed. Afterward, the three women sat in Teencie's sparsely furnished living room. The social worker listened intently as Teencie poured out her heart, anguish and pain evident in her every word. When Karen and the health professional left Teencie's home that night, nothing had changed, but for the first time in a long time, the harried mother knew she was no longer alone.

Through the social worker's connections and some of her own, Karen Eichman scheduled a psychiatric evaluation for Erica Curtis at East Tennessee Children's Hospital in Knoxville. The benevolence of the Wright's Creek congregation provided the financial resources for Teencie to take Erica. Two days of tests and visits with various doctors and psychologists confirmed what this mother's heart had already told her: Erica not only had intellectual disabilities, but the child also had erratic mood swings.

A caring, compassionate doctor in one of the last appointments in Knoxville told Teencie that the most loving thing she could do would be to place Erica in a long-term residential facility. Eight days later, Teencie drove Erica back to Knoxville to a care facility with children close to her age. Thanks, once again, to the loving help of Rod and Karen Eichman and other concerned members of Wright's Creek, caring people subsidized a payment plan for Erica's care. Tears streamed down Teencie's face as she said goodbye to her only child. The drive back to Robbinsonville was long and lonely.

Soon after Erica went to live at the care home, Teencie answered an ad in *The Robbinsonville Times* about a part-time waitressing job at Gravlee's. After two months in the new position, the owner was impressed with her and promoted Teencie to full-time status. Almost every penny the dedicated waitress made went toward Erica's care.

Erica was now twenty-two, and Teencie traveled to Knoxville once a month to see her. This mother had never quite reconciled herself to the fact that her only child lived in a state-run facility, but she also knew she had done the most loving thing she could for Erica: give her the best option possible for a productive life. If it hadn't been for the support and fellowship of her friends at Wright's Creek, Teencie would have lost her mind. Learning to live with a situation that would never have a resolution or a solution was almost more than she could handle. Learning to move forward one day at a time was something Teencie could only do with God's help.

A Bible verse Karen Eichman shared with Teencie on the night Erica attacked her had become a lifeline for the single mother. "*I would have despaired* unless I had believed that I would see the goodness of the LORD in the land of the living." Teencie had learned that David had penned these words while on the run from King Saul, who was trying to kill him. The verse became, for Teencie, a knot that she tied in the rope of her faith and clung to daily. Robbinsonville was, for Teencie, the "land of the living," and God's abundant goodness had saved her from despair.

As he stepped from his truck and headed toward the diner, Keith hoped today's visit might lead to a new beginning for Teencie.

CHAPTER

3

Keith Haliday was on a fishing expedition of sorts. On a recent stop at Gravlee's, Keith picked up on a particular note of dissatisfaction from Teencie. Upon returning to Timothy House, Keith headed straight to Don's office to investigate hiring the woman away from the restaurant. Now, the two had come to Gravlee's mid-afternoon with the pretense of grabbing coffee and a slice of pie but also to determine precisely how dissatisfied Teencie was with her present situation.

The men were seated in the back of the restaurant in a booth that Don frequented. The spot was quieter than others in the diner, where conversations were less likely to be overheard. The corner booth, opposite the door to the kitchen, also had dimmer lighting. Convenient at times when one did not want to be noticed.

Not long after the two arrived, Teencie appeared at the table, a yellow No. 2 pencil stuck in its usual place behind one ear. "Hello, gentlemen," she said with a warm smile. "What can I get for you today?"

"Two cups of coffee to start with would be good," said Don, returning the smile. "How are you, Teencie?"

Keith noticed the slight hesitation in the waitress's usually outgoing personality. Perhaps she wanted a change of employment.

"I'm good," replied Teencie, recovering quickly.

The fact, however, that she chose not to meet their gaze directly—unusual for her—underscored Keith's hunch. "I'll be right back with your coffee," the waitress continued before leaving.

The men looked at each other conspiratorially.

"I see what you mean," said Don, lowering his voice. "I don't ever remember seeing her like this."

"Me, either," said Keith. "You and I are in here at least twice a week. You've lived here for what, forever? I know she's never acted like this in the past two years I've known her. Do you think she'd be interested in working somewhere else? Weren't you telling me that Charmaine's been frustrated lately?"

Teencie reappeared at the table with two steaming cups of coffee. Don had mentioned that Charmaine Jenkins desired to spend more time cooking and developing new meal plans, rather than organizing the kitchen and filling food orders with suppliers. None of the other women on the Covenant Kitchen staff had an administrative flair.

As the waitress placed the coffee cup before him, Keith asked, "What's your pie for the day? I'm starved."

"Is Mr. Don not feeding you enough at Timothy House?" Teencie countered, looking over at the Timothy House director in mock disgust. "Today's selection includes chocolate chess and apple pies. What'll you have?"

Both men practically answered in unison. "Apple pie à la mode!"

Their boyish enthusiasm elicited a smile from Teencie. "Back in a second," she said, then headed for the kitchen.

True to her word, it seemed no longer than a few seconds before Teencie was back at the table with two dessert-sized plates on which sat a generous slice of apple pie, topped with a heaping scoop of melting vanilla ice cream.

"Let me know what you think," she said before leaving to serve another table. Again, Keith noticed the sadness that seemed to accompany her.

Keith would have liked to savor the warm dessert, but the melting ice cream required them to eat quickly. As they ate, the two discussed day-to-day matters of the residential school that required their constant attention. One of those matters included Charmaine's request for a possible assistant manager.

"You know," began Don before wiping a speck of apple pie from the corner of his mouth, "Robert Davis, Gravlee's owner, has mentioned how responsible and efficient Teencie is. If I were to offer her the job, I would want to speak with him first. He's been a generous supporter of the school, and I wouldn't want him to think I was poaching his wait staff." The last of Don's pie disappeared as he placed the fork in his mouth.

"That's honorable," said Keith, sipping his coffee. "Do you know if Teencie would even consider leaving this job? I've heard the stories about Erica and how hard Teencie has worked to provide for her. It's sad to think of a mother having to place her child in a state-run institution."

"It is sad," replied Don, holding the coffee mug. "I wonder if Teencie might have reached the end of her proverbial rope with this job. Not much room for advancement," he said as he downed the rest of the coffee in his cup.

"Why don't you ask her?" asked Keith, suddenly enthusiastic. As he and Don talked, Teencie moved about the restaurant. Her friendly, easy-going manner and efficient service belied the turmoil Keith suspected lay under the surface of her life as the single parent of a developmentally challenged young adult daughter. He also remembered Teencie's many kindnesses to him and Abbie.

"Think I will," countered Don, grinning as Teencie approached the table.

As soon as Teencie placed the order ticket on the table, Don scooped it up. "This one's on me," he said, looking at Keith.

The younger man smiled. "Thanks," Keith said, shrugging his shoulders as he stuffed his wallet into his pocket.

Teencie, who never missed anything, said with surprising wit, "Glad to know I won't have to stop a fight here at Table Eleven." She grinned broadly.

After viewing the amount on the receipt, Don reached for his wallet in the pocket of his slacks and pulled out a twenty-dollar bill. He also took out a business card and handed it to Teencie.

"Keep the change," Don said as he handed her the money.

"Thank you, sir," Teencie said, her smile widening.

As the waitress looked at the card, he leaned toward her and glanced around the room before continuing in a lower tone. "Have you ever thought of working somewhere else?"

She shook her head slowly from side to side.

"When you have time, please call me at my office at the school. I'll let my assistant, Loren, know to expect your call. I've got something important I want to talk to you about."

A quizzical expression crossed her face. "Okay," she said slowly.

She stepped back from the table and seemed to snap back into waitress mode. "Thanks again, gentlemen," she said, "for coming in today. Hope the rest of your afternoon goes well." With that, she turned and headed for the register at the front of the diner.

As Keith and Don slid out of the booth and prepared to leave, Keith asked, "You think she'll call you?"

"I hope so," Don replied. "Timothy House could sure use a Teencie Curtis on its staff."

CHAPTER
4

Taylor Nunley softly closed the bedroom door and stood in the dimly lit hallway for a moment. After placing the fingers of one hand over her mouth, she held them gently against Chloe's door as if to seal it with a kiss. Smiling to herself, she turned and headed back to the kitchen.

When she entered the room, Tim looked up from a group of papers strewn across the breakfast table. "How is she?" he asked.

"She's asleep," said Taylor. "The little lamb couldn't even stay awake to finish the story I was reading her." She reached into the upper cabinet beside the sink and brought out a stoneware mug. After pouring herself a cup of coffee, she joined her husband at the table. From the looks of the stacks of homework assignments, it would be a late night.

"That's understandable," said Tim softly. "Her world's been turned upside down in the last few months."

"I can't even fathom how living with Hope and Kevin Henderson must have been for her," said Taylor as she sipped her coffee. "How people can treat a child like they treated her is beyond my comprehension."

"I know what you mean," Tim replied. After a brief sip of coffee, he set the mug down and reached toward Taylor, who grasped his hands in her own.

"You're doing a great job, Tay," said Tim admiringly, gently squeezing her hands.

Unexpected tears filled her eyes. "That's sweet," she said, wiping away a tear that was making its way down her cheek, "though I'm not sure what I'm doing. What if I can't . . ." Her voice trailed off.

Tim sat silently as she worked to regain her composure.

"What if *we* can't . . ." Taylor tried again, quiet sobs preventing her from saying more.

At this, Tim came around to her side of the table. Moving a chair close to hers, he sat down and pulled his wife into his arms, holding her close as the storm of doubt subsided. He whispered quiet words of encouragement and love, and gently stroked her hair as they sat together.

Taylor sank into the strong arms of her husband. He had always been her rock in times of trouble. Now, in this new season of their life together, she needed him more than ever. After several minutes, Taylor sat straighter and moved upright in her chair, wiping her face with her hands.

Tim grabbed a box of tissues from the nearby counter and handed a few to Taylor.

"I'm sorry," she said once she had wiped away more tears and blown her nose.

"Sorry for what?"

"Sorry for falling apart, I guess," she ventured. "I'm scared," Taylor said with a heavy sigh.

Tim leaned over and kissed her cheek tenderly before getting up. Reaching for his mug, he headed for the coffee maker. "Want some more?" he asked.

"No, thanks," said Taylor, finishing the rest of her now-cooled coffee.

Steam rose from his fresh mug, and Tim nudged his wife with his elbow as he passed her at the table. "Come on," he said lightheartedly, nodding toward their den. "Let's talk. The grading will keep until tomorrow."

Tim knew he had said the right thing when he saw the look on Taylor's face. He chose his wing chair while Taylor found her favorite corner of the couch nearby, pulling a handwoven coverlet from the back of the sofa over her legs.

A slight smile now played across Taylor's lips. "What shall we talk about?"

"Let's talk about doubts and fears, for starters," Tim began. "Tell me what made you cry just now."

Taylor's gaze fell to her lap, where she rubbed one thumb over the edge of the coverlet, the soft fibers seeming to comfort her as she did. "I guess I got overwhelmed tonight," she said, slowly raising her gaze to meet Tim's. "Chloe's only been with us for three months. Sitting in church today, I looked around the sanctuary at the other families near us and started thinking, 'They've had years to build their family unit and get this right. We hardly had any warning and very little time to prepare.' What if we're not cut out to be parents?"

Tim waited for his wife to continue, rubbing his thumb across the etchings in the pottery mug he held.

Tears filled Taylor's eyes once more. "Think how much that would hurt Chloe. What if we fail her?" Her words trailed off, and her gaze plummeted again to her lap.

"Tay," Tim said, as he put down his cup and reached over to lift her chin so her eyes met his. "What have we been praying about for years now, practically knocking down the doors of Heaven every chance we get?"

After a long pause, Taylor replied in a voice barely above a whisper, "Having a child."

Now, it was Tim Nunley who sat without speaking, the hum of a ceiling fan filling the silence between them.

Gently, he said, "There are no guarantees in life. We may well fail Chloe, though I don't think in the way you mean. Because we're fallible human beings, we will sin and make mistakes. What parent doesn't? When that happens, we'll ask Chloe's forgiveness, dust off our pants, and get back in the saddle of parenthood, ready to ride for another day.

"Remember one of our favorite verses from 2 Peter? God has promised He will give us *everything* we need for 'life and godliness.' We are not alone, Tay." Tim took hold of her hand.

Taylor smiled through a curtain of tears, her lips trembling as she offered a brave smile.

"I'm scared, too," he said.

Taylor pulled back her hand and looked at him, surprise written across her face. "You are?"

"Of course I am, silly," he said teasingly. "How do you think I feel now that I'm the head of a household and an instant father to a ten-year-old girl? Parenting isn't opening a packet of instant oatmeal; it's shaping the life of a precious young lady who's experienced only God-knows-how-much sorrow and abuse in her short life. That incredibly overwhelming responsibility will take us many years to accomplish."

Taylor stared at him for a few seconds. "Why, Tim Taylor," she said demurely, feigning a deep southern accent, "I never would have guessed."

Before saying more, Tim reached over and playfully swatted at her leg.

"Do you remember the night a few weeks ago when Don asked us if we would be willing to help Chloe? How we sat up for the rest of the night talking and praying, wrestling with God about what to do? One of the things we told God that night was that we believed He would tell us what to do. Do you still believe that?"

Taylor, now much more serious, looked him squarely in the eye and nodded.

"We don't have to have this figured out tonight, sweetheart," he said. "God gives us only one day at a time. Let's commit to holding tightly to His hand as we live each day fully. Remember what the counselor at the marriage enrichment seminar told us? 'Being the right parent is more about being the right kind of person a child needs and less about biology.' You *can* do this, Tay. *We* can do this."

For a few moments, the tick-tock of the mantel clock was the only sound in the room.

"Come here," Tim said as he patted his lap. "Let's pray."

As soon as she stood from the couch, he pulled her into the chair. Holding her tightly as she nestled against him, he began a petition for this new leg of life's journey they were now on.

"Dear Lord, we thank you for the miracle of bringing Chloe into our lives. She's such a precious little girl and has already brought us much joy. We're scared, though, Lord, as we've never been parents before. You have promised to show us the way, *every* step of it. Help us to hold on to that promise and to lean on You. Make us brave and strong, and keep our fears at bay. Give us patience with Chloe and ourselves. Give us hearts to understand how to be the parents that Chloe needs. Guide us through the adoption process. Bind us together in Your love. Grow the mustard seed of our faith into a towering oak tree of unshakeable trust in You. In Your name, we pray. Amen."

The couple sat for a few minutes, enjoying the security and safety of each other's arms.

However, the striking of the mantel clock, declaring the eleven o'clock hour, brought an unspoken announcement that it was time for bed.

Taylor stood, folding the coverlet and placing it again over the back of the couch. Tim headed into the kitchen, stopping for a few minutes to restore order to the ungraded schoolwork. After turning off the coffee maker and rinsing the carafe, he followed Taylor down the hallway to bed.

The Nunleys enjoyed a restful, peace-filled night's sleep for the first time in a long while.

A light breeze ruffled Abbie's dark brown hair as she left Mistletoe Cottage for a mid-morning walk. The fall semester was underway, and Abbie had found a time slot before classes began and after the five students in the cottage had left for their school day. In this new season, Abbie committed herself to working harder to maintain balance—emotionally, intellectually, spiritually, and physically. It was easy to get absorbed in her work, such as writing and lesson plans, and lose sight of the bigger picture. Looking back on her twelve years at Kent Academy, Abbie supposed that had been one of the contributing factors to her burnout.

The sun had already begun its climb into the morning sky, the looks of which suggested it would be a beautiful day. Making sure she tucked her cell phone into the pocket of her shorts, Abbie headed down the drive toward the front gates of Timothy House. Once on the main road, she turned left and followed the sidewalk as it meandered through a residential section nearby. The daily practice of walking, which Abbie was building back into her routine, had afforded her the time and mental space to think.

One thing to sort through was the hurt and anger of Joe's betrayal all those years ago. Although a believer in Christ and the spiritual discipline of prayer, Abbie knew there were parts of her heart she had walled off from God. Like animals caught in the sharp teeth of a hunter's trap, wounded emotions writhed deep within her, struggling to be free. Abbie also knew that if she and Keith were to have a chance together at any happiness, she needed to face these inner demons and put them to rest, once and for all.

Abbie was also grappling with forgiving Joe for the pain he'd caused her and their son, Drew. God had provided a host of trusted, godly friends in McHenry who had stood by her side and walked with her through the dark times following Joe's death. Lane and Eric Wyatt had introduced Abbie to Timothy House and the possibility of a new career there. Winnie Jeffers had taught her the Target Plan, a simple yet powerful strategy for tackling life's problems one at a time. Beulah Tanner had opened Abbie's eyes to the freedom that comes with putting the past behind you. Audry MacDonald had shown Abbie how to employ courage to step into the future toward which God was leading her. Each, in their way, had shown Abbie how to recognize the Lord's voice more easily. Each had also helped Abbie open her heart and allow God to usher in what only He could—restoration and healing.

Long a student of the writings of Holocaust survivor Corrie ten Boom, Abbie had always been intrigued by the Christian woman's take on forgiveness, especially toward those who had harmed her and her sister while in the concentration camps. Though the exact words of ten Boom's quote escaped her, Abbie remembered that it focused on the fact that forgiveness had more to do with the employment of one's will rather than being guided by how hot or cold one's heart was. Thanks to the Lord's patience and the prayers of her close friends, Abbie was learning to pay less and less attention to the temperature of her heart.

As she walked this morning, Abbie had been intent on silently saying each letter of the alphabet and then thanking God for some blessing in her life. Beulah and Audry had taught Abbie this ingenious way of calling to mind God's goodness many years ago. The Alphabet of Gratitude, as Audry called it, was another spiritual discipline Abbie was trying to reinstate in her life. By divine serendipity, the next letter of the alphabet and the geographic location of this point in Abbie's walk lined up perfectly.

She waited to cross the street to Linden Avenue. While several cars and a delivery van sped past, she reached the letter "L" in her recitation. The tree-lined treasure was a discovery made several weeks ago. From what she could tell, the homes along this street were built in the late 1800s or early 1900s. Architectural styles ranged from Colonial Revival to Georgian to Renaissance Revival to Neoclassical. Although Abbie liked to walk at a steady, fast gait, she often slowed when walking along Linden Avenue to appreciate the beauty before her.

The far end of Linden joined Elm Street at a perpendicular intersection. From Elm, she could reach other streets, also named for trees, such as Oak and Maple. Abbie, however, always walked down one side of Linden to Elm and then crossed the street to head back toward the main road and complete her home tour on the opposite sidewalk. Greer Road, the busier thoroughfare, which Abbie had crossed earlier, was a main transportation artery in this part of Robbinsonville.

Abbie took a right turn at the corner of Linden and Greer. Ahead of her were the grounds of St. Thomas Episcopal Church. According to the historical plaque near the street, the dark red, brick building was built in 1894. Its Gothic design and lead-glass windows caught her attention each time she passed. Although more modern, it was evident that architects had employed careful planning, as the administration and fellowship hall buildings blended nicely with the oldest structure. A small park, with access to Greer Street, lay just past the church. Several stone benches, nestled under towering oaks and elms, offered weary travelers shade and rest.

Looking at her watch, Abbie realized she'd been walking for almost an hour and a half. One of the benches in the park would be the perfect place to stop for a minute and call Winnie. The two had recently been playing phone tag, and today, Abbie was "it." She took her cell phone out of her pocket and dialed her friend's number. When Winnie answered the call, Abbie had just sat down.

"Hello!" Winnie Jeffers's cheery voice sounded over the line.

"Hey, friend," said Abbie, delighted. "Sorry it's taken me so long to get back in touch. I got your message last week but forgot to call you back."

"No worries," said the counselor. "What are you up to?"

"Well, at the moment, I'm sitting on a park bench. I'm out for a walk this morning."

"What about your classes?" Winnie asked, concern evident in her voice.

"I'm enjoying the gift of a day off from my wonderful boss, Don Fielding," Abbie said, smiling at her good fortune. "The seventh-grade class left an hour ago for Oak Ridge on a day trip to the science museum there. They won't be back until late afternoon. I thought I'd get back on track with my walking program this morning."

"Good for you," said Winnie. "I'm proud of you for sticking to this part of the Target Plan."

Abbie smiled. "Yeah, well, we'll see. I plan to walk at least five days a week, although since the semester started, making time for myself has become difficult. However, if every day is like today, my program might succeed. It's a beautiful morning here. What are you doing today?"

As Winnie talked, Abbie listened to her former colleague run down her "to-do" list. Winnie and her husband, Matt, had four sons, ranging in age from fourteen down to seven. As it had been a while since the two friends had chatted, the guidance counselor filled Abbie in on how the family's busy summer had gone. Abbie realized how much she had missed her good friend as Winnie explained how she juggled a schedule crammed with ball practice, trips to the pool, summer church camps, and the annual beach trip she and Matt made with their fellows.

Three years after Abbie had joined the faculty of Kent Academy in McHenry, Winnie came on board as the junior high guidance counselor. Although Abbie was the elder by nine years, she and Winnie quickly developed a solid friendship. In the days, weeks, and months following the shocking revelations after Joe's unexpected heart attack, Abbie had cried countless times upon Winnie's shoulder. Even though Abbie had still seemed mired in the quicksand of confusion and unforgiveness four years after Joe's death, Winnie's common sense, wise counsel had served as a light to Abbie's path, helping her take simple steps that had led her to Robbinsonville and Timothy House.

"Still have that ring on your finger?" asked Winnie, excitement evident in her voice.

"I sure do!" exclaimed Abbie. As she looked at her engagement ring, it seemed to wink in the bright morning sun.

"Have you set a date for the wedding?"

"Yes, we have," said Abbie, hoping Winnie could hear her happiness. "May twenty-eighth is our big day."

"Oh, Abbie," said the counselor, "that's incredible news. You don't know how much I've prayed this guy might be perfect for you."

"I think he is."

"Well, I certainly want to help you celebrate. I want to host a bridal shower for you. We don't have to put a date on the calendar yet, but be thinking of a weekend in the spring that might work."

"Oh, Winnie, that's so sweet of you," said Abbie. "I would love nothing better."

Winnie then steered the conversation in a different direction. "Have you put all your demons to rest about Joe?"

A squeal drew Abbie's attention to a dad chasing his young son around the playground, and she smiled. Finally, she replied, "I'm trying to. There's a part of me, however, that's still terrified Keith will hurt me like Joe did." Abbie was silent for a few minutes while she collected her thoughts. "Keith's certainly not perfect, nor am I. Through our relationship, God has taught me how to trust a man again with my heart. You can't imagine how patient Keith has been."

Tears welled in Abbie's eyes as she thought of this man's great tenderness toward her. "Moving to Robbinsonville has been better than I imagined. Since my students didn't arrive until a few days before the semester began, Mistletoe Cottage was a quiet retreat during the summer. Not only did I unpack all I brought with me, but I also discarded all the emotional baggage I've carried around like a ball and chain . . . or at least I thought I did.

"I'm still wrestling with forgiveness." The intensity of Abbie's tone made her sound harsh and brittle. "I've asked the Lord to help me forgive Joe countless times. Every time I think I have, some hurtful memory or painful emotion bubbles up out of the depths of my heart, and it's like I'm learning about his betrayal for the first time."

"Sweet Abbie," said Winnie gently, "forgiveness can be a struggle. I've found it to be so in my own life. Though there are times you can easily forgive and move on, there are others when it seems like you have to keep taking all the hurt and anger back to God."

Abbie wiped away tears as she listened to her friend's wise counsel.

"I think one reason God asks us to forgive others," Winnie continued, "is because our doing so is an open door through which His mighty power can work. The main reason, though, is that through Jesus Christ,

God forgives our sins. God desires that all could experience that life-changing gift. No one is beyond the reach of His redemption."

Abbie sniffed. "Part of my frustration and unwillingness to forgive Joe is that he was dead by the time all his misdeeds came to light. It was maddening that I couldn't confront him about what he did to me and Drew."

Winnie's comforting voice offered more insight. "What I hear through your words is your desire for vengeance, to be able to make Joe hurt, in some way, for all the havoc he wreaked in your life."

"You're probably right," Abbie said, her tone tightening.

"Remember what God says about vengeance?"

"I know . . . it belongs to Him," Abbie said with a chuckle.

"Abbie, you keep giving to God all these jagged pieces of your pain. Though you still struggle, it is not without purpose. His shoulders are broad and strong. It's time to let the Lord carry this burden of Joe's betrayal for you, once and for all."

"Your godly advice reminds me of something Beulah Tanner told me this past spring. Talking with you today has helped me see that it's time for me to let go."

"Abbie, I'm proud of you." Winnie's sincere words were touching.

"Thank you," replied Abbie. "I'm going to apply the Target Plan you taught me."

"You could be a counselor on my staff any day."

Abbie beamed at the compliment.

A buzzer sounded from Winnie's end of the call. "Hey, Abs, that's my doorbell. I've got to run. Thanks for calling."

"I've missed you, and it's been great to catch up. I'll look forward to planning the shower with you."

"Sounds like a plan," said Winnie. "I'll be in touch soon. Let me know next time you'll be in town so we can plan a visit."

When Winnie clicked off, Abbie rose from the bench and headed back to Timothy House. Along the way, she decided to pick back up with the mental game she had been playing earlier. Moving backward in the alphabet to the letter "J," she thanked God for the blessings of her strong friendship with Winnie Jeffers.

CHAPTER
6

Keith kept his eyes on the road, though he found it hard to do so. Abbie had been chattering like a magpie ever since he had picked her up at Mistletoe Cottage. The couple were on their way to McHenry to spend this November weekend with Abbie's best friends, Lane and Eric Wyatt. Since joining the team at Timothy House, Keith developed great respect for Eric, as he was a member of the school's Board of Trustees, and looked forward to getting to know Eric better.

This trip was the couple's first official outing since their recent engagement. They were excited to have time away from the responsibilities of campus life. The car ride alone offered six uninterrupted hours in which to visit, work on wedding plans, and share the many thoughts they didn't have time to share during the busy weeks at Timothy House.

After what seemed like only a few minutes, Keith's SUV pulled into the Wyatts' driveway. Several owners had modified the ranch-style house, which was built in the early forties, and it appeared to meander across the lawn. Keith hoped to sit on the screened porch, as Abbie had told him stories of many meaningful conversations there shared with Lane and Eric, particularly those following the revelation of Joe's misdeeds.

Throughout their courtship, Keith had not wanted to burden Abbie with questions about Joe Richardson, though he had many which haunted him. He secretly hoped this weekend might provide a chance for him to visit with Eric. Though it had been many years since college, when Keith and Joe had met and become good friends, Keith needed some answers of his own, information that enabled him to walk into marriage with Abbie, better equipped to understand the shadows from her past that might cast a pall over her future.

As soon as the door of the Wyatt home opened, the delicious smell of a roast cooking and the tantalizing aroma of a freshly baked apple pie set Abbie's and Keith's stomachs to rumbling. Lane and Eric had welcomed the couple warmly upon their arrival and helped them move their bags into their respective bedrooms—Keith in one of the extra upstairs bedrooms and Abbie in the downstairs guest suite. As quickly as they could, the two new arrivals entered the kitchen, the heart of the home.

Lane had the kitchen table set up as a buffet, complete with a pitcher of iced tea, as well as appetizers of baked brie and gourmet crackers, mixed nuts, dried fruit, and slices of prosciutto. The four friends filled glasses and plates. Abbie and Keith sat on high-topped chair stools to savor their pre-dinner treats as Lane completed the meal preparations. Conversation began with Eric, Lane, and Abbie doing most of the talking.

As Keith looked around the brick-floored space, he noticed several key design elements. A smartly constructed high-topped counter offered benefits to both guests and chef alike. Turning slightly, he took in the side of the enlarged kitchen that resembled a sitting area, complete with an overstuffed small couch, two club chairs, and a small coffee table centered in front of a river stone fireplace, complete with a dry-stacked stone chase.

Soon the meal was ready, and the foursome moved to the Wyatts' dining room. The table looked like a photo shoot for a magazine. Lane had set it with her formal china and sterling flatware, but the fresh flowers—sunflowers and deep blue hydrangeas—and gingham-checked napkins lent a more casual feel. Each took their place, and Eric reached out both hands to invite Abbie and Keith, seated on either side of him, to take one. In turn, the couple took Lane's outstretched hand in one of theirs, completing the circle.

"Let me ask the blessing," Eric said, and then bowed his head. The others followed.

"Dear Lord, thank You so much for these special friends. We are thankful they're with us. Please bless our time together this weekend. Thank You for this food, and for the hands that prepared it. Equip us to do Your will. Use us as salt and light in this dark world for You. We ask all this in Jesus's name. Amen."

Gentle squeezes passed around the circle as heads raised, and the meal began.

Keith helped himself to generous portions of Lane's food as she passed each serving dish. The perfectly cooked roast lay on a bed of tender vegetables. Twice-baked potatoes came next, followed by bacon-wrapped green beans. A fresh fruit salad and a basket of warm, buttered rolls rounded out the dinner menu. Other than a few comments here and there, the next few minutes were quiet as the four friends relished the fruits of Lane's labor.

However, they sent the dishes for second helpings back around the table, and conversation picked up. Several times throughout the meal, a thrill of excitement shot through Keith when his eyes met Abbie's across the table. Looking at her, he thought about the intensity of emotion she elicited in him. Never in his wildest dreams did he imagine being in love again, especially after the horrific manner in which his former wife and children had died. Watching Abbie laugh and banter with the Wyatts encouraged him to do the same.

Keith's laughter rang out in the dining room, the good old-fashioned kind that rumbled up from somewhere deep in his belly, causing him to almost lose his breath and his eyes to water.

"Eric Wyatt," exclaimed Abbie, trying to suppress another outburst of hysterical giggles. "That is not fair. Please don't tell another funny joke. My sides are aching." The merriment she had tried to hide now escaped in another boisterous chuckle.

Eric had been entertaining Keith and Abbie with jokes for which he was famous. Admired by all his friends and associates, Eric was renowned for his vise-like memory and his ability to recall events. He had a never-ending supply of hilarious yarns and comical puns to share with others when the occasion arose.

Tonight, Keith confirmed his impressions of Eric, developed during board meetings at Timothy House. Eric Wyatt was as solid as they came, and his easy-going manner put others at ease. As Keith listened to the warm exchange between his fiancée and the Wyatts, he prayed that he and Eric would have time this weekend to strengthen their relationship and cement a lasting friendship.

CHAPTER

7

Beulah Tanner, Gladys McLaren, and Muriel Wilson had been working feverishly since eight that morning to ensure their luncheon was picture-perfect. Their junior member, Abbie Richardson, was back in McHenry for a weekend visit and had brought her fiancé, Keith Haliday, with her. These dear ladies loved Abbie like their own daughter, and it had been a while since they had seen her. Happiness had finally arrived for Abbie in the form of this wonderful gentleman, and her three friends could hardly wait to meet him.

Always an early riser, Beulah had readied her dining room table for the afternoon soirée long before Gladys and Muriel arrived. At one end, she placed dessert plates next to the napkins and carefully arranged silver forks on the table's polished mahogany surface. Beulah set out crystal beverage glasses at the other end of the table. An ice bucket and trivet stood next to them, ready to receive the offerings. Fall blooms from Beulah's garden filled a cut-glass vase and were the perfect centerpiece.

After they finished preparing the room, the three ladies gathered in the kitchen to begin the food preparations for Abbie and Keith's arrival.

Standing at the sink, Beulah turned to look at her friends. "I think we've known Abbie for almost twenty years." She turned on the water and filled a pitcher. After turning off the faucet, she stirred the lemonade mixture with a long-handled wooden spoon. "When she joined our Loose Threads quilting group, it was as if she tied up a loose thread in each of us, connecting us through what has become a treasured friendship.

"Drew was in first grade when Abbie joined our merry group. He always wore his Big Bird T-shirt. Hardly ever let Abbie wash it," said Muriel next, as she chopped celery for chicken salad. She sat on a counter stool that looked more like a chair. Working while sitting down enabled Muriel to conserve energy. Since Abbie had moved from McHenry, Muriel's pulmonary condition had worsened, but today, she was determined to enjoy this time with her special friend and Keith. Occasionally, she moved the thin plastic cord of her oxygen tank out of the way.

Gladys finished cutting up tomatoes for open-face sandwiches and added wistfully, "Remember how much we had to teach Abbie about quilting? She was such a novice. Makes me think of the time Abbie was making a quilt for Drew for his eighth birthday. If she hadn't shown us her attempt at piecing the top together, the poor thing would have sewn half the squares together upside down." As she continued slicing the vegetables, she talked about several intricate quilt patterns the ladies of Loose Threads had taught Abbie.

Beulah walked to the refrigerator and took out a bowl of cooked chicken she had cut up earlier. She placed it on the island near Muriel and pulled back the plastic wrap. Nodding toward her, Beulah instructed, "Throw in your celery when you've finished cutting it up."

Muriel nodded, her short salt-and-pepper strands moving in rhythm with her head. The pixie-like hairstyle and her diminutive stature often gave her the appearance of someone much younger. "Abbie loves this chicken salad," she said. "Hope Keith will, too."

"You know he will," Gladys offered. "*All* men like chicken salad."

Beulah and Muriel laughed at their friend's perpetual cheerfulness about any topic under discussion.

Soon, Beulah and Muriel had added all the ingredients for the chicken salad into a sizeable cut-glass serving bowl. As Gladys put together each open-face tomato sandwich, she stacked them neatly on a serving platter. Covering both containers with plastic wrap, Gladys placed them in the refrigerator. Next, she sliced fresh croissants and sealed them in an airtight plastic box until it was time for the gathering. Two cans of nuts—one of salted almonds and the other of cashews—waited to be placed in glass dishes on the island. A tin of fresh-baked chocolate chip cookies waited next to a platter.

"I'm going to look out the window," said Muriel after climbing from the stool. Her petite frame often made her look more like a child. Now she sounded like one waiting to glimpse Santa Claus on Christmas morning. After being in the dining room for only a few minutes, Muriel practically ran back into the kitchen, her oxygen tank thumping along behind her. "They're here!" she said. She stopped and held her hands before her, waving them as she spoke. "And he's so handsome . . ." she cooed. "Keith Haliday looks like a movie star!"

A collective squeal erupted in the kitchen, followed by clapping hands. The excitement was so palpable one could almost hear the crackle of electricity in the air. The ladies of the Loose Threads quilting group were beside themselves with joy and had almost worked themselves into a frenzy with all the preparations for the couple's visit.

They were about to meet Abbie's Prince Charming.

The grand moment was now here.

———

Abbie was mistaken if she thought Keith might be nervous at meeting three older women who thought of her as a daughter. She and Keith had barely rung the doorbell when it opened, and Beulah, Gladys, and Muriel practically dragged Keith and her across the threshold of Beulah's front door. She'd never seen such hugging, back-slapping, and oohing and aahing in her life. Once or twice, her eyes met Keith's as he passed from one hug to another. They had twinkled with delight, and that made her heart soar.

"Where are my manners," said Beulah, running her hand gently over her pearl-colored curls. "You two must be famished. Come into the dining room and fix yourselves a plate." She turned to lead the others from the foyer.

"Miss Beulah," began Keith as he entered the room, "everything looks so beautiful."

"Oh, Keith," Beulah gushed, "it's just Beulah." Her right hand once again found itself gently touching her newly permed hair. Looking at Gladys and Muriel, she continued, "We've been looking forward to meeting you. We've heard so many wonderful things about you."

"Well, ladies," said Keith, ensuring he looked each of the older women in the eye. "I can say the same for you."

Gladys and Muriel beamed from ear to ear as Beulah approached Abbie and placed an arm protectively around her shoulders. "This girl," she said, "is one in a million."

"And don't I know it," said Keith enthusiastically. His concentrated gaze on Abbie made her blush. Breaking the spell, he waved his hand toward the luncheon items arranged on the table. "Abbie, ladies first." He stepped back, allowing his fiancée to be the first in line.

Once seated, the friendly inquisition began.

"Where did you grow up?" asked Beulah.

"How long have you been at Timothy House?" inquired Gladys.

"What sports team do you root for?" quizzed Muriel.

Abbie sat between Keith and Muriel on a deep couch covered in a dated floral fabric. Beulah and Gladys sat in chairs on the other side of the coffee table. *Buddy*, she thought as she watched him, *you can hold your own*. As Abbie listened to the cheerful conversation, Keith's comfort amazed her. *Another reason, sir*, she thought, *why I love you so much*.

During a pause in the conversation, Keith lifted his fork from his plate and announced that he was going back for seconds. Soon, the ladies, including Abbie, followed him to the dining room for more food or to refill their glasses with lemonade.

Once the five sat back in Beulah's comfortable den, the next round of conversation began. This time, Gladys steered Keith through questions ranging from politics to food preferences to matters of faith. He stated his comments on the reelection of President George W. Bush and recent U.S. military skirmishes in Fallujah calmly and without partisanship, bearing witness to a thoughtful and disciplined outlook on the broader world around him.

Muriel and Beulah offered a few inquiries of their own. Again, Keith handled himself with grace and poise and had the most charming, non-offensive way of answering some of the ladies' more challenging questions. Abbie mused as she heard the ladies' views on these varied topics for the first time.

It delighted her friends that she and Keith would soon be married. Not long after Abbie had joined Loose Threads, problems reared their heads in her marriage. As the years passed, the monthly meetings were as much about impromptu therapy sessions as they were about enjoying the fellowship of one another's company. These three ladies knew all too well how much Abbie and Drew had suffered due to Joe's selfishness.

Throughout the morning's visit, Abbie met Keith's eyes across the sitting area of Beulah's home, which had been such a haven of love and encouragement for her for so long. Now, the ladies of Loose Threads welcomed someone she loved more than she thought possible and Keith experienced the gift of friendship the ladies of Loose Threads offered.

Like sleuths in an Angela Lansbury mystery, the ladies watched from the window as Keith helped Abbie into his SUV. A sense of wonder bound together Beulah, Gladys, and Muriel in the realization they had just witnessed a miracle.

As the car pulled away from the curb, tears filled their eyes. Keith Haliday was indeed the answer to the prayers they had lifted for so long to their Heavenly Father.

God had indeed not abandoned their dear friend Abbie.

CHAPTER

8

As soon as Abbie and Keith returned to the Wyatts' home after Beulah's luncheon, final car-loading preparations began for the trip north. Lane and Eric were taking Abbie and Keith to The Resting Place, their cabin retreat nestled in the woods of Johnson's Mountain, two hours northeast of McHenry. Returning to the quaint mountain lodge especially delighted Abbie, as she hadn't been back since she spent a week alone there almost eighteen months ago. The Resting Place was where Abbie took the first steps of her healing journey, allowing the Lord to tend to the dark wounds left in her heart from Joe's betrayal.

The couples took two cars: Lane and Abbie in the Wyatts' car, and Keith and Eric in Keith's SUV.

While Abbie and Keith had been with the ladies of Loose Threads, Lane and Eric made good use of the time, storing food items in Lane's car. Once back at the Wyatts', they performed a final check of the house, and the men loaded luggage and any remaining items in Keith's vehicle.

By mid-afternoon, the two cars were on the road, headed to the mountain retreat. Keith and Eric led the way; Lane and Abbie followed behind.

Autumn was in full splendor in early November in the mountains of east Tennessee. As the four friends made their way toward Johnson's Mountain and the nearby small town of Craggy Bluff, leaves of burnished gold and scarlet offered bright swatches of color through the car windows. The afternoon sun shone through the forest canopy.

As the ladies drove, Abbie shared with Lane the events at Beulah's house.

"You would have been impressed," Abbie began, recounting how the three older ladies practically attached themselves to Keith once he and Abbie arrived. "When Keith started with 'Miss Beulah' this and 'Miss Beulah' that, he had them eating out of the palm of his hand."

Lane kept her gaze on the road ahead. "You can thank his mother for that."

"Keith acted like he'd known these ladies all his life. I've never seen a man so comfortable in a new situation."

"One of the many reasons you love him," ventured Lane, with a smile in her voice.

"You better believe it! I will say," Abbie continued, "the preparation that went into the luncheon was touching, and the food was delicious! Keith kept refilling his plate, which pleased our hostesses immensely."

Abbie sat silent for a few moments, reliving the celebration, before bursting out with the story of the quilting ladies artfully vetting Keith. She could hardly contain her laughter. "You should have seen how Keith handled himself when the interrogation began."

"Interrogation?"

"Yes! It was like Gladys and Beulah were a tag team. Gladys must have worked on her list of questions for a week, because she rattled them off to Keith as if she had memorized them."

"What kind of questions?"

"His political preferences. His favorite foods. How he came to know the Lord. How and why he became a teacher and a coach. She peppered him with queries for quite a long time."

"Oh, my," said Lane thoughtfully.

Smiling to herself, Abbie said, "My Keith answered them all like a champ."

"Speaking of parties," Lane continued, "Winnie called to tell me she's hosting a bridal shower at her house in the spring and asked if I wanted to help."

"What did you tell her?" asked Abbie.

"Well, I said I might be dress shopping that day, but I'd check my calendar and get back to her."

The unexpected quip left Abbie speechless for a few seconds. Finally, Lane's humor dawned on her.

"Ha ha, very funny," Abbie said, her face beaming with the thought that she was the bride to be honored. "Seriously, Laney," she continued, using her best friend's nickname, "thank you!"

"Couldn't let my best girl down," replied Lane cheerily. After glancing at Abbie, she continued. "Have you thought any more about your wedding dress? About how you want to wear your hair?"

"Not really," said Abbie, sounding a bit discouraged. "Although we've been engaged for almost a month, our schedules are so busy, there isn't much free time to talk about the wedding."

"No worries," continued Lane. "When you get back home, why don't you buy a copy of the latest bridal magazine? Find some pictures of dresses and hairstyles you like. Let's set a date for me to visit in the spring. We can go dress shopping and play beauty parlor with your hair."

Abbie tried to suppress a giggle. "Laney," she began, "you sound like the wedding's tomorrow. It's not until May. We've got plenty of time."

"Au contraire," replied Lane, sounding more like a coach prepping her team for a big game. "Your wedding day is May twenty-eighth; it will be here before you know it. Trust me, you'll thank me when you've got all your ducks in a row. The last thing you want to do is wait until the last minute."

"All right," Abbie said, her voice echoing doubts about making plans this far in advance. "It's just that Keith and I are older, and this is a second marriage for both of us."

"All the more reason to make the day as special as possible," was the cheery reply. "Oh, and what about the reception? Have you thought about what you'd like to serve?"

"Not exactly," Abbie offered, "though I've written down a few ideas so I won't forget them."

"I'll call you next week," said Lane, "and we can talk about some food ideas."

"Sounds good to me."

The friends grew silent as bright fall leaves surrounded them in a kaleidoscope of color. Their conversation had afforded little opportunity to enjoy the beautiful scenery of the wooded highway. As they neared Johnson's Mountain, the elevation change brought breathtaking views

of the valley floor below. Abbie thought wistfully of her last visit to
The Resting Place and hoped this weekend's trip would be equally
meaningful.

"Hope you're hungry," said Lane, slowing down to make the turn off
the main road. "I made my special chili for dinner. Thought Keith would
also enjoy it."

"Yum," said Abbie. "He'll love it."

"A big green salad, fresh fruit, salsa, and chips should round out the
meal."

"What's for dessert?" Abbie inquired.

"My grandmother's chocolate chess pie."

"Hooray!" Abbie clapped her hands at this news. "I was hoping you
would make that. Keith's a chocoholic, just like me. That's one of the first
things I noticed about him."

"Well, I made two. Just in case. We'll need it if Keith eats as much
as Eric does."

Ahead, Keith's car navigated the last turn before the drive to the
cabin, and Lane steered along the same path. Both vehicles slowed as
they approached the clearing where the mountain lodge stood under a
broad stand of hardwoods. Lane pulled up behind Keith's Explorer and
turned off the engine. As Lane reached for the door handle, Abbie placed
her hand on her best friend's arm.

"Before we get out," Abbie said softly, "thank you for all you and Eric
are doing for Keith. You will never know how much your support of our
relationship means to me."

Turning to face her best friend, Lane patted Abbie's hand. "Keith
is the answer to the prayer we've been reciting for the past few years.
We're thrilled for you both. Eric has been looking forward to developing
a friendship with Keith. Odd how Joe is the common bond between
them."

"I know," Abbie replied. "But you could have easily kept your distance and not reached out to include Keith. Again, thank you."

Lane quickly hugged Abbie and said, "It's cabin time."

In the waning sunlight, The Resting Place beckoned to the four
friends.

CHAPTER
9

"Quite a cabin," replied Keith as he put his car in park and turned off the ignition.

"Thanks," said Eric proudly. "Welcome to The Resting Place."

Keith peered out the window and admired the stone and timber structure for a moment. Pointing toward the front of the house, he asked, "You and Lane added the screened porch?"

"Yes, that's right." Eric nodded to where several large stone steps rose to meet the porch. "Right about where those steps are was where the stoop, as I call it, was located—a rickety outer entrance to the cabin. Friends referred us to a local architect. We wanted to ensure we didn't compromise the original structure's integrity. Building this porch was some of the best money we've spent. Lane, our sons, and I have shared many special times in those rocking chairs." Eric pointed to a line of rockers visible through the screened porch. "We look forward to making new memories visiting out here this weekend with you and Abbie."

"We can't wait," replied Keith. In his rearview mirror, he noticed Lane's door was open. "Guess we better help the ladies with their luggage."

"Guess you're right," Eric said, reaching to open his door.

"Hey, guys," Lane's cheery voice called out. "Let me get the front door opened." She jingled a set of keys. Making her way up the porch stairs, she pulled open the screen door and unlatched the spring, ensuring the door stayed open.

Abbie, several grocery sacks in hand, followed close behind.

Keith opened the back of his Explorer, and he and Eric grabbed a suitcase with each hand, following Lane and Abbie inside.

The cabin was every bit as charming as Abbie had said. Once through the small foyer, Keith stepped into the great room. The immense stone chase of the wood-burning fireplace on the left wall immediately caught his attention. Smiling, he took the stairwell to the second level and placed his bag in the small bedroom. *Feels like we're at camp.*

Minutes later, he was back outside unloading more items. As he ferried supplies into the cabin, he recalled what Eric had told him on the afternoon trip. He and Lane purchased the place almost ten years ago from an elderly couple who had built the lake house in the forties and had enjoyed it throughout the years. Their declining health conditions forced them to conclude it was time to sell. Eric and Lane were thrilled when their realtor called to say the owners had accepted their offer to buy The Resting Place. She said the sellers knew the couple would take good care of it. From what Eric had said, this place had become special to the Wyatt family.

Eric had also told Keith that this was where Abbie had come almost eighteen months ago to sort out her head and heart concerning a new direction for her life. Keith hoped he could talk privately with Eric, as he had many unanswered questions concerning Joe.

The last item from Lane's car was a small plastic crate filled with food items, including coffee, spices, boxes of crackers, jars of salsa and salad dressings, and bags of chips. Keith brought it into the kitchen and placed it on the small table in front of the side window of the room. This room, though adequate, felt crowded with all four adults in it.

Lane closed the refrigerator door and turned to face the group. "Thanks for bringing in everything." Glancing at her watch, she continued, "Eric, why don't you take Keith for a walk? By the looks of it, we've only got about another hour of sunlight. Abbie and I will work on dinner and let you know when it's ready."

"Yes, ma'am," Eric said, winking conspiratorially at Keith. "Sounds like a plan."

Immediately, the men made their way from the kitchen and toward the cabin's front door. Once on the porch, Eric reattached the spring to the screen door. Keith followed him through it, making sure it didn't slam behind him.

As the two walked past the cars, Eric asked, "Where would you like to go? We can walk around the lake, sit out on the dock, or hunker down on the front porch. I'm thinking," he continued with a wide grin, "as long as we're not inside, the girls won't care where we go."

"A walk sounds great," Keith said, offering a smile of his own. For the past hour, thoughts about Joe had ping-ponged in his brain. *What happened to him? How could he have betrayed Abbie and Drew? Who wouldn't be proud of a son like Drew? How do I help Abbie get rid of the unhealed wounds Joe caused?* Physical activity might help burn off steam. The walk might also be a time for Keith to talk to Eric about his former business partner.

"A walk it is, then." Eric nodded toward his right, where Keith saw a pathway through the trees. Sunlight glistened off the surface of Grant Lake, visible through a stand of hardwoods.

For the next thirty minutes, the men walked around the path that encircled the lake. Sometimes, it ran next to the shoreline; in other areas, it wound through the woods. The air was crisp and cool as Eric and Keith talked about a variety of subjects. As they neared The Resting Place, Keith finally began to relax.

"Want to sit out on the dock for a while?" Eric nodded toward a small pier down the hill from the cabin. "Until Lane calls us, I think we're okay."

"That would be great," said Keith, following his new friend out to the pair of Adirondack chairs waiting for them.

"Remind me of the lake's name?" Keith asked once seated.

"Grant Lake," replied Eric. "A family named Grant settled this part of the mountain in the late 1800s. It's my understanding that the small lake was already here. Over time, the Grants enlarged it. You certainly can't ski on it, but it's a great place to take a canoe, kayak, or small fishing boat. Can't tell you how many mental knots I've untied while out on the lake."

Keith found this last comment the perfect segue into the questions he wanted to ask. Clearing his throat, he began. "I wanted to ask you some questions about Joe."

Eric peered out at the lake for a long while before speaking. "I was wondering how long it would take you to bring him up." Turning toward Keith, he continued, "Abbie has done an amazing job of working her way out from the mountain of guilt, shame, and hurt he piled on her."

"From what she's told me," Keith said, "that's true. One thing I want to know is when Joe changed. We met in college. He was one of the first Christians I met on campus. Though I thought I was walking with the Lord at the time, Joe seemed to be one of those godly role models that had it all together." The hurt in his voice was clear.

The sun sinking low over the lake caught the men's attention. For a time, neither spoke.

Eric, breaking the silence between them, continued telling Keith about his relationship with Joe. "Lane and I met Joe and Abbie at church soon after they moved to McHenry. I don't remember exactly, but they'd only been married a few years. Our sons were in their preschool years—Jason is a year older than Drew, and Jonathan is a year younger. It didn't take long until Lane and Abbie were best friends.

"Joe had recently graduated from law school. I'd been at our firm for only a few years. He and I clicked, although looking back now, I think there was always something about him that didn't square with me. Chad Reynolds, an older attorney who had taken me under his wing, approached me about starting a firm. I told him about Joe, and, as they say, the rest is history. We established Richardson, Reynolds, and Wyatt. Joe was a great partner, won national recognition for his work, and never hinted that anything in his personal life was amiss.

"About a week after Joe's funeral, our firm's accountant called to tell me she had discovered some inconsistencies in the books. It was all I could do not to throw up when she came to my office and brought me the written evidence. Joe had embezzled hundreds of thousands of dollars from seven of his wealthiest clients, not to mention all the money he stole from Drew's college savings fund."

A pause in Eric's comments gave Keith a chance to speak. "Abbie told me how kind you and Murphy Gates were when breaking the news to her, and how helpful you both were in helping her get her business affairs in order."

"Thanks," replied Eric, the pain of Joe's betrayal still evident on his face after all these years. "Abbie's like a sister to me. Telling her what a creep her husband was just about did me in. Joe was one of my best friends. I felt like a total dupe. It's only with God's help that we got through that difficult season, especially Abbie and Drew. I still find it hard to contain my rage at Joe. That's not a godly response, but it's an honest one. Letting go of all the infuriation over Joe's crimes is a subject I'll be talking to the Lord about for years to come, I'm afraid."

"Look," countered Keith, "I feel the same way. Since discovering all this, I've asked myself a million times, 'What did I miss?' Abbie's probably told you, but Joe and I lost touch after college. A note I wrote to him last year, oddly enough, was what initially introduced Abbie and me."

"She told us about your letter," said Eric, his voice slightly less stressed. "For what it's worth"—he looked at Keith—"Lane and I are thrilled for the two of you. Not trying to sound like her dad, but we're protective of Abbie. She's been through so much."

Keith found in Eric's clear, kind eyes honesty and sincerity, qualities he admired in a man. He listened as Eric continued.

"You don't need our permission, but you're the perfect man for her, and we couldn't be happier for you. Drew adores you. He seems to have found a godly role model to follow, and he's thrilled his mother is so happy. My sons have told me many stories about all the heartache Joe caused that boy."

As suddenly as the anger rose within Keith at the mention of Drew's emotional suffering at the hands of his father, it retreated as he offered a silent prayer: *Lord, take this from me, for it's too much for me to carry. Please help me let go of the past and walk into the future you have planned for us.*

A dinner bell clanged from the front porch of The Resting Place. Lane called out, "Dinner's on the table."

Once they stood, Eric placed an arm around Keith's shoulder. "You've got a friend in me you can count on."

As the two men made their way to the old cabin, each knew that the bright light of friendship had been kindled on the hearth of their hearts.

CHAPTER
10

As Eric and Keith walked through the cabin's front door, the savory aroma of chili greeted them. The men washed up for dinner and returned to the kitchen, amazed to find a transformation had taken place in the short time they'd been outside.

A red-checkered cloth covered the small table. Candles glowed on every surface of the small room, lending an air of warmth and intimacy despite the cramped quarters. A large dough bowl sat on the table, filled with a tasty green salad. A bowl of fresh fruit—blueberries, sliced strawberries, and cut cantaloupe—waited nearby. Abbie placed a stoneware chip-and-dip bowl filled with tortillas and salsa on the other side of the table.

Once seated, Eric and Lane, across from one another, took Keith's and Abbie's hands. "Let me ask the blessing," said Eric.

All bowed their heads.

"Dear Lord," he began, "we thank You for this day and especially for these dear friends. We are grateful for this time to get away and enjoy Your beautiful creation and fellowship with one another. Please guide Keith and Abbie on this new journey they are on together. Thank You for this food and the hands that prepared it. All this we ask in Your Son's most holy name. Amen."

As soon as the blessing was over, Lane returned to the stove to scoop large bowls of chili, bringing them to her guests. Serving herself last, she joined the table.

Lane's chili, as Abbie had promised, was fabulous. The men had seconds. At some point, Lane started telling funny stories about Abbie's escapades in the classroom. Keith couldn't contain his laughter, and he added a few tales of his own humorous recollections of coaching young boys in the art and skill of basketball.

Once the noise died down and forks and spoons rested on the plates, Lane said, "Why don't we move into the great room? There'll be more space there. Abbie and I will bring dessert."

After Lane took coffee orders, the men brought their plates to the sink and left the kitchen as the ladies filled mugs and cut ample slices of chocolate chess pie. The best friends ferried the dessert items to the next room using two large wooden trays.

After savoring their dessert and coffee, the four friends visited until almost eleven o'clock. The later the night, the more frequent the yawns, especially from Eric and Lane.

Reaching to place his coffee mug on a table before the sofa, Eric said, "Folks, you'll have to excuse me, but it's past my bedtime." He stood and stretched his back a bit.

Lane followed suit. "It's been a wonderful day," she said, glancing at Abbie and Keith.

"Can we help you clean up the kitchen?" asked Abbie. "Keith and I will be happy to do it for you."

"Well . . ." Lane hesitated and then grinned. "It's a deal. If you're sure you don't mind?" When Abbie and Keith nodded their heads, she replied, "I'd be so grateful." She could barely get the words out before yawning again.

"Cleaning up is one of my special talents," said Keith, winking at Abbie. "It's the least we can do for all the hospitality you've shown us. Head up to bed. We'll lock up before we turn in."

"If you're sure?" Lane asked.

"Laney, we've got this," Abbie said as she rose from the wing chair. "You both look bushed." Walking over to where her best friend stood, she hugged Lane.

"Thanks, you two," said Eric, holding his hand toward his wife. Taking it, he led her toward their bedroom. "See you in the morning."

"Goodnight," echoed Keith and Abbie.

Within twenty minutes, the pair had brought in all the dessert dishes from the great room, scraped the dinner plates, loaded them into the dishwasher, placed leftover food in containers either in the refrigerator or on the counter, and reset the kitchen table for breakfast.

Keith folded a dishtowel and then turned to look at Abbie. "Are you sleepy?"

The candles reflected in her soft green eyes as she replied, "Oddly enough, no. What did you have in mind?"

He took her hand and said, "I thought we'd sit out on the front porch and rock a bit. I've been wanting to do that since we arrived."

"Lead the way," was Abbie's reply.

Before leaving the cabin, Keith turned off all the lights, draping the front porch in almost total darkness. Somewhere out over the lake, a full moon rose in the sky, its silvery glow lending ambient light to locate their chairs and sit. The creaking treads of the rockers sounded like the gentle ticking of a giant clock. Far out in the woods beyond, the hoot of an owl broke the still night.

"Did you and Eric have a good visit?" Abbie asked quietly.

Keith didn't answer for a long time, searching for the right words to share what was in his heart with the woman he loved so much. Finally, he stopped rocking and turned to see her more clearly, their eyes better adjusted to the darkness.

"We did," he began. "We talked about Joe, mostly." He let that sink in for a minute.

"What did you learn?" Abbie's voice sounded small, like that of a child.

"Not much that I didn't already know, from all you've told me," said Keith. "It was good, though, to hear Eric's insights of him. Eric's a good man. You and Drew are lucky to have him as a friend."

"It isn't lost on me." Abbie stopped her chair and turned to face Keith.

"Both of us still have anger issues where Joe is concerned." Keith took Abbie's hands in his. "You and I," he began slowly, "have suffered unspeakable heartache. We couldn't prevent any of it, and that's part of our frustration in coming to terms with it. Neither of us thought we'd ever find happiness, much less love again, but here we are."

Keith brought Abbie's hands to his lips and kissed them gently. "Let's decide tonight that, going forward, we'll leave the past where it belongs—in the past. It won't be easy, but we can do it."

Abbie broke in before he could complete the thought, "With God's help."

"Yes, dear one," Keith said, his voice husky with the emotion welling in his heart. "With God's help. I'm determined *not* to let the past dictate our future. It sounds easier than it will be, but I believe God will honor this request for us."

Quoting a verse from Jeremiah that was special to them, Abbie said softly, "He has 'a future and a hope' prepared for us."

"One that will begin," Keith continued, "in a few months on Saturday, May 28."

Both of them sat for a moment, savoring the promise of their wedding day soon to come.

Keith finally said, "Let's pray and ask the Lord to help us break the bonds from the past. I don't want anything holding us back when we become Mr. and Mrs."

A gentle squeeze of Abbie's hands let him know she wanted freedom from the chains of pain and regret.

"Lord," Keith began, "thank You so much for this time away with Abbie here at The Resting Place. We thank You for the kindness and hospitality of Eric and Lane. Thank You especially that we have in them not only good friends but also fellow believers who see life through the same lens of faith that we do.

"Only You know the extent of the pain caused by Joe in Abbie's and Drew's lives. We ask You to enable them to let go of the anger, bitterness, and resentment that hold their hearts. Give Abbie and Drew the grace to forgive him. Release them from the chokehold of negative emotions.

"Jesus, You also know the deep hurt in my heart. Help me, too, to forgive the drunk driver who killed Genny and our children. I pray the same prayer for myself—that You will cut down the thick hedge that has separated me from experiencing Your love for me.

"Let this day be a new beginning for us. From this day forward, help Abbie and me honor the commitment we make tonight to You and each other to leave the past behind and walk with confidence into the future You have planned.

"Bless us in these next months as we prepare for a new life. Give us the courage to face our fears together, never shrinking back from each other. Enable us to love each other freely and totally, with no lingering torments from the past. Though the love You've given us is more wonderful than anything we could have imagined, we need Your love and power to love one another as You would have us do. We ask all this in Your most precious and holy name. Amen."

The call of an owl, this time closer to the cabin, resounded almost like a second "Amen."

Once they stood, Keith wrapped Abbie in his strong arms and held her close, her heart beating against his own. Before letting her go, he ended their time with a kiss full of tenderness and promise.

As the two made their way back into the cabin, Keith walked Abbie to the door of the downstairs guest bedroom.

Cupping her chin in his hand, he drew her face to his for one more kiss. "Good night, dear Abbie," he whispered. "Sweet dreams."

"Good night, Keith," Abbie replied. She softly closed the door to the bedroom.

Reaching into his pocket, Keith took out a small flashlight before heading for the stairwell and his bedroom above.

CHAPTER
11

Don spent much of his busy Tuesday morning sorting through various file folders. The top of his desk looked like a tornado had landed on it. Folders and multiple pieces of paper lay scattered haphazardly across it. A committee had recently selected the inaugural class of the Tentmaker's Project students, and he was finalizing plans for their upcoming trip to Craggy Bluff, a small town two hours away, where several of the project mentors lived. Don wanted everything to go perfectly when he spoke to the Board of Trustees about the new project in two days.

The ringing phone was a welcome interruption. It was his assistant, Loren Bronson.

"Hi, Loren," Don said, tucking the phone between his ear and shoulder as he rose from his desk chair to grab a paper almost beyond his grasp.

"Mr. Don," Loren said brightly, "a Miss Teencie Curtis is on line one for you. She said you asked her to call you."

"Thanks, Loren," replied Don, immediately losing focus on gaining control of the paperwork. "Put her through."

Don placed the receiver down and waited for the call. He answered it on the second ring.

"Hello, Teencie," he said warmly. "So delighted to hear from you."

"Hello, Mr. Fielding," the waitress replied. "Sorry it's taken me a few weeks to call."

"This is perfect timing," said Don, sensing the woman's nervousness. "I'd like to find a time for you to come see me in my office at Timothy House." He tried to sound upbeat.

"At Timothy House, sir?" Teencie's tone veered toward uncertainty.

"Yes," said Don, a slight laugh escaping. "I want to talk about a job opening at the school."

"A job . . . But sir, I already have a job. At Gravlee's."

"Yes," Don continued, not wanting her to refuse the job before she knew what it entailed. "I welcome the chance to visit with you. After we talk, you can tell me if you're interested."

Don watched the digital readout on his watch click down the time. For a few seconds, he thought Teencie had disconnected.

"I guess that would be okay," Teencie finally said, although she did not sound convinced. "I'm calling you on my break. Would tomorrow morning be a possibility? My Wednesday shift doesn't start until noon."

"How about ten-thirty?" Don said, a surge of expectation buoying his spirits. "You know where our campus is?"

A nervous giggle erupted from Teencie. "Yes, sir," she said. "Everyone in town knows where Timothy House is."

"Good," Don said, feeling for the first time that the conversation had turned in his favor. "Follow the signs to Sanctuary Hall. That's the administration building. Come in through the main doorway. My office is down the hall to the left. My assistant, Loren Bronson, will be expecting you."

"Thanks, Mr. Don. I'll see you tomorrow morning."

"Teencie," Don said cautiously, "if you don't mind, please don't mention this to Robert. I'd rather call him myself and tell him we're going to talk. I'll tell him about the job opening."

Another pregnant pause from Teencie. "You'd do that, sir . . . I mean, talk to Mr. Davis?"

"Of course," reassured Don. "He and I have known each other for many years. He's a faithful supporter of our school. I wouldn't want to jeopardize that friendship."

"Well, thank you, sir," said Teencie, the apprehension still hanging on to her every word. "I'll see you tomorrow morning."

"Great. I hope the remainder of your day goes well. See you soon."

Once Teencie hung up, Don dialed the owner of Gravlee's diner.

"Great to hear from you, Don," Robert said after the head of school identified himself. "How are all the fine people at Timothy House?"

Don smiled as he silently thanked the Lord for his friend's faithfulness. "All are well," he replied, "although I am considering an addition to our staff, which is why I called."

"Must be someone I know," said Robert with a chuckle. "Let me guess . . . Teencie Curtis."

Don was silent for a moment. "You're right on the money, Robert," he said, "though I've said nothing definitive to Teencie. I wanted to talk to you first."

"As a regular customer, you've gotten to know her through the years," said Robert.

"I have. She's a fine, hardworking lady."

"That she is," seconded Robert. "As you're aware, Teencie carries a heavy burden—managing the care of her daughter. I'm sorry I can't offer a more substantial salary. What did you have in mind for her?"

"Well," replied Don, "we direly need an assistant manager at Covenant Kitchen. Someone who could come alongside Charmaine Jenkins and shoulder more of the administrative and organizational duties. Filling this new position would allow Charmaine to focus on her real gift—planning and preparing delicious meals. From what I've seen, Teencie could marshal a military brigade."

"That she could," said Robert proudly.

"Please know," continued Don, not wanting to offend this longtime friend, "that if you have work plans for her, I won't interfere. We both have Teencie's best interests at heart."

Robert paused a minute before replying. "Don, she is a godly, dedicated soul who has worked daily to make the best of a terrible situation. Although I'd hate to lose her, I'm grateful you're considering her for this position."

"She's coming to see me in the morning, and she might turn me down."

"She could, but I don't think so. I've seen a certain weariness come over her this past year, like she was making every good-faith effort to fulfill her work duties, but her heart wasn't in it. I appreciate your courtesy in reaching out to me before talking to her. You have my blessing."

"Thank you," said Don, appreciation in his voice.

"You have my continued support as a Timothy House sponsor," Robert continued. "Let me know how the interview turns out and what Teencie decides."

"I will," Don assured his friend. He held the receiver until Robert disconnected the call. Sitting back in his chair, Don stared at the phone. It was as if God Himself had prepared Robert Davis to hear Don's words.

"Thank you, Lord," he whispered. "Please let Teencie take this job."

At ten-thirty the following day, Loren buzzed Don's office to announce Teencie Curtis had arrived. After asking Loren to show her in, Don crossed to the room's entrance as Loren opened the door. Teencie stood in the doorway, dressed in her waitress uniform. She clutched a small purse as if clinging to a life vest.

"Come in," said Don brightly, extending his arm toward the chairs in front of his desk.

Teencie stepped into the office and took a seat. Before closing the door, he turned to his assistant. "Hold my calls until after our visit."

Once seated behind his desk, the Timothy House director noticed Teencie adjusting her collar as if assuring herself she was properly dressed.

"Teencie, you may be wondering why I've asked you to come see me today."

The woman stared at him, concentrating on his face. A slight nod was the only answer he received.

"The head of our staff at Covenant Kitchen, Charmaine Jenkins, has been with us for fifteen years. She's one of the greatest people you'll ever meet."

"Yes, I know Charmaine. She's a nice lady," offered Teencie. "We both attend Wrights Creek Church."

"That's great to hear," said Don, relaxing a little. "As our school has grown and the needs of our kitchen have increased, the organizational side of Charmaine's position as director of the dining staff has become more involved.

"One of Charmaine's greatest strengths is that she's more than a good cook; she's a chef. She has the gift of tasting a dish once and then returning to the kitchen to replicate it almost exactly. Smells and flavors register with her like one might save data in a computer program. It's amazing."

"I have heard wonderful compliments about her culinary skills," ventured Teencie with a slight smile.

"Charmaine and I spoke recently about adding another member to the dining staff team as assistant manager for Covenant Kitchen. Someone who could take over the business side of running our full-scale kitchen and dining service here at Timothy House. Charmaine suggested I talk to you."

A puzzled look filled Teencie's face, and she tilted her head slightly to one side as if trying to discern a sound she thought she heard. "Me?" she said faintly. "How would Charmaine know about my abilities?"

"Charmaine told me that several years ago, in a women's Bible study, you mentioned your work at Gravlee's. Although you were grateful for the job, you believed you had other gifts and talents, especially related to business management. She said you asked the ladies to pray that God might open a door for you to better use those organizational gifts and talents. Charmaine never forgot that request. You are the only person she would consider for this opening."

"Wow . . ." uttered Teencie. "I don't know what to say."

"Say you'll think about this offer," said Don, capitalizing on this rare opportunity.

Over the next fifteen minutes, the director told Teencie about the Covenant Kitchen staff's general responsibilities, sharing some of Charmaine's specific needs for organization. "Her desire," Don explained, "is to spend more time employing her creative skills to plan nutritious meal and snack offerings, not dealing with vendors and placing food orders." He also explained the newly instituted Tentmaker's Project and how the program might offer partnership opportunities between Timothy House and local farmers in Robbinsonville.

"What do you think so far?" inquired Don, feeling like he was rambling.

"The job sounds fascinating, Mr. Fielding," said Teencie, sounding more confident.

"Please, call me Don," the director said warmly.

"Maybe Mr. Don," said Teencie, a slight smile spreading to the corners of her mouth.

"That's a start," Don said, leaning forward to rest his elbows on his desk. "Your pastor, Rod Eichman, has told me what a warrior you've been for Erica. I can only imagine how hard it's been for you to make ends meet throughout all these years since placing her in residential care."

Teencie lowered her head and wiped both eyes with her hand. "I won't lie, Mr. Don. It's been tough."

Don reached for a tissue box on the corner of his desk and handed it to Teencie. After taking one, she wiped away more tears and blew her nose. Conversation stopped as Teencie composed herself.

"I'm sorry," she finally said. "Sometimes, the emotion is too much to keep inside."

"No apology needed," Don said. "You may or may not know that my uncle, Roger Stevenson, founded Timothy House in 1942, during the early years of World War II. He believed the Lord had blessed him financially, and he wanted to ensure he shared those blessings with others. We offer our employees a full range of benefits, including health insurance and a 401K plan. Would those interest you?"

"Yes, Mr. Don, they would," Teencie said, a glimmer of hope shining in her eyes like she had glimpsed a rainbow in the middle of a thunderstorm.

"That's wonderful to hear," Don said, relaxing. "Why don't you take a few days and consider this offer?

"Thank you, sir, I will," she replied. Suddenly, a look of apprehension crossed Teencie's face. "Mr. Don," she said carefully, "I don't want you to think I don't like my job at Gravlee's, because I do. Mr. Davis and his family have treated me well and have been there to support me through many difficult times with Erica. It's just that he isn't in a financial position to offer the benefits you're offering. And although I enjoy serving our customers, I've spent lots of time thinking about ways to streamline how he runs the restaurant."

Sounds like You're at work here, God, Don thought. "As I've shared, I have the utmost respect for Robert Davis. In fact, I talked to him yesterday after you called."

Teencie's eyes widened, and she drew in a sharp breath.

"He appreciated the call and was delighted to hear about the offer. He said he always felt bad he couldn't offer you a higher salary. I told him I'd let him know once you decided."

Teencie's shoulders relaxed upon hearing this news. She eased the death grip on her purse, and lightly ran the thumb of one hand across its worn surface, much like a small child does to a blanket when seeking comfort.

"Well, okay, Mr. Don," she said. "Could I have until Monday? I'll be seeing Erica this weekend. The drive will give me time to think and pray."

"Sounds like a plan." Don pushed his chair back and stood. "Travel safely. I look forward to hearing from you soon."

"Thank you again, sir." Teencie extended her hand across the desk, and Don shook it in a farewell greeting.

As the younger woman left his office, Don Fielding prayed her decision would be affirmative.

CHAPTER
12

When Abbie arrived, she saw Portia Dockery through the window of the coffee shop. The two were meeting at Darcy's, a popular new establishment on Robbinsonville's main street. A tinkling bell sounded as Abbie pushed open the door and headed inside. Immediately, enticing smells of fine roast coffee and cinnamon greeted her nose. Portia looked up and waved from across the room.

"Hello," said Abbie once she reached the table and pulled out a chair beside the older woman.

"Hello, dear," Portia replied as she patted Abbie's arm. "So glad to see you."

"Sorry I'm running late," Abbie continued. "One of my students had an endless list of questions about a homework assignment. Didn't think I would ever leave campus."

"Bravo for questions," replied Portia with a grin. "That's how most of us learn."

"You are so right," Abbie replied, smiling back. *I see why Keith likes this lady. A straight-shooter. No nonsense. Glad she's a fan of questions because I've got a few of my own to ask her.*

Noticing Portia had not yet ordered, Abbie asked, "Can I get you anything? I'd love this to be my treat."

"Well," said Portia, her grin widening into a smile, "when you put it that way, I'd love a caramel macchiato. Darcy's makes the best in town."

"Wonderful. I'll be right back."

Abbie rose from the table to place their orders. While she waited, she silently thanked the Lord for this kind lady and their new friendship.

A few months ago, Keith had invited Abbie to dinner with Portia at her home. It was the first time she met this older sister in Christ, who reminded her of Audry MacDonald, her dearest friend and a mother figure who had died less than a year ago. Abbie was still grieving her death.

Once the barista announced their flavored coffees were ready, Abbie picked up the drinks and a few napkins and returned to the table where Portia waited.

"How have you been?" Abbie asked before taking a sip of her hot beverage.

"Busier than I'd like," replied Portia after putting down her cup. "This macchiato is excellent, by the way."

"Delighted to hear!" As Abbie took another sip of her latte, lights in the shop caught the top of the diamond in her engagement ring. Portia spotted the glowing stone.

"Let me see it, dear," Portia said, reaching across the table the way a salon manicurist reaches for a client's hand. "I can't believe I didn't grab you when you sat at the table."

Abbie put down her cup and shyly extended her left hand. The diamond practically blinked, it was so bright.

"What a gorgeous ring! Congratulations, Abbie," Portia cooed. "Keith outdid himself. I couldn't be happier for the two of you!"

Still not accustomed to the attention, especially regarding her recent engagement, Abbie blushed slightly and said, "Thank you."

The older woman let go of Abbie's hand and leaned back in her chair. "He called me a few days before he proposed and asked me to pray that you would say yes. I'm delighted God answered those prayers."

Abbie's blush deepened as she looked at the ring finger of her left hand once more.

"Before I forget it," Portia said, switching to another subject, "I wanted you to know how impressed I am and thankful for the critical part you played in rescuing Chloe Minton from the clutches of the Hendersons."

"You are kind to say that. Chloe and I met last summer when I served as a counselor at Camp 4Ever. Some other time, I'll tell you a little of my story. But, for now, because of some events in my childhood, that precious little girl and I bonded. Keith's been in close contact with Chief

Lockhart ever since. The Hendersons' arraignment is scheduled for early next year. What a miracle it was that Taylor and Tim Nunley had filled out the form with the Department of Children's Services so recently."

"God at work," was the older lady's reply, awe and reverence for this turn of events evident in her voice.

The two sipped their coffees for a few minutes.

Putting down her cup, Portia ventured, "I've been thinking about some questions you asked this past summer. How's the 'With God's help' plan going? That you agreed to marry Keith tells me the Lord has moved many boulders away from the door of your heart."

Sudden tears glistened in the younger woman's eyes. "Oh, Mama Dee," Abbie said, calling Portia by the endearing name the older woman had invited her to use. "You will never know what a positive change using that small phrase has made in my life. I still have days when anger about Joe and what he did to Drew and me bubbles up out of nowhere. How do I get rid of that darkness in my soul? I guess I'm not trying hard enough."

Portia giggled softly. "Abbie, dear, there's no trying to it. Don't you remember what I shared with you during our visit? Human endeavor will only take one so far. You can't overcome any temptation, rid yourself of negative emotions or thoughts, or move forward as God desires you to without His help. You keep asking God daily to provide the support you need; He *will* do it.

"One of my favorite writers in the New Testament is the Apostle Paul. He grew up a very privileged man—born by the name of Saul in the wealthy city of Tarsus—a Jewish family member granted Roman privileges, and a student of the renowned rabbi Gamaliel. He grew up to be one of the chief persecutors of the early Christian church. One of the most famous stoning deaths he witnessed was that of the disciple Stephen."

Abbie nodded, listening carefully to Portia's every word.

"Do you remember how God got Paul's attention?" Portia continued. "It was one day on a dusty road as Saul traveled to Damascus. The Lord blinded Saul instantly through a bright light and spoke aloud to him, asking the young man why he was persecuting Him. Four days later, after being taken by his friends traveling with him to a city where they found lodging, the Lord restored Saul's sight. God changed the man's name from Saul to Paul and gave him a new purpose for his life. God's about to do the same thing in your life, Abbie."

A wide smile broke across Abbie's face, and she touched her engagement ring.

"One of the most encouraging stories about Paul's life is in the twelfth chapter of the book of 2 Corinthians," Mama Dee continued. "Paul talked about 'a thorn in the flesh,' some unknown irritation in the man's life that never left him. The apostle explained that he finally concluded that the Lord allowed this irritation in Paul's life so the man would not think more highly of himself than he should—get puffed up, stuck on himself, whatever phrase you want to use. Though I pray God will remove that root of bitterness where Joe's concerned, He may choose not to and use that 'thorn' in your life to draw you closer to Him and change you so that you look more like Him to the world around you."

By this time, several tears trickled down Abbie's face. She reached into her purse and grabbed a tissue to wipe them away.

"What else is bothering you, dear?" asked Portia softly, sensing there were more questions Abbie might want to ask.

"Portia, I love Keith more than I ever thought possible." Abbie stopped for a few seconds, the enormity of this statement sinking in. "Wow," she continued, "I've never uttered that aloud to anyone, not even to Keith."

The older lady grinned from ear to ear.

"What if I can't make him happy? He's been through so much heartache. Losing his wife and children in that car wreck was an unimaginable horror. I couldn't bear causing him more pain."

Portia took hold of one of Abbie's hands. "Dear," she said softly, "take it on good authority that you have brought more joy and happiness into Keith's life than *he* thought possible."

Abbie smiled and suppressed a sniffle.

"There are no guarantees in life. You know that. Remember when we talked about free will? God allows you the freedom *every* day of your life to trust Him or to trust yourself. Choose to believe in Him every day and follow His lead. If Keith does the same, your marriage will surely be happy."

"Thank you, Portia," said Abbie, gently squeezing the woman's hands. "You've meant so much to Keith. I appreciate your kindness to him."

"What's not to love about Keith Haliday?" Portia released Abbie's hand and beamed like the proud mother of a beloved son.

Abbie's smile brightened. "I've not found anything so far. I, too, am grateful for your friendship, Portia. Keith and I look forward to that relationship growing deeper as the years go by."

The expression on the older woman's face let Abbie know Portia felt the same way.

"Now, tell me all about your wedding plans," Portia said in a conspiratorial tone.

For the next few minutes, the two women talked excitedly. Mama Dee's level of joy surprised Abbie as she described the simple ceremony.

"We hope you can be there on our special day," Abbie said sincerely.

"I wouldn't miss it for the world," the older woman replied.

"That's wonderful! Keith will be delighted to hear," said Abbie brightly. "Would you mind if I asked you a huge favor?"

"Not at all."

"Would you mind helping me with some food ideas for the reception? Party planning was never my strong suit."

Portia beamed as if she held the winning ticket at a raffle. "As I've listened to your ideas, a few of my own have sprung to mind. What if I arranged the reception for you? Following your wishes, of course."

Abbie couldn't find words for a few seconds. Portia's generous offer was a huge blessing.

"I don't know what to say. That's a generous offer."

"Say yes, dear," grinned her new friend.

"Yes, indeed!"

After a few more minutes of conversation, the visit ended. Standing by the table, Portia enveloped Abbie in a warm hug, reminding her of the ones Audry used to give.

"Stay close to God," the older friend whispered in Abbie's ear.

"I will," Abbie solemnly replied.

As the two women made their way out of the coffee shop and onto the sidewalk, Abbie whispered a silent prayer of thanksgiving.

God was indeed providing His help.

CHAPTER
13

As the heads around the table slowly lifted after the "Amen," Don Fielding sensed an air of expectation in the room. The meeting of the Timothy House Board of Trustees was now underway. As he looked at the faces of those gathered, he prayed his own silent prayer that God would bless the Tentmaker's Project, a new program about to be initiated into the life of the school. *It's been a long time coming*, thought Don, remembering with gratitude the heavy lifting borne by Chuck Hawthorne and Keith to get the program up and running.

"Well, let's get started," Don began, looking at the faces of caring men and women, some of whom served on the school's board and others who served as mentors for the project.

Heads nodded in agreement. Some attendees drank from water glasses, while others sipped from cups of coffee.

"If you can't tell," Don continued with a smile, "I'm excited about this morning's meeting. Chuck will share the details of next month's retreat for our senior Tentmakers."

Although a few of the trustees could not attend this morning's meeting, Don was pleased with the group seated alongside him. He smiled brightly and took in the faces of those assembled—trustees Portia Dockery, Keith Haliday, Chuck Hawthorne, Lance Tate, and Eric Wyatt, and mentors John Benson, Parker Goodwin, and Elton and Summer Tidwell. *How I wish Uncle Roger could be here with us*, Don thought as he struggled to swallow the lump rising in his throat. *A program like this would have been right up his alley.*

Sensing the pause in the conversation, Chuck picked up where Don's introduction ended. "Well, friends," he said, "this is a momentous day, as Don mentioned. The Tentmaker's Project is one Don and I have been developing for several years. Once Keith joined our team eighteen months ago, the process seemed to accelerate." Turning to look at Keith, Chuck continued, "Thank you, Keith, for all your hard work. Your belief in this program and agreement to come alongside me as the co-director has meant a great deal."

Keith smiled slightly.

"As you know," continued Chuck, turning toward the group, "we recently selected our first students. We hope this program, based on the lifestyle and occupation of Timothy, Paul's younger friend in the ministry, will inspire and equip its participants for a Christ-centered view of work in the wider world."

Chuck picked up a blue folder on the table in front of him. "You'll find in your folders the Tentmaker's program description. You'll also see the names and short bios for our students."

Folders opened and papers shuffled. As Don watched the trustees and mentors peruse the program information, he felt like a proud father introducing his son to the coach of a new sports team. He fervently hoped all present would be impressed with this inaugural class.

"We started with a small group this year," said Chuck, drawing out the paper containing the participant names and bios. "Two young ladies and two young men. These students are from the Robbinsonville area and have been at Timothy House since seventh grade." Chuck nodded toward Don.

"As you may remember from the September meeting," Don began, "the applications were submitted by early October. Chuck, Keith, and I were a bit surprised that all twenty-five students in the junior class applied to the program."

Don then shared how a faculty committee of five had conducted the interviews, remembering how one student struggled to find the right words, feeling the pressure of the meeting. "This is the first time some of these kids have gone through a more formal interview process. All in all, the visits with our students went well. The committee announced the participants' names on October fifteenth. This first group," Don said, looking down at the participant list, "is exceptional, selected from a wonderfully representative cross-section of our student body."

Based on the smiles, those in attendance had positively received Don's message.

"These four participants completed their two-night orientation session last Tuesday evening. This program will be the first time some of our students rub shoulders with adults in the work world. Now, before I turn the meeting back to Chuck, I want to explain how we'll continually develop the relationship between students and mentors. Our mentoring partners have agreed to stay in touch with students by email throughout the coming semester and to make two visits to campus to see their mentees. Our four students will also receive job offers for next summer.

"During their senior year, our Tentmaker's Project students will spend two four-day visits with their business mentors—one in the spring of their junior year and one in the fall of each student's senior year. These individuals have also agreed to write letters of recommendation for our students to accompany college or trade school applications."

Hearty applause broke out across the table. At the sound, all eyes turned toward Portia. "Bravo, Keith and Don," the silver-haired matron said. "Well done!"

Several other board members also expressed their appreciation. Don and Keith smiled.

Chuck then summarized the retreat that would take place over the next four days. "Our group is headed to Craggy Bluff. The town, although small, has a wonderful reputation as a community that supports artisans and merchants alike. Well known throughout the East Tennessee arts community, our students will enjoy a weekend filled with sessions, business advice, and hands-on craft experiences shared with local artisans like Summer and Elton."

Chuck then looked toward the left end of the table, where husband and wife Elton and Summer Tidwell sat. "We owe a special debt of gratitude to these two," Chuck said as he nodded toward the couple. "Summer and Elton have provided us with invaluable advice and creative ideas about how this weekend retreat will run."

As a small round of applause broke out from the group, Chuck seemed to feel a sense of confirmation in the selection of these young entrepreneurs. The Tidwells smiled shyly, looking first at each other and then down at the table. Authentic, hardworking, and humble, they would be role models worth imitating.

"We'll be taking three school vans and leaving tomorrow afternoon around two o'clock," said Chuck as he continued his remarks about the retreat. "Parker and John also serve as Tentmaker mentors. Thank you, gentlemen." Chuck now looked across the table to his right, where these two men sat beside each other.

Parker Goodwin, the owner of Landry's Grocery in Robbinsonville, raised a hand slightly. John Benson, an internist whose wife, Evelyn, was the Timothy House English department chair, smiled at the group. "Glad to help," both men remarked, almost in unison.

"Now I'd like some of our mentors to share their thoughts about how they plan to interact with our program participants," Chuck offered. For the next twenty minutes, all assembled listened as Elton, Summer, Parker, and John expounded on some of their creative ideas for engaging students and encouraging them to think outside the box concerning their future life paths, such as shadowing professionals on their jobs and participating in short-term internships.

Once the mentors' remarks concluded, Chuck took another piece of paper from the blue Tentmaker's Project folder and said, "A good group of adults will accompany the students."

Following his lead, the trustees and mentors pulled out the same sheet from each of their folders, and for a few minutes, all were quiet. The names of adult sponsors included Parker Goodwin, John Benson, Doris and Don Fielding, Lance Tate, and Keith and Abbie. Solid choices in Don's mind. The list included people who could impart their own knowledge.

"As you can see," said Chuck, placing the sponsor list on the table, "Summer and Elton will meet us in Craggy Bluff. Our students will also meet Gurney Tompkins, who owns The Nail's Head, the specialty hardware store in town, and Gurney's cousin, Willow Dean Birdsong, who's a potter."

Directing his gaze across the table from where he sat, Chuck continued, "Eric Wyatt and his wife, Lane, have graciously invited our group for a visit on Sunday to their cabin, The Resting Place, which is only about fifteen minutes from Craggy Bluff. We'll attend a lakeside vesper service that morning, and afterward, the Wyatts are treating us to a cookout. Our group plans to leave right after lunch so students' families can pick them up for Thanksgiving break."

"What an ingenious plan for this special weekend," said Portia, nodding her approval.

"I wish my high school had offered an opportunity like this," Lance shared, his enthusiasm evident.

Chuck concluded his portion of the meeting's remarks by explaining how two local churches provided accommodations in members' homes for adult mentors and students.

"Excellent," said Don, beaming with pride as he prepared to introduce the last details of the new mentoring program. "You can see why we have all been so excited about this project. Our prayer is that the connections made through these mentoring relationships will influence our students' lives for years to come."

For a split second, his uncle Roger Stevenson's face flashed through Don's mind. He would have been so proud, he thought, of this unique way to introduce students to the broader world beyond the gates of Timothy House. Working hard to control his emotions, Don continued, his tone more serious. "I want to thank all the Tentmaker's Project mentors. We appreciate your attendance here today and at the past few board meetings. Allow me to show you out as the board discusses school matters."

Chairs pushed back, and the trustees and staff exchanged handshakes as the mentors said their goodbyes and left the main conference room of Sanctuary Hall.

As Don watched the advisers exit, he uttered a silent prayer that the trustees of Timothy House would be equally supportive of the next item of business on the meeting's agenda.

CHAPTER
14

As soon as the last Tentmaker's Project mentor left the conference room and the door closed behind him, Keith lifted a silent prayer. *Oh, Lord, please open the ears and hearts of these board members to what they're about to hear.* As he looked at his old friend, Lance Tate, Keith knew the man was bringing the same petition before their Heavenly Father.

The group sat in their respective places around the large oval table and turned their attention to Don.

"Thank you for your time today, as this meeting has been a bit longer than usual," the Timothy House director said. "Keith and I have an urgent matter to bring you today, and it won't wait."

Immediately, the faces of those around the table took on more serious expressions.

Meeting Don's eyes, Keith knew this was a pivotal moment for the board of Timothy House. Thinking back over all the second chances that had led him to this place in his life, Keith hoped that those gathered also believed in new beginnings.

"Keith," continued Don, "I'll let you give a word of explanation before I bring in a guest to join us."

Puzzlement flashed across several faces of those in the conference room.

"Thanks, Don," said Keith, nervously raking one hand through his dark hair. Although nearing fifty-five, the passage of time had been kind to him, few gray strands on his head. Taking a deep breath and uttering one more silent prayer, he continued. "I'm about to tell you a story you will not read in the newspapers. To ensure this story is told correctly, I've invited a friend to help me."

At this pronouncement, Don walked to the conference room door. Opening it, he called out into the hallway, "Come on in."

Chief Trent Lockhart entered the room. His six-foot, five-inch frame dwarfed that of Don. Despite his imposing stature, Trent's warm smile and easygoing nature were sure to put all at ease.

"Hello, everyone," he said as he raised a hand in greeting and pulled out a chair on the side closest to the conference room door. "Thanks for having me," he continued as he sat.

Keith grinned at his friend. *Boy, am I glad to see you.* "Trent, welcome. I wanted to wait until you arrived so you could share this story with our board."

Looking around the room, Trent made sure he met the eyes of each board member. After doing so, he began, "As most of you are probably aware, the Robbinsonville Police Department discovered a major drug operation in late September. Four young men were arrested in a routine stop, and our officers discovered drugs in the car when questioning the occupants. Those arrests broke up the most notorious drug operation in this part of Tennessee."

"It has come to our attention," Keith said, "that this drug ring may have targeted students in area high schools. One such student is seventeen-year-old DeSean Matthews. He is in foster care and lives with Max and Edna Smith in nearby Jonesborough. Although this kid comes from a highly dysfunctional family and his story is sad, he has a pretty clean slate. To our knowledge, he also does not smoke, drink, or use drugs. Perhaps DeSean's only crime was that he gave up on himself.

"A senior at Crockett High School, DeSean has been on Coach Jackson Denning's team for the past two years." Upon hearing this comment, many in the room nodded approvingly, as the coach was one of the most storied in Tennessee. "DeSean has incredible talent, but again, his general apathy about life is his Achilles' heel."

Portia interjected when Keith paused in his remarks. "How did you meet this young man?"

"I met him in June at a basketball clinic. Coach Denning invited several of us from Timothy House to help with a skills clinic at the

Jonesborough Community Center. During the lunch break, I took a seat next to DeSean, and we started a conversation. As we were wrapping up our visit, I felt led to give him one of my business cards."

Keith paused after this statement, as he did not want his following words to sound maudlin or fake. After walking many years with the Lord, Keith had learned to recognize the gentle tug of the Holy Spirit in his heart or on his conscience when the Lord had an assignment for him—that day at the basketball clinic in Jonesborough had been one such occasion. Although Keith knew the board members were believers, he also realized they might be at different points in their walk with their Heavenly Father.

Lord, he said, uttering another silent prayer, *please help me explain this in a way these friends will understand and know it is from You.*

In a tone that was now more somber, Keith continued his story. "Although I cannot say why, Crockett High is no longer a suitable fit for DeSean."

No one said anything for a long while. It seemed like an eternity to Keith as this information sank in with the board members.

Looking over at Lance, Keith found his good friend watching. The gentle nod of his head and the expression in his dark brown eyes offered Keith the encouragement he needed to finish his story and ask the board for help.

"Don, Trent, and I have spent many hours over the past few weeks working out different scenarios of how we might help DeSean."

All eyes around the table were on Keith.

"We propose that DeSean become a residential student at Timothy House. Sequoia, the cottage in which Josh Hastings lives, has an extra bedroom, and the young man has agreed to serve as a mentor for DeSean, who would only be on campus with us through the end of next May. Max and Edna, the teen's foster parents, have agreed to help in any way possible, but feel, as we do," said Keith, looking over at Don and Trent, "that DeSean needs a structured environment and tough love. He also needs encouragement."

Portia raised her hand, and Keith stopped when he saw it. "Yes, ma'am?"

"How will this fellow finish high school?"

"We've assigned Stuart Lassiter, a new high school science department teacher, as DeSean's faculty mentor," Keith responded. "Stuart has agreed to work with DeSean in his first few weeks with us and oversee the completion of work DeSean missed in the first part of the semester."

Keith paused momentarily and looked at the school's director. "Don has worked with the senior faculty, and they have graciously agreed to allow DeSean to complete a scaled-down version of what would normally be required. Thanks so much, Don."

Don nodded slightly in response.

"Our school librarian, Bethany Bronson, has also agreed to help DeSean with humanities-based subjects like English and History," continued Keith. "One of our seniors has agreed to serve as a peer buddy for DeSean. Also, Don has offered to allow DeSean to use a pickup truck our maintenance crew has used for years but is no longer driving."

Eric Wyatt asked, "Do we have funds in our school budget to underwrite this expense? What about the upkeep of the vehicle?"

"I'm glad you asked," said Keith. "Bill Howard, the owner of Howard's Tire and Auto here in town, has kindly agreed to provide any maintenance and supplies needed to get the truck in working order. His twin daughters are in our junior class."

DeSean was a juvenile when he was arrested in September, so Keith could not disclose the details of that with the board. He also couldn't share why Bill Howard had made such a generous offer. C.J. Dykes, the leader of the drug ring operation and the one who had coerced DeSean into taking a ride with him and his pals, had worked for Bill for almost two years. Bill often told Keith how terrible he felt that he had hired C.J. Bill never suspected anything.

Keith continued, "DeSean will also have a part-time job as a busboy at Covenant Kitchen a few days a week to help pay for gas."

Eric nodded his approval.

"We hope DeSean might receive the academic and emotional support he needs to help him reach his full potential. Rod Eichman, the pastor of Wright's Creek Community Church, has been a great friend to Timothy House. Josh Hastings is a member of his congregation. Rod's agreed to head up a group of us who will serve as what we're calling DeSean's Barnabas Brothers."

"Barnabas Brothers?" Portia posed.

"You remember the stories in the New Testament, particularly in the book of Acts, of Paul's transformation from the persecutor of the first-century Christians to perhaps the greatest missionary for Christ the world has ever known. His mentee and younger brother-in-faith, Timothy, inspired our school's name. However, long before Paul met Timothy, Paul had many seasons of discouragement and doubt and many dark nights of the soul as he began his new walk with the Lord. Barnabas was an early church leader who believed in the sincerity of Paul's conversion and personally vouched for Paul. Barnabas's name means 'son of encouragement.' That's what we'll be for DeSean—encouragers."

Turning in Trent's direction, Keith said, "I'll let Chief Lockhart share his take on this support group."

The police chief turned his attention to the remainder of the board members. "DeSean Matthews is a young man who's faced disappointment in almost every area of his life. When he was four, his mother died of a drug overdose. Her mother, Lurlene, took the boy in for a while but was too busy trying to pick up men to pay much attention to him. Unfortunately, there's no telling what DeSean saw or heard while he lived with his maternal grandmother."

The board members' eyes narrowed, and several leaned forward to listen to Trent more closely.

"Audie Matthews, DeSean's father, blew up a gas pump the year the boy turned eight. Luckily, no one was killed, although one customer at the gas station sustained injuries when trying to escape from the fire. Audie's in the pen serving a twenty-five-year sentence.

"DeSean entered the foster care system in Tennessee soon after. He's been in and out of about five or six homes. He's lived with Max and Edna Smith since he was fifteen. They're sweet people but are too old to handle the demands of rearing a teenager. However, they are good as gold and have agreed to help us.

"I've gone over DeSean's case with a fine-toothed comb and cannot find any record of his running afoul of the law at any time in his life. What Keith is proposing is a bit unorthodox, I'll grant you that," Trent said, nodding toward his good friend, "but this plan might work. I have a friend who's a police chief in Oklahoma who's used a similar model to support a wayward youth. That young man has completed college, is married with a child, and is a productive member of his community.

"What DeSean Matthews needs most in his life is people who will love him sincerely and stand beside him no matter what. Unfortunately, he's had few people keep their word to him. As Keith mentioned, I will be one of the Barnabas Brothers. Our group includes Keith, Don, Josh, Pastor Rod, and me. We're all excited to have this opportunity to put feet to our faith and show DeSean what real, Christlike love and friendship looks like."

Tears stung Keith's eyes.

"One more name to mention, and then I'm through talking," said Trent with a smile as he glanced at the retired major general. "Lance has agreed to meet with DeSean every few weeks. Turns out the kid has a desire to enter the military. Lance knows the right people to mentor and prepare DeSean."

Soft applause broke out, and a murmur of approval rose from around the table.

Trent then turned his attention to Don. "Your turn, sir."

"Well, friends," Don murmured, "we ask you to approve this rescue plan for DeSean Matthews. We believe he's a young man we can help."

Don looked into the eyes of each board member assembled before ending his comments. "The motto of Timothy House is 'Establishing a Foundation of Faithfulness in a Faithless World.' Please join us in this opportunity to bring those words to life and prove to this young man that we believe in him."

Unanimously, the Timothy House Board of Trustees approved the founding of the school's inaugural chapter of the Barnabas Brothers.

CHAPTER
15

Mother and son talked nonstop on the three-hour drive from Robbinsonville to McHenry. The pair were meeting with Murphy Gates, the attorney and trusted family friend who had also handled business matters for Abbie's late friend, Audry MacDonald. A sense of anticipation and excitement had cheered them throughout the past few weeks as they decided what to do with the generous inheritance Audry had left them less than six months ago.

A letter in Audry's hand explained the gift of two hundred and fifty thousand dollars and how Audry wanted the money split. One hundred thousand was to fund Drew's attendance at a seminary, should he choose, and one hundred fifty thousand went to Abbie with the suggestion to "Grow this money for the kingdom of God." This unexpected bequest was one Abbie still could not wrap her head around.

Abbie smiled as she listened to Drew ramble on enthusiastically about seminary. Joe's critical spirit and demeaning words had nearly extinguished the dream Drew had carried since his early teens. Joe had failed his wife and son miserably, the fallout from his financial misdeeds coming to light only after his death.

To her surprise, hurtful memories, long repressed, sprang to the surface of Abbie's mind, prancing like deer. As if he were sitting next to her, Joe's voice reverberated within the confines of her mind. His cold, denigrating tone when referring to Drew's desire to attend seminary. "Ridiculous" and "idiotic" were the terms her husband had used when belittling their son. Even more painful, though, was the anguished expression on

Drew's face, a look seared like a brand against the backdrop of her mind despite the passage of time.

The deep wounds caused by Joe's betrayal added insult to injury from those suffered in Abbie's childhood due to the neglect and emotional abuse from her alcoholic mother. God, however, had not abandoned her. The faithfulness of supportive friends—Lane and Eric Wyatt, Arthur Patterson, Winnie Jeffers, Beulah Tanner, and Audry MacDonald—had rescued Abbie from the depths of desperation and despair. These same stalwarts had restored Abbie's faith in her fellow man.

A glint of sunlight flashing across the top of the large stone in Abbie's engagement ring caught her eye, reminding her of another of God's provisions. Keith Haliday's unexpected arrival on the horizon of her life opened her heart to new possibilities. Like Abbie, Keith had suffered enormous losses, though in a much different way than Joe's betrayal. In one terrible, heart-stopping instant, one careless decision by a drunk driver to get behind the wheel of a car snuffed out the lives of Keith's wife, son, and daughter.

Abbie said a silent prayer as the sunlight showered the car's interior with multicolored light refracted from the top of her ring. *Thank You, Lord, for holding on to Drew and me throughout these difficult years. Show my son Your path for him to attend seminary. Guide me as I seek to further Your kingdom with the money Audry left me. How grateful I am, Lord, that You have not abandoned us.*

A question posed by Drew brought Abbie back from her thoughts. "Mom," her son asked, "what happens to the money Audry left me since I haven't decided on a seminary?"

"Let's see what Murphy says. I'm sure he'll answer your questions," she said as she entered the parking lot next to Murphy's law firm.

Drew sighed as he seemed to relax. "You're right," he said, raking his hand through his sandy blond hair. "It's just that this is still surreal. When I made those visits to the seminaries in July, that was me attempting to step out in faith. Depending on what Mr. Gates says today, I *really* may go to seminary."

As Abbie glanced at Drew, her son's face filled with pure wonder and astonishment. *Christmas may have come early this year*, she thought as she put the car in park.

Once inside, it was like a homecoming as Wilma Jennings greeted Abbie and Drew with warm hugs. Years ago, Abbie had taught one of Wilma's daughters.

Wilma ushered mother and son into the conference room. "If I remember correctly," said Wilma, "you like your coffee blond and with Sweet N' Low." The secretary moved to a coffee service atop a sideboard beside the table and picked up a china cup.

"That's right," said Abbie. "Great memory."

After placing the coffee in front of Abbie, Wilma looked at Drew. "What will you have, young man? We have Mountain Dew and Sprite in the fridge."

"Mountain Dew would be wonderful, Mrs. Jennings," Drew replied.

A few minutes later, she placed a cold bottle of Drew's favorite beverage in front of him.

"Enjoy!" was Wilma's last greeting before closing the conference room door.

Abbie and Drew waited only a few minutes before Murphy entered the room. After exchanging hugs and handshakes, the three sat for their meeting.

Murphy looked at Abbie with a wide grin. "I hear congratulations are in order."

Abbie smiled broadly as a blush crept up her cheeks. "Thank you. They are." As she held out her left hand, her attorney gently took it in his and pulled it closer to see the engagement ring. "I still can't believe it," Abbie cooed as Murphy turned her hand slightly, the diamond sparkling in the office light.

Releasing his client's hand, Murphy turned his attention to Drew. "What do you think, son?"

"About Keith Haliday?" Drew asked. "He's the greatest thing that's happened in Mom's life in a long time." The tone in his voice was sincere and proud, almost as if he were the father of the bride-to-be rather than her son. "I couldn't be happier for both of them."

"Terrific." Murphy reached into the breast pocket of his coat and pulled out a pair of reading glasses. "Let's get down to business," he said with a twinkle in his eye as he opened a sizeable legal folder before him. Inside, packets of paperwork, silver clips situated just so, waited in neat stacks. "Well, Abbie," he began, "it's been a while since we've discussed Miss Audry's gift. Have you and Drew decided how to spend this money?"

"Well, one of us has," Abbie said, glancing at her son. "I'll let Drew tell you."

As Abbie and Murphy listened, Drew shared his longstanding desire to attend seminary, speaking with the confidence of a man many years his senior. As Abbie listened, tears glistened in her eyes as she remembered the countless nights she had stood outside Drew's room, hearing him as he poured out his heart before the Lord about his dream. He explained his process of finding the right seminary to attend.

"What happens to the money if I don't know where I'll be attending school?" Drew queried. His grip on the table tightened as he waited for the attorney's reply.

"That's an easy question to answer," said Murphy. Looking at Drew, he continued, "Your mother can open an account with the First Trust and Savings Bank in Robbinsonville, where Miss Audry's money has been held since before her death."

Abbie looked quizzically at Murphy. "Since before her death?" she whispered.

"Yes, dear Abbie," said Murphy with the tenderness of a father for a daughter. "Miss Audry asked me to visit her in the assisted living facility a few days after she moved. Her instructions were clear. I believe she knew she didn't have long to live and wanted you to be taken care of. As I've told you, she thought of you as the daughter she never had."

Tears welled in Abbie's eyes as she clasped Drew's hand. "Oh, my," she said, her voice breaking.

"Drew, one hundred thousand dollars is Miss Audry's bequest to you."

Looking back at Abbie, Murphy continued. "I'd suggest you create two accounts at the bank—one for you and the other for Drew. One hundred thousand dollars will go to Drew's account; the remaining one hundred fifty thousand, Abbie, will go in your account. Drew, once you transfer the money, it can sit in the account as long as needed until you decide which seminary you'll attend." Murphy turned his attention to Abbie. "There's one provision in Audry's careful planning that I need to share with you."

Abbie looked at the older man, wonderment rising within her. "Another provision?"

"Miss Audry placed her financial gift to you in a savings account rather than a regular escrow account. As such, the principal balance of two hundred fifty thousand dollars has gained interest during this time—an additional twenty-four thousand dollars."

As she had last March when seated in this same office with Murphy, Abbie could not quite believe what she was hearing.

"Since this amount is not part of the principal," Murphy continued, "I suggest we cut you a check for this amount earned through interest. It would be a great nest egg with which to plan your wedding."

Abbie nodded, still too moved to speak.

Murphy spent a few more minutes explaining how to establish the accounts at the bank in Robbinsonville. As he spoke, he gathered several papers from the sheath in the file folder and slid them across the table to them. "These will help you when you get to the bank."

Abbie took the documents.

"Have you decided how you want to spend your inheritance?" Murphy inquired with a grin.

"Not exactly," said Abbie, still feeling like she was in some beautiful dream. "I'll use this interest money to cover my wedding expenses."

Drew and Murphy both smiled at this.

Abbie continued, "Although I've not worked out all the details, I'm interested in establishing a scholarship, maybe even two, at Timothy House in Audry's memory. Perhaps one for a male and one for a female student." Abbie stopped for a moment, lost in thoughts of Audry. Recalling all the dear older friend had done for her, her heart warmed with the knowledge that Audry's legacy of loving care would continue into the lives of others.

After a few minutes, Abbie continued. "Maybe . . ." she began, a slow smile spreading across her face, "we could offer the scholarship as a lump-sum gift, a sort of promise for a deserving student's future."

"Sounds like a plan to me," concluded Murphy. "Let me know when the accounts in Robbinsonville are ready, and I'll wire the funds. Putting together the plan for a scholarship might take some time. Don't worry if it doesn't happen right away. The main thing is that you have an initial game plan about how you want to invest Audry's gift. Let's meet again in about two months." Looking down at a notepad before him, the attorney verified Abbie's address. "You can expect a check for the additional interest by the end of the week."

Abbie smiled at this.

"Also, I'll be happy to drive to Robbinsonville for our next meeting," Murphy offered. "I'd like to see the famous Timothy House campus that's made such a difference in your life, and I want to meet Keith Haliday."

Abbie beamed at the mention of her fiancé's name. "I'd like that very much. I'll be in touch soon."

The group stood and said their goodbyes. As they left the conference room, Wilma extended a warm farewell to Abbie and Drew.

As soon as Abbie's car cleared the city limits of McHenry, Drew was fast asleep. They had both gotten up early to make the trip, and the idea of Audry's financial gift was still overwhelming. *I'll need a nap myself,* Abbie thought, as she stole occasional glimpses of her now-grown son. Her heart swam with the knowledge that God had indeed made a way to bring one of Drew's biggest dreams to life.

Memories of happy times shared with Audry MacDonald flashed through her mind as beams of afternoon sunlight shone through the trees. Car rides in the country. Nights spent sewing with the Loose Threads. Running errands to the post office and garden store. Meaningful conversations shared while enjoying a meal together. "Thank you, Audry," Abbie whispered, wishing she could thank her dear friend in person.

The unexpected interest money would allow Abbie to make a few purchases for her wedding, including a dress. She had also wanted to repurpose Audry's engagement ring, which she'd left to Abbie. Only a few days ago, Abbie visited a jewelry store in Robbinsonville. The owner made several creative suggestions about placing the diamond solitaire in a pendant.

Before she knew it, a highway sign told her they were only a few miles outside Robbinsonville. Thinking back over the meeting at Murphy's office, Abbie's heart was full of gratitude for the Lord's provision and yet another sign that God had not abandoned her family or her.

CHAPTER
16

As the Smiths' dark gray Honda sedan pulled up the drive of Timothy House, DeSean could see Coach Hastings waiting on the cottage's front porch. The teen swallowed hard to tamp down the irritation rising within his spirit. The older model car creaked over the dips and sways in the driveway but seemed to hold its own. When Max pulled into the space and put the car in park, Coach Hastings walked down the stairs to meet them, offering a bright grin and a helping hand.

"Hello, Mr. Smith," the man said, extending a hand toward the older man in greeting as soon as Max stepped out of the car.

Max Smith took it and shook it vigorously.

"It's nice to meet you," said Max. "My wife and I appreciate you allowing DeSean to bunk with you for these next few months."

"You're welcome, sir," replied Coach Hastings as DeSean clambered out of the car. "We'll take good care of him. You can count on that." He flashed another smile at Max.

Irritation rushed through DeSean. *I'm not a baby*, he thought as he listened to the coach talk to his foster dad.

"Hey, DeSean," continued Josh, looking toward the wayward teen. "Glad you're here."

DeSean lifted a hand in the semblance of a greeting but uttered no words. He wasn't in the mood. He reached into the car, drawing out a bulging garbage sack. After slinging it over his shoulder, he walked onto the front porch of the cottage.

Coach Hastings turned his attention back to DeSean's foster parent. "Mr. Smith, there are a few people DeSean and I need to see on campus this morning. You can meet us back here a little before noon."

"That'll be fine," Max said. DeSean watched Mr. Smith glance across the top of the car at where he now stood on the porch. The man had a strange look on his face, like he might as well have been looking across the Grand Canyon.

"Have a good morning, DeSean," the older man said, looking a bit timid, like he wasn't quite sure how the boy would respond.

"Later," said DeSean. His expressionless face matched his lackluster response.

Max Smith's shoulders sagged. Turning around, he walked back to where he had parked his car.

Josh and DeSean waited in silence as the car started and then drove away.

Now that it was just the two of them, the moment seemed awkward. Bounding up the steps two at a time, Coach Hastings stepped past DeSean and opened the front door. "Come on, man," he said, waving his arm for DeSean to follow him.

The door to the bedroom closed quietly. As DeSean dropped his bag onto the bed, he surveyed the simple space. In less than twenty minutes, he put away all his earthly possessions in the spare bedroom of Sequoia Lodge. Named for the famous redwood trees that reached heavenward and lived long years, the house undoubtedly had stories to tell, although DeSean's spirit wasn't receptive to them.

Once the teen unpacked his clothes, he walked over to a bedroom window that looked out into the woods beyond Sequoia Lodge as dappled sunlight filtered through the trees. Soon, his mind wandered back to an incident before the ride with C.J., his pals, and the subsequent arrest.

DeSean had ridden with the Smiths to a doctor's appointment for Edna in Johnson City. When they arrived at the clinic, Max stopped the car under the covered drive-through so Edna wouldn't have far to walk. As he helped his wife out, DeSean also got out of the back seat. As Edna gathered her purse and sweater, Max gave the young man the car keys, handed him a fifty-dollar bill, and told DeSean to buy a few things he would like at the Old Navy store in the shopping center across a busy boulevard from the medical office. Max told the boy to return to the physician's office in one hour. DeSean could hardly believe his good luck.

Once the Smiths were inside the lobby of the brick-and-glass medical facility, DeSean pulled onto a side street where he could catch the traffic light. As he waited for the light to turn green, he glanced to his left and noticed an Army recruiting office a few doors down from the clinic. On the spur of the moment, he switched the blinker from the right arrow to the left, and when the light changed, he guided the car into the parking lot and parked. After getting out, DeSean headed toward the front door.

A polite staff sergeant greeted him once inside. The man introduced himself to the boy and extended his hand. DeSean looked the man squarely in the eye, firmly clasped the man's hand in his own, and told the soldier his name. One benefit of living with Max Smith was that the teen had learned some of the finer points of basic etiquette. His confidence, however, was another matter. After hemming and hawing for a few minutes, DeSean managed to ask for a recruitment brochure. By the time he returned to the car, his hands were clammy and his mouth dry.

Why am I always so nervous? he thought as he headed to Old Navy. *The man must have thought I'm a lightweight.*

DeSean was often his own worst enemy. Before exiting the car for a second time, he reached into the back seat and shoved the brochure into the seat pocket. He'd need to remember to take it out when they returned home from her appointment.

For the next week, DeSean had practically memorized the recruiting brochure. There were five requirements for enlisting in the U.S. Army: show proof of U.S. citizenship, be between the ages of seventeen and thirty-five, meet the required standard on the ASVAB, possess a high school diploma or GED, and prove medical, moral, and physical competence.

After careful study, DeSean deduced he already had three of the five qualifications in the bag. One of the few possessions he treasured was his birth certificate, which stayed folded in a white envelope he kept tucked into the back of his sock drawer. DeSean probably had his grandmother, Lurlene, to thank for that, although that may have been the only thing he could thank her for. The document was critical for enlistment success.

He met the age requirement and figured his medical, moral, and physical condition was as good as the next guy's.

The last two requirements, however, would be a challenge. First, DeSean had no idea how and where one took the ASVAB. Second, if DeSean didn't buckle down and apply himself, he might not graduate. Now that he had changed schools in the middle of the first semester of his senior year, he had no idea of his future.

The sound of a door closing in a nearby room drew DeSean out of his daydream. Opening the bedroom door, he headed into the den to meet Coach Hastings.

After a brief tour of the cottage, Josh and DeSean returned to the house's main living room. DeSean had said little during the introduction but seemed to listen. However, he buried his hands in his pockets.

Now Josh sat on a weathered velour sofa. DeSean plopped onto a faded plaid recliner nearby.

"Hey, man," Josh began, "all of us here at Timothy House are excited you'll be living with us for a while."

DeSean shrugged.

Although young, the coach had seen some challenging teenagers in his short career. *This kid may be one of the toughest of all to reach*, he thought, looking at the seventeen-year-old. *Lord, You have to help me here.*

In a recent meeting, Trent Lockhart had filled in all the members of the Barnabas Brothers and provided them a summary of DeSean's short but disappointing life. From what Josh understood, just about everyone who was anyone in the boy's life had either died, tried to get rid of him, walked out on him, or given up on him. The last two years with Max and Edna Smith had been the most stable the boy had enjoyed. Although DeSean seemed apathetic toward his foster parents, as witnessed that morning, the coach knew enough about the boy to surmise that his aloof nature was a cloak of protection, a defense mechanism DeSean used to protect himself from being hurt. *This kid's got a lot to learn*, Josh thought as he looked at DeSean.

Taking a deep breath and hoping for a lucky break, Josh posed a question. "Want to tell me a little about yourself?"

"Not much to tell, I guess," said the teen, shoving his hands deeper inside his jeans pockets.

"Oh, I don't believe that," countered Josh, offering a grin. Watching the boy, Josh thought, *This pocket thing must be a comfort mechanism when this kid's nervous.*

"Well, you can believe it or not," DeSean replied, his stare cold and hard.

Josh tried again with another warm statement. "I'm glad you're here, and I look forward to getting to know you better."

The boy shrugged and stared at a spot on the floor somewhere past Josh.

When the brief, awkward exchange ended, Josh knew little more than when the question-and-answer session began. If using the fewest number of words meant anything, DeSean indeed won. Josh had done all the talking.

Glancing at his watch, Josh realized they were due in Don Fielding's office in Sanctuary Hall in ten minutes. "Well," he said, again trying to sound as cheerful as possible, "we need to get going. Some gentlemen are looking forward to a visit with you." Josh stood, and DeSean followed suit. As they left the cottage and headed toward the central part of the school grounds, the campus was quiet.

During the walk to Sanctuary Hall, Josh wondered if the teen was questioning his decision to come to Timothy House.

CHAPTER
17

When Josh and DeSean reached Don's office, they could already hear a conversation underway. Once at the open door, Josh knocked on the casing. Four men turned toward the noise.

"Good morning, DeSean," said Don brightly as he stood and approached the young man.

One by one, the other three men—Trent Lockhart, Keith Haliday, and Rod Eichman—followed Don's example and extended their hands in greeting. DeSean shook each man's hand and greeted them as politely as you please. *Miracles never cease*, Josh thought. *Maybe we can reach this kid after all.*

DeSean sat quietly as Don began the conversation.

"As you might remember, DeSean, the men gathered here are looking forward to getting to know you and building solid relationships with you. I hope you got settled in at Sequoia Lodge. After our meeting, Josh will walk you through the campus.

"The admission plan we've put together for you includes a free room in the cottage, meals in Covenant Kitchen, the use of a renovated pickup truck, and the moral support of all of us in this room."

Though he had not said a word, DeSean appeared to be glued to Don's every word as he sat forward in his chair and listened attentively.

Next, Keith spoke. "The five of us refer to ourselves as the Barnabas Brothers. Do you know who Barnabas was in the Bible?"

The teen shook his head slowly and said, "No, sir, I don't."

I don't believe this, Josh thought. Only minutes before, while back at Sequoia Lodge, DeSean had been anything but polite with Josh. Sullen. Withdrawn. Aloof. Now, the teen's demeanor had totally changed.

"His name means 'Son of Encouragement.' Barnabas was a young man who was a great encourager to Paul, the author of many of the New Testament books. That's what we want to do for you. To encourage and strengthen you. We'll do this is by meeting with you every week."

Though Keith's smile was bright, the firm look in his eye seemed to convey that these meetings were non-negotiable.

Rod Eichman, seated next to DeSean, spoke last. "I'm here to offer you a warm invitation to Wright's Creek church. Many young people your age can't wait to meet you."

A look of puzzlement crossed the teen's face.

Nodding across the circle, Rod continued. "Josh has told the group great things about you." Reaching into his shirt pocket, the pastor retrieved a business card and handed it to DeSean. "Call me anytime if you need anything."

The teen accepted the card handed to him. "Thank you, sir. I will."

Are you kidding? Josh thought. Flabbergasted by the teen's Jekyll and Hyde behavior, the coach missed his cue for his part of the meeting. An awkward silence followed until Rod caught Josh's eye and nodded slightly toward DeSean.

"Oh, yeah," Josh said sheepishly. "My turn."

Everyone laughed.

"DeSean, I am glad to have you with me in the lodge. I hope you will make it your home for the next several months. One of my goals for you in the coming semester is to help you succeed academically. I'll be serving as your tutor. I hope we'll get to know each other well. Mr. Stuart Lassiter, one of our high school science teachers, will be your faculty mentor. He's a great guy, and he's excited to work with you. You'll meet him next week when you return from break."

DeSean flashed a brief smile in Josh's direction, and for an instant, the coach glimpsed a hint of sincerity. *This kid is starving for love*, Josh prayed silently. *Please, Lord, let him respond to Yours.*

Chief Lockhart was the last of the five Barnabas Brothers to speak. "DeSean," Trent began, "I hope you realize you've received a second chance through the kindness of the men assembled in this room. We believe in you. We will do everything we can to help you succeed, but we expect you to give your best throughout the next few months."

DeSean, acting like a perfectly mannered teenager, now looked like a frightened little boy. His face had taken on a strange pallor. From where he sat, Josh saw fear in the teen's eyes, but couldn't make sense of the cause.

A few of the men made additional comments after Trent concluded his remarks, and they gave DeSean their business cards, all containing their cell numbers. One by one, the men stood, their posture signaling the meeting's end.

Stepping from behind his desk, Don approached DeSean and put his arm around the teen's shoulder.

"Hey, guys," said Don, trying to catch the group before anyone left the office. "I'd like to pray for DeSean and our special group before we leave."

The four additional Barnabas Brothers formed a circle next to Don and DeSean. Following the older man's lead, they, too, put their arms around each other's shoulders. Josh found himself standing next to DeSean. The coach was surprised to feel the teen lean toward him a bit when he placed his arm over the boy.

"Dear Lord," said Don, his voice earnest and strong. "We thank You for DeSean Matthews and his presence here at Timothy House. We thank You also for the fellowship and friendship of those of us gathered in this room this morning. Equip us, like You did Barnabas, to be encouragers of one another and especially of DeSean. Give this special young man a sense of purpose and direction. Help him see and understand how very much You love him. As the great repairer of the breaches in our lives, we ask that You redeem the circumstances of DeSean's past. We know You have a plan and a purpose for his life. Show it to him in ways too unmistakable to ignore or pass off as chance or circumstance. Give us all Your love, joy, and peace. Amen."

After brief goodbyes, the Barnabas Brothers disbanded and left Don's office. Josh and DeSean were the last to leave.

As they reached the doorway, the teen turned back to Don. "Mr. Fielding, sir," the boy stammered as he worked to get out what he wanted to say. "I know all of you must think I'm a total loser, but I want to be a better person. Thank you for all you're doing for me. I promise I won't let you down."

Josh stood behind the teen, his mouth gaping. *Where did that come from?*

Don smiled and approached DeSean. "Thank you for saying that. We want you to remember that God, your Heavenly Father, loves you more than you could ever imagine and will *never* give up on you. Don't ever forget that." The director wrapped the tall boy in a bear hug as a holy hush fell over the office.

As Don met Josh's eyes over DeSean's shoulder, the coach saw tears glistening.

———

Walking back from Sanctuary Hall, the coach and teen shared small talk. Maybe it was his imagination, but Josh sensed a change in the boy's spirit during the meeting. As the path wound around a small copse of trees, Max Smith's Honda came into view outside the stone and timber cottage. The engine exhaust created a hazy cloud in the chilly morning air.

Nearing the car, Josh stopped and turned toward DeSean. "I'm glad you're a part of our Timothy House family, and I'm looking forward to getting to know you. He clasped DeSean's shoulder, slightly squeezing it.

"Thanks, Coach Hastings," said DeSean. "You too."

"I'm here for you, buddy," Josh said warmly.

The teen looked over at him. "I know that, sir. Thank you," he said, with as much sincerity as Josh had ever heard in the young man's voice.

While DeSean climbed into the car's front seat, Josh greeted Mr. Smith and waved a final goodbye.

As the car drove down the drive toward the front of the Timothy House campus, Josh smiled to himself.

Lord, You are surely up to something good.

CHAPTER
18

Stuart Lassiter glanced up at the clock hanging on the wall beside his office door. An administrator from a former school had told him the location was helpful in managing one's time.

Ten more minutes, he thought, as he walked to a nearby file cabinet to retrieve a notebook atop it. Stuart was in his first year at Timothy House, although not his first as an educator. Now forty-three, he'd been in the classroom for almost twenty years. As he looked out the window of his third-floor office in Sanctuary Hall, the science teacher reflected on his family's move a few months ago to eastern Tennessee. Life in a large, midwestern city had left Stuart and his wife, Hannah, frazzled and worn out. His last principal, at a large public high school in Illinois, wasn't especially interested in building bridges with his faculty members. The man's practice of leaving teachers to fend for themselves generally left Stuart feeling abandoned and defensive, especially with contentious students and parents. The science teacher did his best to ignore the lack of administrative support and threw himself into his work, trying to make his science classes fun and exciting.

However, after one of his sons experienced a harrowing bullying episode in middle school, and after Stuart's principal left him high and dry over a disagreement in classroom policy, Stuart realized it was time to leave. Never again would he leave his children in an unsafe school environment nor compromise his personal beliefs for political expediency.

Stuart was delighted to be at a school with an outspoken commitment to bettering the lives of its students. He relished this new opportunity to work at the same school his sons—Ryan, Paul, and Tim—attended.

Daughter Sara was still at home. Their children especially enjoyed tromping through the several acres surrounding their home on the outskirts of Robbinsonville.

DeSean Matthews was due to arrive at his office in four minutes. Last week, Don Fielding had asked Stuart if he would serve as a faculty mentor for the teen and provided information about DeSean's background. Don had handpicked Stuart for this assignment because of the thoughtful questions Stuart had posed during the recent new-faculty orientation. Perhaps the teacher and the teen, both newcomers, could support one another during their first year at Timothy House.

Movement in the office doorway caught Stuart's attention. He looked up to see DeSean Matthews standing in the hallway, looking as if he wanted to either cry or run away.

"Hello, DeSean," said Stuart, rising from his chair. Motioning with his arm, he continued, "Please come in and have a seat."

As DeSean entered and sat before the teacher's desk, Stuart closed the office door. While settling back in his chair, Stuart noticed DeSean still looked uncomfortable. *We'll have to do something about that*, he thought, then plunged into what he hoped would be an inspiring chat.

"So," Stuart began, "Mr. Fielding tells me you're our newest senior at Timothy House."

"Yes, sir." The reply was flat and uninterested.

"Tell me a little about yourself. What are your favorite subjects? What do you like to do in your spare time?"

DeSean looked at his shoes for a minute. As he raised his head, Stuart was relieved to see that the teen met his gaze squarely. *Well, that's a start.*

"I don't have a favorite subject. School's been kind of hard for me. Just trying to get through this part of my life and on to the next."

"Fair answer," said Stuart, watching the boy for his response. Deciding to take another tack, the teacher commented, "I hear you are the newest basketball team member. Congratulations!"

DeSean's face reddened, and a shadow of a smile crept over his face. *We're getting somewhere, at least to a subject he likes*, thought Stuart.

"Coach Haliday told me you're one of the best talents he's seen in a long while," continued the teacher.

"Thank you, sir, though I'm not sure about the truth of that statement. The coach has only seen me play once."

Honest, and either humble or discouraged. Maybe it's too soon to tell, Stuart thought.

"Well, you impressed him—enough to offer you a position on the team. Coach Haliday doesn't give out those jerseys to just anybody. Anyway, Mr. Fielding suggested a plan we think will help you succeed and graduate with your class in May. You and I will meet three times a week while classes are in session: Mondays, Wednesdays, and Fridays. Later in the afternoon is better, but because of basketball practice, that might not be a convenient time for you."

"Uh, you're right," DeSean stammered. "Practices are usually from four until six every afternoon in the preseason and from four until five three days a week once the season begins."

"I see," said Stuart, grabbing his desk calendar. He flipped to the pages for the upcoming months. "Do you have any open spots in your class schedule?"

DeSean pulled out a crumpled piece of paper from his jeans pocket. Unfolding it, he studied it for a few minutes. "I have a free slot from one until two forty-five every day, right before my last class."

Stuart rubbed his chin, considering his teaching schedule. "That might work . . ." He shuffled through a stack of documents until he found what he was looking for: his weekly schedule. "Bingo," he said, smiling at DeSean. "Looks like that will work. Today's Tuesday. Why don't we start Monday? That will give you the rest of this week to adjust to your classes and find your way around campus. Know that I'm here to help you, though Mrs. Bronson, the librarian, will handle most of the subject tutoring or else a senior peer student who volunteered to help you.

"You may not know it, but I'm new here, too, DeSean, and I could use a friend. I want to use our time each week to discuss whatever you'd like. If you hit any snags or run into problems on campus, those visits will be the time to tell me about them and help you figure out a solution. How does that sound?" Stuart prayed the boy would accept the plan.

Again, the direct gaze. "I think that sounds good, sir," said DeSean, this time sounding more polite than he had the entire time he'd been in Stuart's office. The teen's next comment caught Stuart off guard. "Why are you doing this?"

"Well, first, because Mr. Fielding asked me to." Stuart wanted to be forthright with the young man and not sugarcoat anything.

"Could you have told him you didn't want to do it?"

"Yes, I could have. Mr. Fielding is not a dictator. I've chosen to spend time with you."

"Is there another reason?" the teen asked, this time sounding timid, like a boy far younger.

This break in conversation was what Stuart had hoped for. "Once upon a time, I was a boy of seventeen. My family was extremely dysfunctional, and I had little support at home. I know how hard it is to try to make it on your own. Maybe, in time, you'll see we have your best interests at heart here at Timothy House. I pray God will teach you many wonderful things as a student here."

DeSean soon leaned back in the chair as the science teacher talked. If body language were a teller, Stuart believed the first encounter with this wounded young man had gone well.

"Is there anything else you want to know?" Stuart asked, bringing the conference to a close.

"No, sir," said DeSean. The boy stood.

"Well, have a good day, DeSean," Stuart said, extending his hand across the desk.

Surprisingly, the boy took it. "Thank you," he said, turning to leave. After opening the door to Stuart's office, the teen turned back and said, "I'll see you soon, sir."

"Take care, DeSean."

While he watched the boy walk down the hallway, Stuart knew only the Lord Himself could provide the care DeSean so desperately needed.

CHAPTER
19

Keith checked again to ensure his bag contained all he needed for the Tentmaker's Project retreat. *How can it nearly be the end of November,* he thought. Keith smiled, realizing how much he had looked forward to this special student weekend. As he zipped shut his duffel bag and slung it over his shoulder, his smile widened, thoughts of Abbie filling his mind. This weekend away with the four new students selected for the Tentmaker's Project would provide another chance to spend time with his fiancée in another school setting. Stopping only to lock his front door, he remembered how Abbie's arrival at Timothy House five months ago had seemed natural, like slipping one's foot into a shoe that fit perfectly. *I hope the road ahead for us will be equally so.*

In less than ten minutes, Keith reached the front steps of Covenant Kitchen. As he rounded the side of the building, he saw Chuck Hawthorne and Lance Tate talking on the front porch. The remainder of the Project sponsors and mentors gathered around the four students selected for the program. Just as Keith was about to step onto the porch, a familiar voice caused him to stop and turn around. It also made his heart skip a beat.

"Hello, Keith," said Abbie, her face flushed with what Keith hoped was the excitement and joy of seeing him.

Keith beamed at her. "Hello, beautiful," he murmured, not wanting the others to hear his remark. Although their wedding date was six months away, he found it more and more challenging to be without the woman he had come to love so dearly.

The blush on Abbie's face deepened. "Stop it," she said playfully.

Bounding up the stairs, Abbie stepped ahead of Keith and joined the group gathered around the students. She seemed as if she needed something to divert her attention.

Keith followed her cue and headed over to greet Chuck and Lance.

Keith drove one of several eight-passenger vans which Timothy House had purchased a few years earlier, expressly for trips like this one. Along with him rode Lance, Parker, John, and Tentmaker's Project students Andy Beason and Davis Landrum. Although a committee had voted for the selection, Keith felt a small pride in these outstanding young men who were also on his basketball team. Ever since meeting Andy, the teen reminded Keith of his late son, David, the Timothy House student's resemblance to him uncanny. As such, Keith had made it a point to invest in the young man's life and had come to admire and respect the student.

Chuck drove the second van. Passengers in this vehicle included Don and Doris, Abbie, and the two female Project selectees, Julie Adams and Heather Phillips.

The trip to Craggy Bluff took over two hours, including two pit stops and sitting on the highway for twenty minutes while police cleared traffic after a three-car pile-up. By the time the two vans pulled into the parking lot of the Koinonia Fellowship Church, the sun had already set. The church's lights blazed against the dark, chilly November night. A small crowd stood near cars parked in front of a building. As the vans pulled up, a figure from the group stepped forward.

"Don," a man called out as Don Fielding exited the second van.

"Thompson," Don replied, equally as enthusiastic.

A large-framed man with long hair and a bushy beard stepped into the beam of the van headlights as he greeted Don. The two men hugged like long-lost brothers, drawing back to look at one another and guffawing. By the time the men finished their lengthy greeting, the occupants of both vans were out of the vehicles.

Don turned back to all from Timothy House who had made the journey to Craggy Bluff. "Friends," he called out, "this is my good friend, Thompson Manning, the pastor here. He and I go back many years."

"To the Dark Ages," the good-natured minister shouted out as the others laughed. From what they could see, he looked more like a lumberjack. His plaid flannel shirt and quilted down jacket only added to the illusion.

"Welcome," continued Thompson as he gestured toward the door to the Fellowship Hall. "Come inside. Let's get you all out of the cold."

In a short time, the group assembled in a combination gym and meeting space. The small group of Koinonia members exchanged greetings with the visitors of the Tentmaker's Project.

"Folks, welcome," said Thompson after clinking a spoon on the side of a small glass.

The room instantly quieted.

"All at Koinonia are delighted you're here in Craggy Bluff this weekend. Our church is happy to have this opportunity to partner with Timothy House in this Tentmaker's Project retreat weekend."

Throughout the next several minutes, Thompson introduced the various members of his congregation who would house members of Timothy House in their homes. During this time, he also distributed a sheet of paper containing the same information.

After everyone had a copy of the paper, the pastor continued, "If you will, please bow your heads while I ask the Lord to bless our food and this weekend."

A hush fell over the group.

"Dear Lord," said Thompson, "we thank You for this day and this opportunity to share Your love and hospitality with these friends. Thank You for bringing them safely to us. We ask for Your special blessing on these four new members of the Tentmaker's Project. May You show Yourself to these young men and women in a real and personal way during this weekend. We thank You for the hands that prepared this food and ask that You use it to nourish our bodies as we seek to do Your work. In Jesus's name, I pray. Amen."

Delicious smells filled the air as the blessing ended. Soon, all were seated in a previously unnoticed area. Portable partitions cordoned off a section of the fellowship hall into a cozy space. Candles gleamed from small centerpieces on each round table. White cloths draped the tables, and red-checked napkins stood in front of each chair. Filled glasses of water and tea waited at each place setting.

No sooner had everyone taken their seats when the church's hospitality committee appeared. Donning fall-colored aprons, the ladies carried plates heaping with steaming chicken pot pie, mashed potatoes, herbed green beans, and hot rolls. A small salad plate containing a mixed fruit medley sat beside each place setting. Warm slices of homemade chocolate pound cake followed, topped with scoops of vanilla ice cream.

Before long, the meal was over. The Timothy House visitors shared hearty thank-yous with the hospitality staff. After pulling on their coats and jackets, the group returned to the vans. Within an hour of leaving the church parking lot, the twelve members of the Tentmaker's Project were delivered safely to their respective hosts' homes.

Doris, Don, and Keith were guests of Marge and Harvey Stallings, an older couple in Thompson's congregation. Their home was simple yet comfortable, and it was evident Marge had gone to great pains to ensure her guests would have everything they needed. After taking bags to their rooms, the couple invited their guests for a visit in the home's den. After only a few minutes and feigning sleep, Keith excused himself.

Once in bed, it took a while before Keith could close his eyes to sleep. Thoughts of Abbie filled his mind. This weekend's retreat would be one of the first opportunities for them to serve together, side by side, as Timothy House staff. Everyone in their group knew the two were engaged, and Keith was mindful that many eyes would be watching them. Although he desperately wanted to spend time alone with Abbie, his heart was more concerned that his actions, and hers, were pleasing to the Lord.

"Guide us through this weekend," he whispered. "Help us be an example of what a God-centered relationship looks like. Please help me be the godly leader Abbie needs. Mainly, Lord, may all we say and do honor Your name. Amen."

After sending his prayer heavenward, Keith turned over and fell sound asleep.

CHAPTER

20

The Tentmaker's Project team gathered early Friday morning in Fellowship Hall. If yawns were any indication, some were still trying to wake up. However, from the laughter and upbeat conversation, it sounded to Keith like everyone in their group slept well and had pleasant experiences with their host families.

The visitors from Timothy House didn't have to wait long for the Koinonia team. As they had the night before, the church's hospitality committee again donned their signature aprons to offer a hearty breakfast. Pans of sweet rolls, eggs, cheese, sausage wraps, orange juice, and coffee greeted them. The tables quickly filled as adults and students made their way through the food line.

Once everyone was seated, Thompson stood in the middle space between the tables in front of a microphone on a stand, then took the mic from its holster. "Good morning," he said, waiting until the conversation died and he felt like he had the group's attention.

"Good morning," was the response.

"I hope all of you had comfortable beds, a restful night, and sweet dreams."

As Keith sat with the group, he was drawn deep in thought as he tried to reclaim snatches of a dream about Abbie he had had the night before. The soft applause of some in the group broke Keith out of his reverie. Thompson laughed. "Glad to hear. Let us pray." Everyone bowed their heads as the pastor blessed the food and their plans for the day. As soon as his "Amen" sounded, the eating of breakfast commenced in earnest.

The hospitality committee stayed busy refilling beverage glasses. Several in the group filled their plates a second time from the buffet line.

After a sufficient amount of time, Keith stood and clanked his spoon against his ceramic coffee mug. Once he had the group's attention, he took the mic.

"Before we get started this morning, let's give a warm Timothy House thank-you to the hospitality committee."

Applause rang out in the fellowship hall. A few of the ladies blushed while others waved shyly.

"I also want to thank Pastor Thompson for all you've done to make sure this weekend is a success."

Thompson beamed broadly and raised a hand as more clapping followed.

"Today will be a special day. This morning, we'll spend time with Elton and Summer Tidwell, the owners of Posie's, a local art gallery a few blocks from here. As small business owners, they'll have a wealth of information to share with you.

"Lunch will be a treat at Hungry Jack Café. Known for its barbecue specialties, you'll find something delicious on the restaurant's menu. After lunch, we'll walk two doors down to one of Craggy Bluff's retail treasures, The Nail Head, a hardware store owned and operated by Mr. Gurney Tompkins. He also supports local artists at his store. One of them is his cousin, Willow Dean Birdsong, who's a potter.

"Mid-afternoon, we'll go to the warehouse where the magic of throwing and firing pottery happens. You may even get a turn on the wheel."

At this, two of the Project students high-fived each other.

"We'll gather back here at five thirty for dinner. I hear another generous group from the Koinonia congregation will serve tonight's delicious meal. Today's activities will end with a discussion session with four businessmen also serving with the Tentmaker's Project. You'll hear their stories and hopefully glean useful information from them."

After checking his watch, Keith glanced back up at the group assembled. "You've got about fifteen minutes before we leave. Don't be late."

Summer and Elton were waiting on the sidewalk when the vans pulled up. The Timothy House team made its way into Posie's a little after nine o'clock. Keith had purposefully set this start time with the Tidwells because it would offer them close to an hour before their regular retail day began. Once the last of the visitors was inside, Elton locked the front door. Settling on an open space on the gallery floor, the program sponsors formed a semi-circle around the four students—Andy, Davis, Julie, and Heather. The Tidwells now stood at the front of the store with Keith beside them.

"Folks, can I have your attention?" Keith began, clapping his hands together a few times. At this, the chatter died down.

"We are thrilled to be here this morning at Posie's Gallery. To my right are Summer and Elton Tidwell, who own and manage the shop."

Polite applause greeted the owners. The Tidwells smiled slightly. Summer raised a hand in greeting.

"The Tidwells," continued Keith, "were the first business sponsors to join our program. They possess a wealth of knowledge about running a small business. Without further delay, I will turn it over to Elton."

Keith stepped over to join the group from Timothy House, turning back to face the speakers.

"Welcome to Posie's and Craggy Bluff," Elton said. "Summer and I are delighted you're with us today." He peered at the students, looking each in the eye before continuing. "It's especially interesting that you would want to learn not only about our craft as potters but also a little about the ins and outs of running a business. One aspect of the Tentmaker's Project that impressed Summer and me is that the practice of apprenticeship is a component of the program. Can any of you tell me what an apprentice is?"

Davis Landrum raised his hand.

"Yes, sir," said Elton, pointing toward the teen.

"It's a program," explained Davis, "where you learn how to do something—like making pottery or building furniture—by working with someone who performs that skill for a living. Apprenticeship is more about hands-on experience and less about book-learning."

Looking toward Timothy House's head of school, Elton ventured, "Wow, Don." He then nodded to Davis. "I couldn't have said it better myself."

Don turned his gaze toward Davis, raising his chin and signaling a silent attaboy through his smile.

Davis, seemingly pleased he had answered well, returned the nod to his administrator and then turned his attention back to Elton.

"I learned how to make pottery by spending time with my grandmother. We named the shop after her. Much of what I know about the wheel and glazing and firing pottery I learned from my Posie. By the time I was fifteen, I had made pieces for sale and even received a few commissions, requests by paying customers to make a certain item for them."

Somewhere during this exchange, Keith noticed Abbie standing at the back of the group. She looked lost in thought. Once or twice, he saw her attention drawn to a particular painting nearby.

"Now, I'm going to let Summer do some of the talking."

The sound of the man's voice drew Keith's attention back to the group.

"Well," she began, "we're delighted you're here. Elton's in charge of what we make—type of item, size, color, glaze finish, and quantity. Though I'm also a potter, my attention was captured years ago by how artisans market and distribute their work. No matter how good a product may be, if the rest of the world doesn't know about it, you probably won't sell much of it."

Gesturing around the gallery, Summer continued, "You can see different merchandise displayed in various parts of the shop."

The items in the gallery ranged from felted wool pieces, to paintings in multiple mediums, to hand-turned wooden bowls and objects, to the pottery of various local artists. Gift-type, manufactured items—greeting cards and knickknacks—completed the retail mix.

Summer gestured toward an open doorway behind her. "Let's go in the back of the store where we'll talk a little about sales and distribution."

The antennae of Keith's heart told him that something was bothering Abbie. Knowing Summer would be talking to the group for at least another twenty minutes, Keith walked to the far side of the gallery.

For now, Abbie was his primary concern.

CHAPTER
21

Abbie had been among the last in the Tentmaker's Project group to enter Posie's. Not wanting to call attention to herself, she found a place along the gallery's far wall near the framed art. Though she didn't believe in déjà vu, Abbie had the same sensation one sometimes has when reliving a dream. This store was where she first laid eyes on Keith and Don. How could she have known where that chance meeting would lead? How strange to stand in the same place today with Keith's engagement ring on her finger!

From across the room, Keith stood in front of the student group and sponsors. An enormous sense of pride filled her as she watched him do what he did best—encourage others and help them reach their full potential. *I hope Don knows what a fine man Keith is*, she thought as a group of paintings nearby captured her attention.

As Elton and Summer welcomed the students and sponsors of the Tentmaker's Project, Abbie found herself lost in thought. Last summer, during her week's retreat at The Resting Place, she had driven into Craggy Bluff and spent a wonderful afternoon exploring the town. Posie's was one of those stops. Abbie recalled how she had hidden behind a display rack to peer at Don and Keith. In fact, Keith and Abbie had made eye contact that day as he and Don had left the store. His deep velvet blue eyes captured her from the moment she saw them. *Sad eyes*, she'd told herself that day. Now, those eyes sparkled with joy, in part because of her. *Oh, what a difference a year makes*, she thought, touching a price tag on a painting that had suddenly captured her attention.

Keith's hand on her shoulder caught Abbie off guard, and she jumped. She turned to face him. "You scared me, silly." Her smile was bright and inviting.

"I've been watching you, ma'am, from across the room," he began.

"Oh really, sir," she teased. "Did you think I was in distress?"

"I couldn't be sure," Keith said, and though his tone was light, the look in his eyes told Abbie that he was worried about her.

"I'm wonderful," she began, then waved a hand toward the space around them. "I've been traveling down memory lane to last summer. I've never forgotten that day."

For a few seconds, Keith didn't say a word. He appeared to be concentrating on some thought, as if trying to fit the last piece of an intricate puzzle together. Suddenly he exclaimed proudly, as if he'd won the winning card in a bingo game, "*This* is it. *This* place is where I saw you!"

"What do you mean?" Abbie exclaimed, still clueless about Keith's train of thought.

Looking sheepish, Keith tried to explain his comment. "Ever since we met, I've had this sense that I knew you somehow. I hadn't seen Joe since our college years, so I knew it wasn't with him. Even when we *officially* met at Don and Doris's home during Camp 4Ever, I still couldn't quite put my finger on it." Keith's eyes twinkled with delight.

He stared at Abbie for a long moment as if sizing her up. Finally, in a comical voice, he said, "So you *knew* that night at the Manse that I was the one?"

Blushing a bit, Abbie took a step back. "I'm . . . I'm not sure . . ." she stammered. "I know that seeing you at Posie's and then meeting you a few weeks later at the dinner piqued my curiosity. That night, when you told me you knew Joe, I suddenly understood the mystery of the letter you wrote to him. Though I wasn't sure how, I had an uncanny sense that I would get to know you better."

Keith took Abbie's left hand in his. Running a finger over her engagement ring, he murmured, "I'd say you've definitely gotten to know me better."

"You *could* say that," said Abbie coyly. She hoped her smile and the look in her eyes conveyed all the love and devotion she felt for the man, but she couldn't adequately express it at that moment.

Suddenly, she became aware that the students and program sponsors were nearby. To keep her emotions in check, Abbie changed the subject. Turning toward the side wall of the gallery where the paintings were displayed, she drew Keith's attention to one in particular.

"Look at this fabulous painting," Abbie said, pointing to a detailed landscape nearby. "I can barely take my eyes off it." Two figures, a man and a woman, stood in the foreground, their backs to the viewer, facing a ridge of mountains rising in the background. The couple stood in shadow as if enveloped in semi-darkness. Their attention seemed fixed on the road that stretched before them, one that became smaller and narrower as it wound its way through the mountains, finally disappearing over the top of one of them. Light had been skillfully employed by the artist to illuminate the towering peaks.

Abbie stood silently and allowed Keith to inspect the painting. As he did, the group from Timothy House followed the Tidwell's through a doorway into the back of the shop.

Finally, unable to contain her excitement, Abbie stepped forward and pointed to a price tag beside the picture's frame. "Did you notice the title of this painting?"

"No," said Keith, seeming a bit confused by this impromptu exercise in art appreciation.

"*Higher Ground*," she replied. "Can you believe that? It perfectly captures our relationship."

"I'm not following you."

She made a fist and playfully punched her fiancé in the arm. "Silly . . ." Her voice trailed off as a laugh rose in her throat. "Notice how dark the colors are in the foreground?" Tears suddenly flooded Abbie's eyes as she grew quiet.

"What's wrong?" asked Keith, taking Abbie's hand.

He waited patiently for Abbie to find the words she seemed as if she were trying not to say.

"The darkness . . ." Abbie fought to regain her composure.

Swallowing hard, she continued, "The darkness of how angry I still am at Joe. It comes over me out of nowhere." She clenched her fists as she blinked back tears. "I have to let go of this ball and chain of Joe's financial betrayal once and for all. I thought I'd forgiven him, but looking at the dark hues in the painting's foreground reminds me of the gloomy hold my unforgiving spirit still has over me."

Keith stepped closer to Abbie, placing his arm protectively around her shoulders. "Abbie, I still wrestle with forgiving the driver who killed my family. Some days, I feel like a dog, running back to the spot in the backyard where I buried a bone and am now digging it up again."

Abbie drank in his every word.

"I know all those platitudes about not forgiving others—that it's like drinking poison and expecting the other person to die. But honestly, I've had to bring my pain and anger back to the Lord time and time again."

Reaching over, he thumbed a tear from her face. Nodding toward the painting, Keith continued, "Not once has Jesus ever chastised me or shamed me for asking for help with my inability to forgive. Instead, it's been like He's gotten down on His knees right next to me, put His arm around me, and whispered to my heart, 'We'll do this together. I'll help you.'"

A slight laugh escaped from Abbie. Pushing back hair behind one ear, she said, "That's so beautiful, Keith, and so encouraging to know you struggle with this, too."

Keith pulled her closer.

Reaching up to wipe away more tears, Abbie continued, "I want to give all of myself to you when we marry. We can start fresh. Keith, please pray I can settle this matter within myself before our wedding day."

"I will, dear Abbie," Keith said gently, giving her shoulders a firm squeeze.

Dropping his arm, he turned back to scrutinize the painting. "So . . . tell me again why this painting reminds you of us?"

Like a museum curator proudly extolling the symbolism in a priceless seventeenth-century Vermeer, Abbie motioned toward the bottom of the painting. "That's where we were before we met, separated and lost in the darkness of our devastating experiences."

Moving her hand up slightly, she gestured toward the painting's upper composition. "Together," she said with a smile, "we're moving into the light of a new path on which God has placed us. He's moving us to higher ground."

When Abbie turned back to look at him, the tender look in Keith's smoky blue eyes told her he perfectly understood the comparison she'd been trying to make.

———

Laughter erupted from the gallery's back room.

"Higher ground, hum?" queried Keith.

"Yes," Abbie whispered and then moved toward the back room of the gallery.

"I'll be there in a minute," said Keith, before turning back to the painting.

Staring at the landscape, the knowledge that God had used the elements of color, perspective, light, and darkness to provide a visual representation of great inner turmoil overwhelmed him.

Stepping closer to the painting, Keith removed the sales tag. Carefully placing it in his pocket, he turned to rejoin the group.

22

Lunch at the Hungry Jack filled the bill for the famished group. The café's owner had a large table waiting for the visitors from Robbinsonville and even had printed small menus featuring two salad selections, a pair of entrée choices, and a duo of dessert options to expedite the meal's service quickly. Noisy chatter filled the small space as students and sponsors took their seats.

Within minutes, food and drink orders were taken and, soon after, the meals were served. As the Hungry Jack's customers satisfied their hunger, the room became quieter.

Keith wiped his mouth with a napkin, a feeling of satisfaction warming him. Across the table, Don and Chuck seemed to be enjoying their lunch. Comments from both the Timothy House Head of School and the patron who introduced the Tentmaker's Project to the school indicated that both men were enormously pleased with the retreat so far.

Every aspect of the retreat—from the food to the warm, welcoming homes where the students and sponsors stayed, to the visits with various business owners and artisans—was running without a hitch.

Twenty minutes later, the group headed out onto the sidewalk. Walking less than a block, they arrived at their next stop, the town's hardware store.

Keith held open the door of The Nail's Head as the group members filed through the entranceway. The tinkling of the bell against the door's glass pane was just as Abbie had described it from her visit to Craggy Bluff the year before. He peered through the front window and saw the Radio Flyer tricycle exactly where Abbie had said it would be—suspended above one of the front sales counters. Through the open doorway, Gurney was easy to spot—worn jeans held up by suspenders, a plaid shirt, and his trademark Atlanta Braves baseball cap. *This ought to be interesting*, Keith thought, as he stepped across the threshold of the hardware store.

Gurney stepped forward, his chest out and his head held high. "Welcome, folks," he began, his voice marked by a distinct drawl. "This here's The Nail's Head, as your leader, Mr. Fielding, probably told you. I've been running this here business for almost fifty years. I hear you're on this trip to our fair city to learn a little about running a business. There's lots of ways to do that, you know."

Gurney paused to survey the faces of the teens standing before him.

Waving a hand in the direction of the hardware store's shelves, he continued. "You could own a retail store like this one here, or you could work out of your home like my cousin, Willow Dean."

As soon as Gurney mentioned her name, his cousin stepped out from behind the main counter. Willow Dean was tall and slender, like a reed along a creek bank, with wiry silvery strands of hair plaited in a thick braid coiled atop her head. To Keith, she looked more like a school librarian than a potter.

Gurney brought his hands together in front of him and steepled his fingers. "Willow Dean's going to tell you about her pottery business. After that, Mr. Fielding told me you can look around the store and shop for a little while. How's that sound?"

Stepping closer to the group, the older woman picked up a small pottery dish from the counter. Holding it, she began, "I learned how to throw pots from an old woman who lived on the mountain near me." As she spoke, she looked wistfully at the bowl.

"I was about eleven years old. Miss Ella, as I called her, had seen a pottery demonstration at a local fair. One of the most important lessons I learned from Miss Ella was not to let looks deceive you. Although her small home was modest, she had what mattered most—family, good friends, her health, and a strong faith in God. She never married, and seemed perfectly content to live alone. An older brother lived in the clearing on the other side of the woods from her house, and he and his family did a good job of looking in on her and making sure she had what she needed. Though no one knows for sure, an inheritance from a family member brought her financial stability, leaving her free to pursue her passion for pottery.

"My mother knew Miss Ella and brought me with her one day on a visit to her home. I wandered into a spare bedroom she'd reclaimed as a studio, and in it, I found her pottery wheel. Well, Mother and Miss Ella realized I was no longer with them, and they searched through the house for me, only to find me staring at the wooden shelves along the sides of the room, brimming with bowls and vases, trays and small dishes this wonderful artisan had created. My mother told me not to touch anything for fear I would break something, but Miss Ella must have sensed in me a natural curiosity. I'll never forget how she picked up a small, white-glazed bowl. 'This is for you,' she said.

"Miss Ella told my mother that she would happily give me pottery lessons every week. There were very few lessons I missed over the next few years. By the time I was sixteen, I was selling my pottery in galleries throughout this part of Tennessee. A few years later, Miss Ella passed away. My family and I were shocked when a small truck appeared at our house one day with the wheel and the kiln inside it. The driver gave us a sealed letter Miss Ella had left with her lawyer, explaining that she was leaving her pottery equipment to me. That simple act of passing on what mattered most to her has led to a lifetime of enjoyment and purpose for me. My life's never been the same."

Keith was mesmerized by Willow Dean's story. Seemed the others were, too, as no one spoke a word.

"My advice to you," she said, "is to find something to do in this life that brings you joy and do it. Though money is certainly a concern, working at a job only because of the financial compensation is a rather shallow way to lead one's life." She pointed to the glass counter nearby. "Over there, you will find four bowls I made for each of you in this new Tentmaker's Project group."

The four students gasped in surprise. Keith smiled as he watched their unexpected reaction. *Perhaps they will learn some valuable lessons during this weekend*, he thought.

"Let these little clay vessels remind you that if you allow Him, God will use all in your life—even what you think may be your most glaring shortcomings or greatest failures—to fashion you into people who will live purpose-filled lives and bring honor to His name." Once she finished speaking, Willow Dean stepped back toward the side of the store.

Don stepped forward and turned to face his students. "What marvelous gifts! What do you tell Miss Birdsong?"

A chorus of thank-yous accompanied the applause.

"Ladies and gentlemen," Don continued as the applause died down, "Gurney has a special announcement for us. After he's finished, you'll have twenty more minutes to shop in the store, and then we'll head to the vans. We're due at the Tidwells' workshop by three."

Gurney waved a hand from behind the front counter. "Willow Dean and I enjoyed having you stop by today. As a way of saying thanks, all purchases made by your group will receive a ten-percent discount. Take your time and look around. You might find a few things to take home with you." Leaning over the top of the counter, he waved his hand toward the shelves beneath, stocked with an assortment of candies, like an emcee beckoning a stage curtain to open. "Don't forget to look down here for something to soothe your sweet tooth."

Activity in The Nail's Head picked up. Keith watched as the four students made selections around the store. The girls each chose small pottery crosses, slightly similar but with distinctively different finishes. Davis held a leather-fobbed keyring, while Andy decided upon a small camping flashlight. Moved as he had been earlier by the students' wonderment, Keith was pleased to witness the seeming care given to their purchases.

Gurney waited on customers who had entered the store as Willow Dean entertained questions from a few in the group.

Several of the Tentmaker's Project sponsors lined up, their arms filled with pottery bowls from Willow Dean's collection whose glazed ceramic finishes reflected the store's lights.

Keith caught Don's eye across the room and smiled. He wondered if his boss was pleased with the latest experience for the Tentmaker students. The lift of Don's chin seemed to indicate approval. Glancing over at Chuck, Keith felt validated as he, too, seemed to confirm the success of this outing with a thumbs-up and a grin of his own.

Ten minutes later, the students and sponsors said goodbye to Gurney and Willow Dean and headed out to their waiting vans, parked along the sidewalk in the next block. The drive to the Tidwell warehouse would take only a few minutes.

As he opened the driver's door to the van, the bright expressions on the faces of his passengers matched the sense he had about the new student program so far. It was all too easy, within the course of a school semester, to allow the routine of the everyday to consume a teacher's time and sidetrack the direction of a class. Glancing into the back of the van, Keith watched as Julie, Heather, Andy, and Davis talked excitedly with one another, seemingly oblivious to his presence. This experience of gaining a new perspective on the world beyond the gates of Timothy House was already bearing fruit.

As he climbed into the van, Keith thought, *Chuck's Tentmaker's Project idea is terrific.*

CHAPTER
23

The size of the Tidwell warehouse was impressive, especially considering that Posie's was a mom-and-pop operation. The gallery in town had a manager and two part-time employees who assisted with daily operations. Though Craggy Bluff was a sleepy little mountain town, Summer and Elton had established quite a reputation in the regional artisan community. Several galleries throughout the southeast carried the Tidwells' work.

Keith watched Abbie, who seemed captivated by the comments of the young woman who assisted Summer with applying glazes and firing the items.

"The heat of the kiln is what makes the pottery strong," the assistant said while leading the group over to the opening of a walled-off section of the warehouse. Peering into the large doorway, the female apprentice pointed to four large kilns, each looking like a large chrome, decagon-shaped tower.

Just like you, Lord, to have put each of us through Your refiner's fire, thought Keith.

As if she sensed his eyes upon her, Abbie turned and looked across the ample space, her soft peridot eyes capturing his in their loving expression.

"The finer the object," the woman continued, "the hotter the temperature of the kiln."

As the students asked a few questions regarding temperature and time required to fire various pieces, Keith knew the love he and Abbie shared had survived suffering's fiercest heat, yet emerging unlike pottery but as forged steel, strong enough to endure any adversities still ahead on the path of their lives.

Andy, Davis, Julie, and Heather enjoyed hands-on demonstrations with the pottery wheel. Summer provided each of the four with oversized canvas smocks, which looked more like aprons, to protect their clothing. Once tied up in their new garments, Summer and Elton led the students through a turn at the wheel. Surprisingly, Davis and Julie were the most adept at handling the clay.

Keith watched as each student experienced how quickly disaster can strike if one doesn't position the clay right or if the design under construction gets off balance. He joined with the laughter of the other group members and good-natured ribbing that followed each clayform disaster. While the lessons continued, memories of the night, only eight months earlier, when Keith had declared his love for Abbie, flooded his mind. Wryly, he remembered how that one declaration could have spelled disaster for them, like a shaped vessel disintegrating into a soggy mush on a potter's wheel. He silently thanked the Lord for keeping them together.

Though the Timothy House students tasted humble pie as their primitive clay creations fell apart on the wheel, their sponsors were happy to see how well they handled the foibles. The ability to laugh at one's own mistakes was a bonus lesson taught that day by the Tidwells.

Later that evening, the students and sponsors from Timothy House sat back at Koinonia, listening to Thompson Manning. He must have been telling one of his trademark jokes, because laughter bubbled up from several in the group.

Lance Tate, Chuck Hawthorne, John Benson, and Parker Goodwin were the speakers for tonight's program. Sitting next to them, Keith looked toward the four men and winked.

"Here we go," he said.

Standing up to quiet the group, Keith walked to the middle of the circle. "Folks," he began, "you're in for a real treat tonight. You'll hear four business leaders in various occupations share their insights on solid business practices and how they've integrated their faith into their professions. These men serve either on the school's board of trustees or the Tentmaker's Project board. They are committed to ensuring your futures are bright and that you have all the tools you need to succeed in the wider world."

Chuck Hawthorne was the first to speak, telling the group about his business consulting firm. Most of his time, however, was spent explaining how the Lord had given him countless opportunities to integrate his faith into his work.

"I would not be where I am today," he said, "if it were not for two older men in the Richmond, Virginia, business community who reached out to me in my early thirties and came alongside me as friends and business guides. Those two not only showed me the ropes in the business world but, more importantly, they helped me to grow in my faith. Tom, the older of these two gentlemen, taught me the importance of prayer and of making sure I ask for help from God first before asking others. Steve, the other friend, has modeled for me godly character—honesty, humility, and integrity—in the way he relates to his colleagues and customers."

Looking over at the four students, he concluded his remarks. "We are so proud of you and are excited you're a part of this new program. Know that the adults around you are eager to walk alongside you."

Keith joined in the round of applause that followed as Chuck sat back down. Thinking over the events of his professional life, Keith knew, without a doubt, he was where God intended for him to be. Working for a purpose greater than his own satisfied Keith, bringing meaning to his life as none of the years spent in pharmaceutical sales had ever done.

John Benson was next. "Once upon a time," he began, "I was a high school junior."

A few laughs filtered through the group. Keith chuckled to himself as he remembered his high school years and what a pivotal season it had been in his life.

"One of our neighbors, Dr. Kelly, was an internist. He was also a family friend, and he and his wife frequently visited our home. When he discovered I had an interest in the medical profession, he took me under his wing. He allowed me to shadow him for two summers. His nurses taught me the rudimentary elements of gathering a patient's vital signs—height, weight, temperature, and blood pressure. What Doc Kelly modeled for me during those summers is what I've set as the standard of care in my internal medicine practice—treat patients like I would want my family members to be treated."

Keith noticed that Andy and Julie, both interested in pursuing medical careers, leaned forward as if to grasp John's every word.

John continued, "Know that if any of you would like an opportunity to shadow me and my staff, you have a standing invitation to do so."

The students and sponsors clapped as John rose from the speaker's chair and sat again with the group. Keith knew that John's invitation to visit him at his office was not lost on Andy and Julie. He hoped that one day the two teens would indeed have the opportunity for John Benson to shape their medical careers.

Parker Goodwin then made his way to the front of the group. "My dad started Landry's Grocery when I was four years old. Seeing a need in the community for another grocery store, he wanted to provide a market where local farmers and ranchers could sell their produce and stock.

"An important facet of Landry's corporate philosophy is to improve the lives of others. Toward this end, we partner with Mountain Gleaners. Once a week, this company gathers all unsold produce, meat, and dry and canned goods near the end of their shelf life and distributes the food items to needy families in a tri-county area of this part of Tennessee."

Keith nodded approvingly, knowing full well the value of faith-based lessons that come from caring for others.

"Giving back to the community is of vital importance to all of us at Landry's," said Parker, looking earnestly into the faces of the young people before him. "If any of you are interested in interning with the grocery, I'd be honored to teach you the ins and outs of the grocery business."

As before, with Chuck and John, a hearty round of applause followed Parker to his seat. Davis Landrum seemed to clap the loudest. Keith knew of the teen's interest in the retail business as the teen's uncle owned a health food store in Knoxville.

Lance Tate was the last of the business mentors to speak. The group grew silent as he settled into his chair to begin his remarks. "Mr. Haliday may have told you how he and I have known each other since college."

Suddenly finding himself at the center of attention, Keith knew he needed to shine the spotlight elsewhere. What better choice than to aim the beam back at Lance?

"Do I even look old enough to have gone to class with this fellow?" said Keith, a look of mock disgust on his face.

With that, a series of chuckles rippled throughout the group, and as they died down, the attention turned once more to Keith's college mate.

"Service in the U.S. Army was my career path," Lance continued. He then explained how, through a college ROTC program, he discovered a fulfilling life's work that included a grueling selection process for service as a Green Beret, through twenty-nine years of military service, and his retirement at the rank of major general.

"One of the greatest lessons I learned while in the military was that supporting a cause greater than yourself can be incredibly fulfilling. Much of the rhetoric you hear from the world encourages you to focus solely on yourself, at all costs. While that may work for some, it isn't a satisfying way to go through life.

"Military service, though an excellent fit for me, is not for everyone. Find a career path to make a difference in this world. Be the best person you can be—in thought, word, and deed. This world is desperate for solid, principled leaders, especially in business. Commit yourselves to being stalwarts of honor, honesty, and integrity. Let compassion and humility be the garments you wear every day.

"The only way I've found true fulfillment is through a relationship with Jesus Christ. There came a point in my early twenties when I knew I needed to decide—my way or God's. Mine wasn't working well, so I gave God a chance. He's *never* let me down. As the Old Testament leader Joshua suggested, 'Choose for yourselves this day whom you will serve.' Give God the keys to your life," the general concluded in a quieter, more serious tone, "and He'll lead you where He wants you to go."

As Keith watched Lance return to his seat, he knew how fortunate Timothy House was to have a patron and supporter of the caliber of this major general.

Keith motioned for Thompson to join him at the front. "Students," Keith began, "I hope you were inspired by what you heard tonight from these four gentlemen.

The students broke out in whistles, whoops, and loud clapping, as Chuck, John, Parker, and Lance grinned.

Once the noise died down, Keith continued. "Would you please join me in thanking the Tidwells?"

The Timothy House students and sponsors gave an equally robust round of applause as they expressed appreciation for the artisans from Craggy Bluff. Summer blushed slightly, and Elton lifted a hand in greeting.

Once the noise died down, Keith continued, "This program offers you an opportunity, while in high school, to rub shoulders with business leaders, develop friendships with them, and begin thinking now, not someday far out into the future, about what you might want to do with your lives."

Putting an arm around Thompson's broad shoulders, Keith said, "Pastor Thompson's going to end tonight's program with a word of prayer."

Thompson stepped forward, bowed his head, and closed his eyes.

"Dear Lord," he began, "thank You for this day and especially for these business leaders—Summer, Elton, Gurney, Willow Dean, Chuck, John, Parker, and Lance—who have generously allowed us a glimpse into their lives and their hearts today. Bless these terrific young people from Timothy House—Andy, Davis, Julie, and Heather—and show them the path they are to take. You, Lord, instituted work for man to complete. We ask that You guide each of these students and make obvious to them the path for their life's vocation. We ask all this in Your Son's holy name. Amen."

Don and Chuck were standing in the parking lot when Keith exited the building.

"Keith," said Don, pride obvious in his voice. "Today couldn't have gone any better. Thanks for your hard work in coordinating all this. I am proud of you and the way this program has begun."

"Let me second that sentiment," Chuck added.

"Thanks, guys," said Keith, a bit bashfully. "I think what you saw today resulted from all the prayers we've said for the Tentmaker's Project."

"Amen to that," said Don.

The three men climbed into the van to join the other passengers. As Keith drove out of Koinonia's parking lot, he glanced up to see the cross on the church's steeple illuminated in the light of a full moon.

Lord, he thought, *thank You for constant reminders of Your faithfulness to me and to these students.*

CHAPTER
24

As Keith turned onto the drive leading up to The Resting Place, sunlight danced in and out of the trees, bearing promise of the beauty of the day. As the lake came into view, Keith spotted Grant Lake shrouded in a foggy veil. Folding chairs peeked out through the mist wafting up from the lake shore, evidence of Eric and Lane's hard work.

Once parked, Lance and Parker retrieved black cases from the van's open hatch. Both guitar players had brought their instruments. Though new to playing with each other, the two had found a few spare minutes to run through several selections. As the group found their seats, the men strummed the hymns "Amazing Grace" and "The Old Rugged Cross."

Julie, Heather, Andy, and Davis sat together. The girls seemed entranced by the lake while the guys murmured to one another. As the gentle strains of the time-honored songs continued, the sponsors joined them. The chilly morning air was invigorating. From across the lake, the fingers of the rising sun poked through the gauzy mist as it dissipated.

At eight-thirty, the service began.

A light breeze rippled across the lake's surface as Don offered a prayer.

Seated near the back of the group, Keith bowed his head, soaking in the serenity of this hour. Gratitude blanketed his heart for all the Lord had done throughout the weekend—developing camaraderie within the group, building bridges between the sponsors and the students, and deepening the spiritual commitments of all.

Afterward, Thompson led the group in singing two praise songs. Once the music ended, the pastor took his seat.

Keith once again stood before the group. "Before Thompson gives the message this morning, I've asked each of our Timothy House students to come forward and share Bible verses written by Paul to his young charge, Timothy."

As he returned to his seat, Keith well remembered the long hours Chuck, Don, and he had spent selecting the verses that would serve as the foundational statements for the Tentmaker's Project. The men had purposefully chosen scriptures that not only reflected the spirit of the school's namesake—Paul's young protégé, Timothy—but also would empower and equip the teens selected for the program with God's boldness and confidence. He could not wait to hear how these same life guides had impacted the hearts and minds of these four students.

Heather Phillips spoke first. Her voice, though quiet, was confident and sure. "First Timothy 4:12 says, 'Let no one look down on your youthfulness, but *rather* in speech, conduct, love, faith *and* purity, show yourself an example of those who believe.'"

Davis Landrum was next. "'For God has not given us a spirit of timidity,'" he read, "'but of power and love and discipline. Second Timothy 1:7.'"

Julie Adams was the third student to share her scripture. "'Be diligent to present yourself approved to God as a workman who does not need to be ashamed, accurately handling the word of truth.' Second Timothy 2:15."

Andy Beason was the last Tentmaker's Project student to stand and speak. "First Timothy 1:5 says, '. . . the goal of our instruction is love from a pure heart and a good conscience and a sincere faith.'" When he finished, the students sat together.

Thompson rose again. "The apostle Paul, as you know, considered Timothy a son. The two met while Paul was on the second of three, perhaps four, missionary journeys he would make. About fifteen years Timothy's senior, Paul saw in this younger man the hallmarks of leadership and integrity, character traits he rarely saw in those he met. Paul also found in his student a young man with an earnest, inquiring faith, determined to make a difference. That's the challenge I want to give to you today."

Looking directly at the four students, Thompson continued. "Each of you—Heather, Davis, Julie, and Andy—has just read a portion of God's Word that Paul wrote specifically for Timothy. Though he was probably a little over twice your age, he was nonetheless the student as he traveled with Paul, learning the ins and outs of his faith and how to defend it. Timothy's legacy is now yours. Heather, you read 1 Timothy 4:12, which outlined five ways believers are to be examples—in speech, behavior, love, faith, and purity."

Heather shyly tucked her chin a bit.

"Though written to the young, this verse is good advice for every believer in Christ. It covers the waterfront in terms of how you are to behave. Your words, your conduct, the actions of your heart, and how you live as a person of moral standing in a fallen world. I challenge you today to follow Paul's guidance: 'Set an example.'"

Thompson now moved his attention to Davis. "Your verse talked about timidity or fear not coming from God. It also explains what God gives us to combat fear—'power and love and discipline.' In some Bible translations, the term 'sound mind' is substituted for the word 'discipline.' As believers in Christ, God's Spirit lives within you. His power is available to you at all times. His love, though not a love we can adequately understand this side of Heaven, fills your hearts. That same love is what this old world so desperately needs. God's Spirit will also guard your mind and guide your thinking. Let Him do that every day."

Julie blushed as the pastor called her name.

"You read us 2 Timothy 2:15," Thompson said, "which spoke about a workman or student that does not need to be ashamed of their work. This verse is often used to encourage young people your age. I want to focus, however, on two other parts of that verse. In the opening statement of verse five, Paul said to be 'diligent' and 'to present yourselves approved to God.' Diligent means persevering or working hard at something, ensuring you get it right. It also means you will need to work on whatever you're attempting to do *daily*. Diligence is an ongoing action, never stopping. Making sure you're 'approved to God' means that God should be the one you look to for approval every day and not your best friend or the kids in your English class or popular culture around you."

Lastly, Thompson turned his attention to Andy. "Your verse, 1 Timothy 1:5, focuses on the three aspects of our lives that are guided by the love of God within us—'a pure heart and a good conscience and a sincere faith.' You cannot be pure, good, or sincere on your own. However, when you allow the Lord to guide your life, He'll equip you to live lives of purpose and meaning, which will positively impact others.

"Know that the adults around you today, sponsors of this program and administrative leaders of Timothy House, believe in you and are committed to helping you be the best young men and women you can be. We pray that this experience in this inaugural class of the Tentmaker's Project will be life-changing and inspire you to lead lives of service to others in Jesus's name."

As the music began, the students and adults rose. The relaxed, soft sounds of the guitars made the lyrics of the familiar hymn written by Frances Havergal even more poignant. Tears stung Keith's eyes as he sang the first two lines, "Take my life, and let it be, consecrated, Lord, to thee." This plea reminded him of the attitude that anchored Abbie's character, this woman he loved so much.

The words of the fourth stanza almost took Keith's breath away.

> *Take my will, and make it Thine,*
> *It shall be no longer mine.*
> *Take my heart, it is Thine own,*
> *It shall be Thy royal throne.*

Myriad memories flooded his heart as he thought over how the Lord had used all the pain and suffering of these recent years to mold Keith into the man he now was. His position at Timothy House fulfilled him in a way no other work had before. More recently, his relationship with Abbie had been an unexpected blessing, one he never thought possible. Bowing his head once more in surrender, he prayed, *Lord, You know I only want what You want for my life. Nothing more.*

As the strains of the guitars faded away, Thompson bowed his head. The others in the service did the same.

"Dear Lord," the minister began, "how grateful our hearts are for this special time You've given us this weekend. We thank You for these four students in this new Tentmaker's Project. We also thank you for the business partners who've agreed to walk alongside them and serve as guides in this endeavor. I ask for a special blessing on Timothy House School, its leadership, and its student body. Equip and empower these individuals to be Your salt and light in this very dark world. Give Heather and Julie and Andy and Davis a special sense of Your presence, and shine bright the light of Your divine guidance onto their paths. Let their lives, Lord, be consecrated, be made holy, and set apart for You. All this we ask in Your name. Amen."

God's peace blanketed Keith's heart as he and the others walked to The Resting Place from the shore of Grant Lake. The future God had prepared for him was here today—with his sweet Abbie, dear friends like the Fieldings and the Wyatts, and his rewarding work at Timothy House.

He knew beyond a shadow of a doubt that the Lord was leading him to higher ground.

CHAPTER
25

Although unsure of what had awakened her, Doris Fielding lay for a few minutes in the darkened bedroom, working to clear the cobwebs of sleep. Perhaps it was a subconscious thought about wishing their children, spouses, and four grandchildren could join them for Thanksgiving, only four days away. Though she and Don would miss them terribly, they would all be together for Christmas in a few short weeks.

Only yesterday, Doris and Don had returned from the weekend Tentmaker's Project retreat in Craggy Bluff. The long drive had offered Doris ample time to look through several of her favorite cookbooks she had brought. The turkey was in the refrigerator thawing, and Doris would begin the brining process later that morning. There was also the chopping and mincing of the many vegetables for the dishes she would prepare.

Suddenly, any lingering sadness about who would or would not be at their dining table disappeared as Doris became vividly aware she was not hearing her husband's telltale deep breathing. Reaching across the bed in the still-darkened room, she reached out to feel for him on the other side. Her outstretched hand only found a slight depression in the mattress where he once lay, the bedsheets cool to her touch. Don had a habit of waking at all hours of the night when consumed with matters of the school or of some student who needed help. Tonight, however, felt different.

How long has he been up? she wondered. Doris glanced at the digital clock on her bedside table. Two forty-seven. Now alert, Doris threw back the covers and wrapped herself in her robe. Once she stepped into her slippers, she crept into the hallway, the faint glow of a lamp downstairs beckoning her like a trail of breadcrumbs.

Quietly, Don's wife padded down the stairwell and followed the trail of light until she found it burning brightly from a floor lamp next to her husband's wingback chair. She smiled as she stood in the darkened doorway, watching Don's robed figure. He faced away from her, but his posture let her know his thoughts had taken him a million miles away. She watched him for a few minutes more and then entered the den. The movement as she sat on the sofa across from him caught his eye.

"Oh, hi, honey," he said sheepishly, lifting a hand in greeting. "I'm sorry to wake you."

"You didn't, actually," said Doris, pushing a wayward strand of hair back from her face. "I was going over recipes for our Thanksgiving luncheon in my mind. Then I discovered you weren't beside me and decided to come find you." She smiled tenderly at her husband and waited for him to tell her what was on his mind.

Doris learned long ago to allow her husband the space to choose his way of opening up. She had paid careful attention throughout the almost forty years of their marriage, carefully learning the steps of the dance of give-and-take required. Instinctively, Doris knew Don was grappling with some inner turmoil. As she watched him gather his thoughts, she realized he had been quiet for some months, only she had been too busy to see it. *Strange, the contrast light brings to the darkness*, she thought, waiting patiently to hear what her husband might share.

Finally, Don turned to face her. "I think it may be time for us to leave Timothy House." Once the words left his mouth, he looked relieved, like several hundred pounds had suddenly lifted from his shoulders. He sank back against his wing chair and waited for her response.

"Oh, Don," was all she could muster.

The striking of a grandfather clock from the front hall of the Manse sounded like a bell tolling in the small den. Three fifteen.

"People have always remarked that I'll know when it's time to retire," he said, pulling the shawl collar of his robe closer to his neck. "For the past few months, I could not get this thought off my mind."

Feeling guilty that she had not picked up on his angst before now, Doris said, "I apologize that I've been so busy this semester. I'm sorry I didn't notice you've been unhappy."

Don stretched out a hand in the dimly lit room. Leaning toward her husband, Doris instantly grasped hold, his warmth immediately making her feel safe.

"My plan worked," said Don, smiling slightly.

"Your plan?"

"Yes," he continued. "I didn't want to bother you with this until I worked it out myself."

"You know I'm here for you," said Doris quietly. "Always." Her voice trailed off as she waited anxiously to hear what he would share.

Don squeezed her hand and then let it go to pat his knee. "Come sit here."

Doris left the couch and sat at Don's feet. This place in the den was one of her favorite spots, her seated on the floor before him, her head resting on his knee, his hand gently stroking her hair. This was also where their most meaningful talks as husband and wife had taken place, especially during their thirty-two years at Timothy House.

Don lifted his wife's chin until she looked at him. "The time we've had together at Timothy House has been wonderful."

Doris nodded slightly, her eyes filling with tears as she so wanted to encourage and support her husband.

"For the past nine months, I've had this tugging in my spirit that God was leading me away from here, that perhaps it was time to pass the baton of leadership on to someone else."

"Keith Haliday?" Doris posed.

Don nodded slowly, his expression relaxing as if he had finally set down a backpack of great weight carried interminably within his soul.

"When Keith joined our staff almost two years ago, I found in him a confident, strong friend with whom I instantly connected. Although older, he reminds me of our Wilson."

Doris smiled, silently agreeing with her husband about the many similarities between Keith and their son.

"Then I remembered our school's motto. 'Establishing a Foundation of Faithfulness in a Faithless World.' Uncle Roger coined it when Timothy House opened its doors."

Doris's mind immediately went to the carved truss in the vault of the main dining room of Covenant Kitchen. She had walked beneath its words every day.

"Roger and Marie believed that living the Christian life was possible, even in a fallen world, and that students could learn this concept at this school," continued Don. "Although I share this belief, I've never found anyone who worked with me who seemed wholeheartedly committed to this concept. Until I met Keith.

"Everything you and I have done, Doris, while living in Robbinsonville, is to unconditionally love the students here as we keep our eyes focused on the three primary purposes for Timothy House: to build up solid young men and women in Christ and to equip them for His purpose in the world; to provide an excellent education, preparing students for the wider world; and to bind up the wounds of mind, body, and soul that might hinder our students, in any way, from realizing their full potential in Jesus Christ. That last purpose is the most important for our students, binding up wounds that only God Himself could heal. Keith is a man who has experienced this life-changing healing in his own life."

Doris nodded silently, her eyes brimming with unshed tears as she thought of the horrific loss of Keith's wife, son, and daughter.

"Although Keith's life is full of confirmations of the many ways in which God has healed his broken life, it wasn't until he met Abbie that I knew God's plan included a new family and a chance to start again."

"They certainly seem a match made in heaven," murmured Doris as she pulled herself onto her husband's lap.

Don wrapped his arms around Doris and drew her close to him as four strikes of the grandfather clock broke the stillness of the room.

As the last chime of the hour sounded, Don sat back in the chair. "Let's move to the couch. These old bones tell me we'll both be more comfortable."

Doris laughed as she stood, and together they settled on the nearby sofa. Don sat at one end, his wife nestling close beside him, his arm securely around her. Doris pulled the blanket from the other end and spread it over them to ward off the chill of the early morning in the old stone Manse this time of year. With her snuggled close beside him, Don continued to share why he believed Keith was the man to lead Timothy House into a new season of its history.

After what had only seemed like minutes, the chime of the old grandfather clock and the faint gleam of light outside the den windows signaled seven o'clock.

As Doris looked over at her husband, the soft glow of the floor lamp revealed certainty and confidence on his face, a look she had not seen in a long while. She knew, without a shadow of a doubt, that God had made clear to her beloved husband His next steps for continuing to establish His foundation of faithfulness at Timothy House.

As their conversation ended, Don and Doris bowed their heads and, with hands clasped, prayed to their Heavenly Father that He would confirm this same plan in Keith Haliday's heart.

Winter has arrived, thought Abbie, as she stepped out of her car. Drawing her jacket closer to her, she rushed into Timothy Hall, tiny puffs of air visible with each breath. Once in the building, she took the stairs to the third floor to meet Chloe Minton. While waiting outside the student's last class of the day, Abbie reflected on all the events since her leap of faith in coming to Camp 4Ever a year ago as a timid new counselor in Cabin Five. Bonding immediately with Chloe, one of her campers. Discovering she and Abbie had both come from dysfunctional backgrounds. Seeing Chloe months later at the Timothy House Christmas Pageant. Reuniting with Chloe this past summer. Chloe's unsettling disclosure during share time in the cabin. The meeting with Chief Lockhart and investigator Hayley Collins. The forensic interview with Monica Forster. Tim and Taylor Nunley's miracle of potentially having a new daughter in Chloe. The Nunleys' adoption process currently underway.

Though His ways were often mysterious, Abbie did not doubt God Himself had orchestrated these past sixteen months to bring Abbie and Chloe to this afternoon's visit. Abbie had been looking forward to this moment all day. Tim and Taylor had heartily approved Abbie's request to take Chloe for a walk around Serenity Cove before taking the girl home.

The clang of a bell signaled the end of the class period, pulling Abbie from her thoughts. Realizing she'd been leaning against the wall on the other side of the classroom, Abbie stepped across the hall to see Chloe the minute she walked through the door.

As soon as she did, the child's eyes lit up with delight. "Miss Abbie, Miss Abbie," she said, rushing over to where Abbie stood.

"Hey, Chloe," she said. Abbie wrapped the child in her arms and gave her a tight squeeze. "I've got a surprise for you," she continued as she straightened.

The child's eyes were wide with wonder. "What is it?"

"Well . . ." said Abbie, hoping to keep Chloe in suspense a little longer, as she knew the child liked surprises. "I talked to the Nunleys, and they said we can spend the afternoon together."

"Oh, goody," clapped Chloe, delight written all over her face.

"Let's put your backpack in my car, and then we can walk around the lake. I brought some bread so we could feed the birds. Would you like that?"

The child's head bobbed up and down, her dark hair moving with the motion of her head, her face like a china doll's.

Abbie didn't have to worry about what to say, as Chloe chattered incessantly from the classroom, down the stairs, and out to Abbie's car. Once Abbie placed the child's school bag on the back seat of her SUV and retrieved the loaf of bread, the pair headed out along the walkway that wound behind Sanctuary Hall and out to Serenity Cove, the lake on the back of the Timothy House campus. This spot, one of Abbie's favorites, was one of the first Abbie claimed as a peaceful place to retreat to upon her arrival at Timothy House.

As they walked, Abbie reminded Chloe to zip up her puffed jacket. Early December in the mountains of eastern Tennessee could be a chilly time of year. The last thing she wanted to do was send Chloe home with a runny nose.

Once they reached the lake, Chloe stood near the shoreline watching a gaggle of geese floating nearby. *Oh, if only life could be this simple and carefree*, Abbie thought. She watched with pleasure as the child reached into the bag of bread and brought out a slice. Tearing the bread into small bits, Chloe tossed them onto the water's surface. The geese paddled over immediately, snatching the soggy treats from the water before the next one could get it.

Chloe laughed at their antics.

Pulling out a few more slices, the girl tossed them onto the water. Continuing to watch her, Abbie silently prayed that these beautiful birds would help her convey what her heart wanted to share with this precious child. Abbie well remembered her childhood and the pain of abandonment she felt because of her mother's neglect due to alcoholism. She had only been a few years older than Chloe when she went to live with her Aunt Caty and Uncle Scott.

"Chloe," Abbie began. "How do you like being with the Nunleys?"

At this, Chloe turned her attention from the hungry geese to Abbie. The look on the child's face was like that of an angel. "I love it, Miss Abbie. It's the best thing that ever happened to me." Her smile was electric.

Abbie waited to speak until the knot in her throat lessened and the tears in her eyes evaporated. "That is such wonderful news. Many people have prayed for you, hoping the Nunleys could be your new parents."

"When I lived with the Hendersons, I had *Cinderella* hidden under my bed so they wouldn't find it. Every time I read it, I prayed for a fairy godmother to bring me a real family someday. I never stopped praying that God would do that in my life."

Abbie could hardly speak. She looked at Chloe and then patted the space on the bench next to where she sat. "Come sit with me for a minute, sweet girl."

As if sensing this moment was not to be missed, Chloe turned from the shore of the lake and sat next to Abbie. She looked up at the teacher with deep blue eyes glistening like sapphires in the afternoon sun.

"I love you, Chloe," Abbie began, her heart filled with the many emotions this precious child stirred within her. "You are such a special girl, who means a great deal to me."

At this, the child wrapped her arms around Abbie and hugged her tightly. Abbie returned the embrace.

"I love you, too, Miss Abbie," the girl said as Abbie held her close.

Stroking Chloe's hair, Abbie continued, "I want you to know that Mr. Keith and I are here for you. We will *always* be a part of your life."

Pulling back to see Abbie's face, Chloe exclaimed, "You're my fairy godmother, Miss Abbie!" Her smile was as bright as sunshine.

Abbie wasn't sure how to respond to this comment, and two geese chasing each other along the shore interrupted her thoughts.

Laughing softly, she replied, "Oh, Chloe. You know, there is no such thing as a fairy godmother. They exist only in fairy tales. Besides, God is the one who's in charge of this world and who makes the plan for our lives."

"Well," Chloe said, "He sure made a great plan for me."

"God's plans are *always* the best ones, Chloe," said Abbie, smiling down at this dear child.

A sudden gust of wind blew across the lake. Abbie and Chloe shivered.

"Oh, my," said Abbie, pulling Chloe up as she stood. "It's time to head home."

As the pair made their way back across campus to the car, Abbie knew without a doubt that God had answered a colossal prayer in this child's life. While Chloe buckled into the back seat, Abbie turned on the car, adjusting the temperature on the heater when she did. Once out of her parking space, she headed toward the front gates of Timothy House and out onto the main road, toward the Nunleys' home.

Glancing in the rearview mirror at Chloe, she thought, *How thankful I am, Lord, that the details of my life and Chloe's don't depend on the whims of a make-believe fairy godmother but rather are in Your very real, capable hands.*

Abbie and Keith arrived early at Lime Tortilla, where Drew had asked them to meet him. The waiter, polite and enthusiastic, directed the couple to a booth in the back corner of the restaurant. Abbie hoped it would be a quieter spot. Once the waiter placed the menus on the table, he left.

"I hope Drew's drive from Dallas went well," said Abbie, looking nervously across the room toward the front door. "What do you suppose is keeping him?" Abbie looked at her watch for the fourth time in as many minutes. Drew was twelve minutes late.

"He'll be here," said Keith, eyeing her with a suppressed smile and patting her hand. "He's a grown-up, and I'm sure the visit to the school went well."

"I know, I know," replied Abbie, trying to calm the storm of butterflies that beat their wings incessantly in the pit of her stomach.

Her son was on his way home from a visit to Dallas Theological Seminary. Drew had dreamed of attending seminary, but until recently, that aspiration had seemed as attainable to him as flying to the moon. That is, however, until Audry MacDonald.

Suddenly, from across the room, Abbie saw what looked like Drew. *Is that him? The five-day trip to Texas changed him somehow*, she thought. Making his way through the crowded restaurant, her boy, now a man, looked like an entirely different person. He seemed to stand straighter and taller, as if freed from some spell cast over his soul that had formerly crippled his spirit. She watched with delight as he approached. Once he reached their table, Abbie jumped from the booth to hug him.

"Hello, son," she exclaimed, throwing her arms around his neck. "I'm so glad you're home safely."

Drew kissed his mother on the cheek and returned the hug. "Me too, Mom," he said, sitting in the booth across from Abbie and Keith.

Keith reached across the table, and the two men quickly shook hands. "Welcome home, Drew," Keith said warmly.

"Thanks," replied Drew, settling against the seat cushion. Running a hand through his hair, he continued, "Sorry I'm late. It's been a long day. Ran into heavy truck traffic coming through Knoxville. I almost stopped and called to tell you I'd be late, but thankfully, I could thread my way through the needle of vehicles. Boy, I'm glad I stopped in Little Rock yesterday. A good night's sleep made a world of difference."

Picking up his menu, Drew stopped talking for a few minutes to make his selection. At that exact moment, their waiter appeared.

Once the dinner guests had ordered and a basket of seasoned tortilla chips and bowls of salsa and queso were before them, Abbie leaned forward in anticipation, like a child waiting for Christmas morning. "Well," she said, "don't keep us in suspense. How did the visit go?"

Drew sat silently for a moment, then sipped his iced tea. When he finally spoke, his eyes twinkled with excitement. "It was great! Mrs. Jefferson, the admissions counselor, couldn't have been more helpful. She scheduled all the appointments I requested."

At that moment, the waiter arrived with their orders and placed a large steaming platter of fajitas between Abbie and Keith, and a plate brimming with a steak chimichanga with Spanish rice and refried beans before Drew.

Keith asked if he could bless the food, and the three bowed their heads. Once the "Amen" was voiced, the trio reached for their forks.

As each at the table began to eat their meal, Abbie noted Drew's excitement, as he hardly touched his food before him.

"I had no idea you could cram so many meetings into a two-day visit," Drew said excitedly after wiping his mouth.

"Did you meet everyone you wanted to?" asked his mother.

"Did I ever," replied Drew gleefully, taking a long sip of his drink. "My first appointment on Monday was with my faculty advisor, Dr. Jeremiah Henry. He's also the head of the theology department. He looks like he's in his early sixties."

Drew reached for a tortilla chip and dipped it in the queso before popping it into his mouth.

Abbie looked at her son and smiled. Silently, she thanked the Lord that her son's long-cherished dream might be coming true. Despite Joe's constant belittling of Drew, the young man had overcome the discouragement and persevered. *Bravo, Drew*, Abbie thought.

"Tell us more," Keith prompted.

"Mrs. Jefferson's schedule said I was to spend only twenty minutes with Dr. Henry. It's hard to describe, but he's someone I felt like I'd known for a long time. He shared some stories about his struggles during his time in seminary. His honesty encouraged me to share how I'd always wanted to become a pastor, but Dad always squelched it. I've hardly told that to anyone before."

Abbie winced inside as she listened to Drew talk so candidly about the pain his father had caused. She still grappled with guilt, as she was at the moment, about having married Joe in the first place. Though she had chased this rabbit down this trail many times before, Abbie knew full well that without Joe, there would be no Drew. Looking at her precious son, Abbie knew the suffering and pain that they had endured was worth it in the end. They had each other. Abbie would not trade her son for anything in the world.

"By the time we finished talking," said Drew, "I'd been in Dr. Henry's office for an hour and a half."

"Impressive," said Abbie as she piled some peppers and chicken onto her tortilla. "How kind of him to spend so much time with you."

"I'll say. Dr. Henry even bought me lunch in the campus cafeteria," replied Drew before gulping down a large forkful of rice.

"Nice," said Keith.

Drew continued, "Afterward, Dr. Henry walked me to the admissions office for my afternoon appointment. He gave me his card." Looking like a child who had unwrapped a much-anticipated birthday present, Drew exclaimed, "He even gave me his cell phone number and told me to call him any time I needed him."

"I look forward to meeting Dr. Henry," said Abbie. A sense of gratitude filled her heart about how well the campus visit had gone. Though Drew would now be moving away, this mother could see God's hand at work. The knowledge that there would be good people in Dallas to continue molding her son into a godly person soothed her soul.

"Mrs. Akers is my contact in admissions. I took all the paperwork Mr. Gates gave me about Audry's gift."

Abbie smiled at the mention of her late friend's name. *Wouldn't Audry love hearing Drew tell this story?* The older woman had been such a dear friend to Abbie over the years, filling the emotional void left by her alcoholic mother and self-centered, dishonest husband. From his early elementary years, Drew became the apple of Audry's eye. The generous inheritance left to Abbie and Drew was a mute witness to Audry's largesse of spirit and her fierce love for the two.

"Mrs. Akers assured me that Audry's financial gift would more than cover the cost of tuition, books, fees, and housing for my seminary degree."

God, Abbie thought, *more evidence of Your provision.*

"Any luck finding a place to live?" said Keith after the waiter refilled their glasses.

"Not exactly," replied Drew, "but I have some promising leads. I met with a real estate agent on Tuesday who works closely with the seminary. Dan was the man's name. He picked me up at my hotel that morning and drove me by four apartment complexes within a five-mile radius of the seminary. The rates the agent quoted sounded reasonable."

"Terrific," said Abbie.

"Did Dr. Henry guide you on the degree path you might take?" Abbie continued before taking another chip from the basket. She dipped it in the queso and popped it into her mouth.

"Yes, he did," said Drew after wiping a spot of cheese from the corner of his mouth. "Since I'm unsure which direction I might want to take in ministry, Dr. Henry suggested I pursue a Master of Theology. Within each degree program, students have to focus on a ministry track within that niche of study. He felt interdisciplinary studies would provide me with a broad overview of topics while offering foundational courses that would benefit me regardless of the ministry path I take."

"That's wonderful," said Abbie. God had answered many prayers on her son's behalf.

"Well, it is wonderful," continued Drew, "but I still have to complete the admissions process. I'm scheduled to sit for the GRE and complete and file my admissions packet in January. The school requires each applicant to submit three personal character reference letters. Pastor Rod, Mr. Fielding, and my college history professor have offered to write them on my behalf. Mrs. Jefferson said I should hear about admission from the school by late April."

"You'll be busy, young man," said Keith.

"Sure," interjected Abbie, "but I know he's ready to dive in." She offered a bright smile to her son.

"Yes, sir, I am," replied Drew. Putting down his fork, he looked at his mother and her fiancé with a serious expression. He hesitated for a moment before continuing. "It's just that . . . I'm not really sure which direction I want to take once I complete my degree. I had this dream for so long, but I don't know about the rest of my life plan."

Abbie felt Keith's eyes on her. Turning to him, she sensed his asking her permission, a silent request to allow him to reassure Drew. A simple nod was the encouragement he needed.

"Drew," Keith began, "you don't have to have your life figured out today. You obeyed God and followed him through what looks like a door to seminary. Believe me when I say many people will never darken the door of a seminary class because they lack the financial means. Miss Audry's gift hasn't simply opened that door for you; it's knocked it right off its hinges. Your mom and I believe in you. God will show you the next step to take."

Drew leaned back and seemed to relax. Smiling slightly, he said, "I guess you're right."

"How about dessert to celebrate your successful trip?" Abbie offered.

Her son's smile immediately brightened. "Let's order their sopapilla, Mom," he said. "Remember how good it was last time?"

Less than ten minutes after ordering, the warm, powdered sugar-coated pastry sat in the middle of the table.

Before taking the first bite, Drew held up his fork in the air. "Here's to marching orders!"

Abbie and Keith raised their forks and returned the salute.

CHAPTER
28

Teencie was the first to arrive for work on this crisp December morning. After hanging her coat in her new office, she walked back to the enormous prep kitchen in Timothy House's dining hall. She went over to the large industrial sink, in front of which was a sizeable multi-paned window. Despite the chilly weather, the glow of a new winter's day bathed the world beyond the warm kitchen in a rosy hue. Standing there, she thought back over the past few weeks' events, still marveling about her new job. She could hardly believe all that had transpired since that morning only weeks ago when Don Fielding handed her his business card and told her he might have a job for her.

The appearance of two figures on the walking path caught her attention. As they drew closer in the early morning light, Teencie saw Charmaine Jenkins and Lynette Meeks, a cook, approaching Covenant Kitchen. The two women waved, little puffs of air appearing with their every breath.

Turning around, she went over to the coffee machine. Since organizing was one of her strong suits, one of the first revisions Teencie made in the kitchen was instituting several "systems," as she liked to call them, to make life easier and more efficient in Covenant Kitchen. One of these was to make sure she placed fresh coffee grounds—regular and decaf—in the filter compartments of the kitchen's large machine before leaving work each day. Then, all one needed to do was add the water, turn on the device, and voila! Freshly made coffee in a matter of minutes.

"Hey, Teencie," called out Charmaine's cheery voice.

"Morning," said Lynette, looking like she was still trying to wake up.

Turning around, Teencie greeted her new friends, "Hey, ladies."

"The early bird again, I see," continued Charmaine.

Blushing, Teencie waved a hand before her as if to shoo a bug. "Today will be busy, as the Tentmaker's Project banquet is tonight. Figured I'd get a jump on the day."

"You won't hear any argument from me," said Charmaine as she and Lynette pulled off their coats to start their days.

Lynette headed toward the enormous commercial refrigerator and pulled out eggs, a quart of milk, butter, and a thick package of bacon to set about with initial breakfast preparations. Charmaine filled a travel mug with steaming hot coffee, then headed into her office.

Calling out from her desk, Charmaine said, "Teencie, when you have a few minutes, let's go over the details for the banquet one more time."

"Headed your way. Let me grab my planning notebook and pen from my desk, and I'll be right with you," was the prompt reply.

Teencie quickly poured herself a cup of coffee, flavored it with creamer and sweetener, retrieved the items from her desk, and joined Charmaine in the kitchen manager's office. She knew what a big day this would be, and she did not want to disappoint Charmaine or Don.

"Would you mind closing the door?" Charmaine asked before Teencie had a chance to sit. "The other cooks ought to be here soon. Although the breakfast preparations are music to my ears, the pots-and-pans symphony sometimes makes it hard to carry on a conversation."

After accomplishing her small task, Teencie took her seat, placing her coffee mug on the front of Charmaine's desk, then opened her notebook to a blank page.

As the kitchen manager and her new assistant discussed the evening's Decision Banquet, Teencie quickly filled one page and then another with notes. They'd carefully planned the menu for this special evening—sirloin steaks, sweet potato soufflé, tossed green salad, baked fruit, rolls, and Charmaine's famous chocolate cake. The kitchen manager confirmed several off-campus errands Teencie should make that day. Teencie likewise went through a list of items that required Charmaine's advice or approval.

Once Charmaine had covered the plans for the day, Teencie closed the notebook. As she put the cap on her pen, Charmaine said, "There's something I'd like to talk to you about."

Perplexed, Teencie sat back in her chair. Had she not met Charmaine's expectations? Would she be let go? She took a long breath and waited to hear what her boss would say.

"Teencie," the manager began, "even though you've only been on this staff for less than a month, I want you to know what a marvelous difference you're already making at Covenant Kitchen." Her smile was warm and sincere.

Teencie slowly exhaled as a flood of emotions washed over her, but happiness and joy in knowing she was making the grade in this new position stood out strongest.

"I've been in this industry for a long time, and believe me when I say I've not seen many individuals as dedicated and talented as you. I can hardly believe how organized the kitchen is. Your systems have greatly benefited the ladies preparing the food. I hope, in time, they will convey to you the compliments they've already shared with me. Know that I'm pleased with your wonderful job."

Feeling a bit more composed, Teencie replied, "Thank you. I'm humbled by your kind words. For a minute there, I was afraid you'd tell me I'm fired."

The kitchen manager laughed. "Not a chance, Teencie. You're a keeper."

As Teencie nodded, her red curls gently bounced. Rising from her seat, she hoped again to keep her emotions in check. "Much to do today. I'm about to head out on errands and should be back by ten."

"Sounds like a plan."

"Thanks again," Teencie said, hoping her boss could see the gratitude in her eyes.

Raising a hand in farewell, Charmaine smiled warmly. "See you soon."

As the newest employee of Covenant Kitchen left the manager's office, she glanced through tear-filled eyes at the landscape of the kitchen's expanse spread before her. *I could have never imagined this*, she thought.

This sense of accomplishment and God's purpose for her life was a recipe of sweet blessings for which she was developing a taste.

CHAPTER
29

Wonder rendered Abbie speechless as she pulled open the door to Covenant Kitchen. Never had she seen the space looking so lovely. Countless strands of twinkle lights crisscrossed the rafters in the large dining hall. Starched white cloths covered each table. Charmaine's staff had placed fresh sprigs of evergreen and sprays of holly adorned with plump red berries along the wide, red-plaid ribbon that ran down the center of each. Evenly spaced large votive candles flickered against the ribbon to complete the festive centerpieces for tonight's Decision Banquet.

At the sound of laughter and cheerful conversation, Abbie turned to see students and faculty spilling into the room. Once the Timothy House school family took their seats, Don rose and blessed the meal. No sooner had the "Amen" sounded than the kitchen doors opened, and the dining staff streamed through, large trays of filled plates balanced in their hands. Each wore a white blouse tucked into a long red skirt. A festive holly-green apron completed their attire. With all the activity, Abbie felt more like she was at a winter resort than a school dining hall.

As promised, Charmaine Jenkins's meal selection was delicious. The steaks were tender and moist, the sweet potatoes warm and creamy, and the salad delicious with its Christmas-themed assortment of spinach, almonds, and cranberries tossed in a light vinaigrette.

Once the assistant manager gave the signal, the kitchen staff cleared the dinner plates and removed the roll baskets and butter plates from each table.

Don rose once more as the swinging kitchen door settled behind the last of Charmaine's staff. Lifting his water glass, he clinked his spoon against the side of the beverage. Immediately, the hall quieted.

"Folks," he began, "this meal has been delicious, but our most important part of the evening is soon to begin." After glancing at his watch, he continued, "The Tentmaker's Dedication Service will begin at seven-thirty in Peter's Chapel. Once you've completed your meal, please head toward the back of campus. I hope this night will begin a wonderful, new tradition here at Timothy House. Doris and I look forward to gathering with each of you soon."

Abbie stepped through the doorway of Covenant Kitchen as Keith followed close behind. Once on the porch, he reached for her hand and enveloped it in his, strong fingers telegraphing warmth and security. Pulling her to him, he bent down and softly kissed her cheek. "I'm so glad you're here with me," he said, his voice thick with emotion.

"I am, too," Abbie said, feeling a bit shy due to his display of affection. "I'm incredibly proud of you," she said softly, wishing there was time and opportunity to say more as dinner guests spilled through the doorway onto the building's broad porch. She and Keith had enjoyed several lengthy conversations recently about the importance of the Tentmaker's Project and the valuable contribution it would make to the culture of the school.

Soon, Chuck found his way to them.

Never letting go of her hand, Keith led her down the steps. The couple walked alongside Chuck. Abbie listened as the men chatted while following the path that led to the old stone chapel. As they neared, the glow of candles lit the stained-glass windows, making each look like a kaleidoscope of color against the dark winter night.

Once inside, Abbie and Keith followed Chuck into a pew near the front. Abbie immediately noticed Doris's handiwork on the platform. A carved wooden podium stood centered near the lip of the stage, a plump, leafy fern, flanked by pots of bright red poinsettias in front of it. Off to one side, Lance Tate and Parker Goodwin sat in chairs and softly strummed their guitars, the strains of various hymns filling the room as the Timothy House student family filed into the chapel.

"Welcome, all," Don said, holding out his hands. "Tonight, we begin what we hope will be a treasured tradition here at Timothy House, the Tentmaker's Program Dedication Service.

As Don's welcome continued, Abbie happened to catch the eye of Chloe Minton, who was seated nearby. It thrilled her to see the girl grin like the Cheshire Cat when Abbie waved at her.

The Nunleys were seated next to Chloe, and the sheer joy on their faces moved Abbie deeply. Like Chloe, Abbie knew the deep pain of abandonment and the feeling of not fitting in that one experiences when a member of a dysfunctional family. Though never having adopted a child, Abbie was enormously grateful to Tim and Taylor, who had opened their home, but more importantly, their hearts, to bring Chloe close into the circle of their love. Abbie could think of no better gift for this Christmas season.

After a few minutes, the ovation subsided.

Don said, "Let us begin this service with a word of prayer. Dear Lord, how grateful we are to gather in this place tonight. How good it is to be a part of such a wonderful extended family at Timothy House. You have blessed our school in many ways, and we pray You would never lift Your hand of protection from us. We are especially grateful for the lives of these new Tentmaker's Project students—Julie, Heather, Andy, and Davis. Be their Guide and Mentor on this journey as they seek Your direction for the path You want them to follow. Make Yourself known to them. Equip them with the skills, talents, wisdom, and knowledge needed for the road of life ahead. We wait expectantly to see what You will do in the lives of these young people. All this we ask in Your holy name. Amen."

As soon as the prayer ended, Don said, "I'd like to ask Josh Hastings to come forward and lead us in a few hymns."

As Josh approached the podium, Lance and Parker began the opening phrases of "O Come, All Ye Faithful." The cross-country coach signaled for everyone to stand. Then, raising one arm like a maestro, Josh directed the congregation to join him.

While the sounds of music reached the rafters of Peter's Chapel, Abbie glanced at Keith as he sang. A lump formed in her throat as she remembered the many special moments God had provided for her here in this chapel. Her first Christmas Pageant when Chloe made her the cross-stitched picture. Doris's explanation of how Marie Stevenson had imported the stained-glass windows of the chapel from England as a way to impart beauty and culture to the first students attending the school in the late 1930s. Attending the school's Christmas vesper service, after which Keith asked her out on their first date. The particular Good Friday when Keith declared his love for her and his willingness to wait for her.

Keith turned to look at Abbie as if he could sense what she was thinking. His tender gaze let her know he could imagine the thoughts running through her mind. He smiled and then turned back toward the front of the chapel.

After the melody, the congregation sat as Don returned to the podium.

"Tonight, we're in for a treat," he began, looking down at the four juniors seated in the chapel's front row. "Patterned after the husband-and-wife New Testament team of Priscilla and Aquilla, Paul's co-workers, the Tentmaker's Project hopes to offer students access to career guidance through a mentoring program based on apprenticeship and friendships developed with adults in the business community.

"The weekend before Thanksgiving, the Project sponsors and the first students traveled to Craggy Bluff, where members of the Koinonia Fellowship Church hosted them, and they were greeted warmly by members of the local artisan community. A few of those craftsmen are here tonight." Looking to his right, Don motioned for Summer and Elton Tidwell to stand. "Please give a warm Timothy House welcome to the Tidwells." Applause broke out and then settled. "I've asked each student to share how the retreat impacted them."

Julie Adams was the first in the group to speak. As she made her way to the podium, her ponytail of long blond hair swayed as she walked. Once she reached the stage, she placed a sheet of paper on the podium. She addressed the audience with her eyes before speaking.

"I'm excited to be a new Tentmaker," the student began. "My dream is to one day pursue a career in the medical field." It took her a moment to locate John Benson toward the back of the chapel. Once she found him, she waved in greeting. "Dr. Benson, I want to thank you for sharing a little of your story with us at the Saturday night session of our retreat. Your words have inspired me to devote myself and work as hard as possible to pursue my dream. I believe God will help me do this."

Having accomplished her speaking task, Julie folded the paper and left the podium.

As the applause followed the student back to her seat, Abbie was transported to her junior year of high school. What a tremendously positive difference the influence of her English teacher, Miss Frances Thompson, made in her life. Abbie knew she had witnessed the same miracle in Julie's.

"Thanks so much, Julie," said Don, smiling broadly at the teen. He then returned his gaze to those assembled before him. "Next, we'll hear from Heather Phillips."

Tall and slender, Heather's strawberry-blond hair glinted in the chapel's candlelight as she climbed the steps to the podium. Though soft-spoken, her bright blue eyes bore evidence of a maturity far beyond her years.

"Poetry has been my main interest for many years," Heather said, referring to the index card in her hand. "Writing is hard work and often unrewarded." Looking across the room at the Tidwells, Heather continued, "Thank you, Miss Summer, for the time you spent talking with me during the weekend of our retreat. You helped me see that one blessing of being creative is discovering the simple joy in whatever that creativity may be—composing a poem, making a quilt, or throwing pottery on a wheel—rather than being sidetracked by the lures of money or fame. You've encouraged me to hone my craft and leave the results to God."

Heather placed her hand over her heart in a silent gesture of thanks. A round of warm applause accompanied the student back to her seat. As she had while watching Julie, Abbie thought of all the lessons God had been teaching her about letting go of the past and letting Him lead her on a new path to His future for her. Abbie so longed for the joy of simplicity that Heather spoke about.

Don stood in front of the pew. Looking at the students seated nearby, he said, "Please welcome Andy Beason."

While the tall, dark-headed student made his way up the podium steps, Abbie remembered how Keith had once said that Andy reminded him of his son, David.

Andy placed a hand on either side of the podium and leaned toward the mic. "Until this year, playing on the basketball team has been what I've liked best about being a student at Timothy House. No offense, Coach," he said, looking over at Keith. "But being selected for the Tent-maker's Project is a close second."

Keith called out, "Good with me, Andy!"

The audience erupted in laughter.

Once the noise died down, the young man continued. "Though I'm interested in a possible career in medicine, I know now, after the retreat, that whatever I do, I want it to provide a way for me to serve others."

Looking over at Lance Tate seated nearby, his guitar across his lap, Andy continued, "Mr. Lance, you inspired me to make sure I'm the right man on the inside, as that will direct what type of man I am to the rest of the world. I'm determined to lead a life of integrity and honor, no matter my career."

Lance gave a small salute as clapping rang out as Andy returned to his pew.

Once more, Don stood. "Last but certainly not least, we'll hear from Davis Landrum."

At this, the redheaded young man stood on long legs and headed to the podium. As had Heather, he carried an index card in one hand. "Thank you, Mr. Don," he said, appearing nervous to stand before so many. "Working in some type of retail business has always interested me."

As had Andy, Davis looked toward the guitar-playing adults but directed his comments toward Parker Goodwin. "Thank you for sharing the story of your family's grocery business with us. You've helped me see how the simple act of helping others buy food at economical prices is also an excellent way to serve the greater community. I look forward to learning more from you during my apprenticeship."

Parker Goodwin smiled and nodded at his student protégé.

Picking up his index card from the podium, Davis walked down the platform steps, his freckled face reddening in response to the audience's hearty applause.

Don approached the podium one last time. "Well, if these students' testimonies are any indication, God is already at work through the Tentmaker's Project. Let me close us before we head home."

As a hush fell over the chapel, Abbie felt God's confirmation of her decision to establish a scholarship for Timothy House faculty and students.

Don's strong, sure voice rang out with a prayer to close the service.

"Lord, thank You for all we've heard tonight, both in song and from the reports these students gave, of Your faithfulness and desire to fit us for service in Your kingdom. Make us worthy vessels to bear Your image. We ask that others might see in our lives a reflection of You. We ask all this in Your strong and precious name. Amen."

When the dedication service ended, students and faculty streamed from the pews, heading for the chapel door. Abbie patiently sat as Keith, Don, and Chuck visited, listening to the snippets of conversation she overheard.

"What an inspiring service."

"I hope more students will be selected for next year's program."

"I had no idea this program would make such a huge impact on the students' lives."

"I'm going to contact a business owner in town who might want to serve as a mentor for the program."

Knowing how hard Keith, Don, and Chuck had worked to implement the Tentmaker's Project, Abbie couldn't wait to share with Keith the positive feedback tonight's attendees expressed.

Catching Keith's eye across the room, she told with a nod of her head that she was walking back to her girls in the cottage. He waved goodbye and then turned back to his friends.

Pushing open the heavy front door of Peter's Chapel, Abbie glanced once more at Keith. Her heart swelled with pride as she watched her fiancé do what he did best—build strong relationships with others.

CHAPTER
30

Don had a great deal on his mind this morning. He checked his watch and knew Keith would arrive at his office any minute. The director of Timothy House had already been up five hours, his eyes opening themselves at three o'clock as if connected to the strings of a marionette puppeteer. He had diligently tried to go back to sleep, but after fifteen minutes of tossing and turning and not wanting to wake Doris, Don had slipped out of bed and headed to the bathroom to grab his robe. Minutes later, in his wing chair in the den with a steaming cup of coffee, he sat with his Bible open before him. Don spent the following hours talking to the Lord, searching for direction in His Word.

Like clockwork, Loren, Don's assistant, buzzed on the phone, announcing that Keith Haliday was there for their morning meeting. As Don neared the office door, he uttered a silent prayer within his heart. *Lord, please give me the words to say.*

The men shook hands as Keith entered Don's office, then Don closed the door and headed to his chair behind the desk. After a few volleys of pleasantries—"How are you?" and "How was your week?"—Don knew he needed to cut to the chase.

After clearing his throat, he began. "Keith, this has been a momentous fall for you. August marked your eighteenth month with us at Timothy House, and then came your engagement to Abbie, which we are all pleased about. The Tentmaker's Project couldn't have gotten off to a better start, and, if memory serves me correctly, this current basketball season has been the best in the past ten years. What's your record so far, 7–3?"

"Yes, sir, you are correct," replied Keith, "though I still can't figure out how we pulled out a win Monday night against Oaklawn."

"Good coaching and determined young men," said Don.

"But . . ." Keith hesitantly inquired, "you didn't ask me to come see you today about the school's basketball record, did you?"

Now it was Don's turn to sport a wide grin. "Haliday," he said, slapping his desk playfully, "I can't get anything past you." Becoming more subdued, Don sat straighter before continuing. "Yes, I have an important matter to discuss with you."

Keith remained quiet, his eyes fixed on his boss.

Don leaned back in his chair and raked one hand through his hair. "You know I love Timothy House with every fiber of my being. I spent much of my happy childhood on this campus—countless hours romping through the woods, running through the fields, and fishing in Serenity Cove. Uncle Roger hired me the summer I turned fourteen to help the campus handyman, and I lived and worked here every summer afterward until I graduated from college in 1961.

"I sought a career in education because Roger influenced my life. I saw firsthand the positive difference he and Aunt Marie made in the lives of the children who came to school at Timothy House, and I wanted to make that same kind of difference in others' lives."

Keith's silence made Don wonder if there was some chance his protégé would not be interested in running the school.

"Do you remember when we first met?" Don inquired.

"Like it was yesterday," replied Keith, a grin dawning.

"At the Harrisburg Leadership Forum," both men practically said in unison.

"Jinx," Don said playfully. "What I see in you today, my friend, is the same thing I saw in you all those years ago—integrity, a teachable spirit, and a servant's heart."

Keith looked at his hands. When he looked back up at Don, tears filled his eyes. "But that was before I came to know the Lord," he said softly, his voice barely above a whisper.

"I know, son," said Don. "But even then, with all the shortcomings you believed you had, I recognized the hallmarks of a truly great man. Since you were saved, those qualities have only grown stronger."

After a pause, Keith continued, seeming to regain his composure. "Looking back, Don, I believe God sent you to me."

"Well, that's one way to look at it," said Don, smiling back at his younger friend.

"There may be other viewpoints," continued Keith, "but that's the version of my story I'm sticking with. Had I stayed in pharmaceutical sales, I surely would not be here with you at Timothy House today."

Don sat as Keith struggled to find more words.

"When our paths reconnected at the men's retreat, where I was saved, that was a watershed moment in my life," the younger man said. "It wasn't long after that you offered me the position at the school."

Breaking from the younger man's gaze, the director shuffled some papers on his desk. Looking back at Keith, Don continued, "These thirty-two years Doris and I have spent at Timothy House have been some of the richest of our lives. Our children grew up here. Wilson and Valerie were four and almost one when Doris and I moved into the Manse. She and I have spent a lot of time talking about our lives, work, and future, and we've concluded it's time for me to leave this post."

Don grinned slightly, noting a look of concern on Keith's face.

"We think you'd be the perfect man to lead Timothy House into the next season."

The grin on Don's face widened as he watched Keith's face surrender to an expression of total disbelief.

Don held out a packet of papers, letting it fall on Keith's side of the desk. "These are my thoughts about how this transition might take place. I've also included some financial information related to Uncle Roger's trust fund to cover all school operating expenses."

Keith slowly leaned forward and took the paperwork from Don. "I don't know what to say," he said as if in a daze.

"You don't have to say anything now," said Don, laughing slightly, "but you do need to think about this long and hard, and you will certainly need to see what Abbie has to say about this. She might not want this type of life."

Keith nodded, still too moved to say much.

"We've got two more days in this semester before the Christmas break," continued Don, a fatherly tone in his voice. "Why don't we plan to follow up on this in early January? That would give you and Abbie a few weeks to roll the idea around in your minds and talk about it."

"Sounds like a plan," said Keith.

Don slid his chair back from his desk and slapped both hands on his knees before standing, a telltale sign that this meeting was over. Keith stood from his chair, rolling the sheaf of papers carefully.

As they reached the door to the outer reception area, Don placed his hands on Keith's shoulders. "I've prayed about this matter for months now. Your name is the *only* one that keeps coming to mind. But for it to be right, we have to arrive at the same conclusion. Ask the Lord what He wants you to do. He'll let you know."

The younger man nodded and hugged Don tightly.

"Thank you, Don," Keith said, tears in his eyes. "Your confidence in me truly humbles me. Once Abbie and I talk, I'll be back in touch."

As Don watched his second-in-command depart from the meeting, he silently prayed that God would confirm with Keith the choice He had already made clear to Don.

CHAPTER
31

Keith and Abbie sat at their favorite table at Giuseppe's. Abbie looked around the candlelit room as they waited for their server. As Keith watched her, he could tell the Italian restaurant's red, green, and white color scheme enthralled her. Her expression was like that of a child on Christmas Eve, full of expectation and wonder. Soon, the waiter arrived and handed them menus artfully written in calligraphic script.

The drive to Kingsport had been a great way to unwind. The last month of the year was always busy, but this particular December was especially jam-packed with programs, deadlines, basketball games, and papers to grade. There was much Keith needed to tell Abbie. Her response to his news might well determine the direction of their future.

"How is it possible that today is the last day of the year?" Abbie exclaimed, looking up from her menu.

When Keith didn't respond immediately, Abbie touched him on the arm. He seemed absorbed in his menu.

"Are you okay?" she asked.

"Uh, sure," Keith stammered, realizing he had not disguised the preoccupation of the matter weighing on his mind.

Abbie then posed her original question another way. "Can you believe this is the last day of the year?"

Not wanting to pique Abbie's curiosity and trying to appear calm, he continued, "No, this year has flown by too fast. We're more than halfway through the basketball season. I can hardly believe it."

After they ordered their meals, Abbie had plenty to talk about concerning wedding plans. As she chatted, Keith tried to pay close attention.

Internally, however, his emotions were swirling. Keith had thought of little else than Don's offer to pass on the mantle of leadership of Timothy House. Between basketball practices and games, class preparations, grading end-of-semester exams, and spending time with Abbie, he spent all other waking moments seeking God's direction about this momentous, unexpected fork in the road of his life. Keith desperately wanted to know what Abbie thought about the news that would potentially change the direction of their future. The waiter's arrival at the table, entrées in hand, meant Keith would soon have his answer.

Keith took Abbie's hands in his and blessed the food. As they picked up their forks to enjoy Giuseppe's fine Italian cuisine, Abbie was still reporting on wedding news between bites of her chicken piccata. However, this latest conversation dealt with a bridal shower that several friends, including Beulah and Lane, wanted to host for her in McHenry. Keith smiled, trying to listen yet concentrating more closely on finding a break in the conversation to make his announcement.

Finally, when Abbie reached for a second piece of focaccia, Keith made his move.

"Abbie," he began casually. "Don and I had an interesting conversation recently."

"Really?" said Abbie, focused on dipping her bread in herbed olive oil. "I'm sure he's relieved that the holidays are here. Running a school must be an exhausting job."

You have no idea, Keith thought, immediately sending an SOS to the Lord. *You'll have to help me with this*, he prayed silently before plunging into the conversation.

Putting down his fork, he looked at Abbie, hoping she would receive his news with an open mind. "He's thinking about retiring, and he talked to me about taking over as the next Timothy House head of school." Relief flooded through him as, at last, the cat was out of the bag.

Abbie stopped chewing, her mouth still full of the bite she'd just taken. She looked like he had thrown a glass of water in her face. Suddenly, seemingly realizing the food must be swallowed, she completed the bite and chased the bread down with a large swig of her iced tea.

"Don wants *you* to become the next head of school?" The tone in Abbie's voice matched her expression. Incredulous.

Smiling a bit, Keith said, "He does." She might as well have asked him if he could fly into outer space, the skepticism within her palpable.

Abbie idly wiped her mouth with her napkin, a dazed look on her face. Carefully placing the cloth back in her lap, she looked directly at Keith and asked, "What exactly would that entail?"

Grateful for this open door, Keith walked through it, sharing the details of his conversation with Don. "I was as surprised as you," he told her. "Never in a million years would I have guessed this offer was possible." Reaching into his shirt pocket, he pulled out a carefully folded list he'd written, containing the pros and cons of accepting the offer. After opening it, Keith read the list aloud. "I've had so many sleepless nights following my meeting with Don, and I've prayed for God's guidance and direction."

As he had before blessing their dinner, Keith reached out to hold Abbie's hands. "I want to hear from you. If we're not united on this decision, then the answer's no."

Her peridot-green eyes filled with tears. "You mean that?" Her bottom lip quivered slightly.

Keith squeezed her hands tightly. "You bet I do." Leaning over the table, he drew her left hand to his mouth and kissed it tenderly. "Abbie," he murmured, "you are my world. I still have to pinch myself when thinking about how God has brought you into my life. I never thought I'd find happiness again, much less love."

Abbie's gentle grip tightened on his hands, lending Keith the courage to continue.

"As much as I love you and look forward to our life together, I cannot shut myself up in our house and live solely for myself. I believe God has a purpose and a plan for my life, an avenue in which He wants to employ the gifts and talents He's given to me to encourage the lives of others, share His love, and bring honor and glory to His name. I could do that— *we* can do that—in this leadership position at Timothy House."

Keith ran his thumbs across the tops of Abbie's hands. She said nothing for a long while but stared into his eyes. After giving his hands a quick squeeze, Abbie pulled away from Keith and placed her hands in her lap.

Looking across the table, she posed a question of her own. "What about my continuing to teach? Though I love it, this past semester was quite a challenge."

"That would be your decision," Keith said with a protective tone in his voice. "You've more than served your time in the classroom, especially this past year."

Abbie grinned. "Serving as housemother has been more than I bargained for." She reached for her glass and took a long sip. Her fingers played with the beads of condensation collecting on its surface as she placed the glass back on the table. "I'm grateful for Don's plan to bring Teencie into the cottage as the new housemother. But that leads to my next question. If you take this job, where would we live?"

"In the Manse," Keith replied, watching Abbie's reaction. "Don will announce his retirement within the next few weeks. He will leave the position in May, at the end of the school year. He and Doris plan to move to Nashville to be closer to their children."

"Wouldn't living in Don and Doris's old home feel strange?" Abbie inquired.

"Maybe," he said and then grinned at the seriousness of what Abbie had asked. "Yes, a bit, I guess, but there's a housing stipend included in my financial packet that would allow us to renovate the place and add our unique touches to it."

Abbie sat for a minute as these words sank in. Keith couldn't quite discern the look in her eyes.

"Where would Drew stay when he came to visit us?"

"The Manse is a three-bedroom home. There will *always* be room for Drew."

At this, Abbie seemed to relax. Leaning back in her chair, she spoke barely above a whisper. "I'm sorry if I haven't reacted to this news correctly." She brushed away a tear that had trickled down one cheek.

Keith reached across the table, tenderly wiping away another. "I'm not sure there is a right response," he said softly. "This is life-altering news."

"I'll say," Abbie said, a bit of humor evident in her tone, though it seemed she was still working hard to control her emotions. "This scenario is not one I could have envisioned in a million years."

"Me neither."

Both sat silently together in the enormity of the moment.

"Did you ever see yourself as the head of Timothy House?" Abbie ventured.

Keith shook his head. "Never," he replied as a wry grin broke across his face. "And to think I came to education through the back door of alternate route certification."

"Proves that where it's God's will, He'll make a way." Abbie reached over and patted Keith's hand.

Sitting back in her chair, she leaned her head to one side as if listening for a particular sound. "So . . ." Her voice trailed off for a second. "Let's go back to your list of pros and cons."

"Okay," said Keith, his tone patient and steady.

"How would filling Don's shoes affect your role as the head basketball coach? You adore coaching your young men."

"I do indeed," replied her fiancé, as memories of the last several basketball seasons crowded in like guests at a birthday party. "I think, however, that I may have to take off my letter jacket. Coaching, however, will still be in my playbook; it just won't be taking place from the sidelines, but rather in my office."

Abbie looked a bit surprised but did not comment.

"You've asked a question. Now, it's my turn," Keith said.

"Ask away," replied Abbie, smiling back at him.

"Let's go back to the question you asked a few minutes ago about you teaching."

Abbie sat quietly and looked down at her hands, as if carefully composing her answer. "For almost two years now," she began, "I've been trying to solve the riddle of the disquiet and unrest within my spirit. Seeking the answer to what has caused that is part of what led me to Timothy House."

Moving her hands to the table top, Abbie moved the fingers of her right hand across her engagement ring, watching the stone sparkle as she twisted the gold band back and forth. "Falling in love with you was something I never dreamed possible."

As he listened, Keith reached across the table and took hold of her left hand.

"Teaching has been my passion until this past year." Tears glistened in Abbie's eyes as she continued. "However, trying to juggle the responsibilities of full-time classroom teacher and housemother to five precious but very precocious seventh-grade girls has about taken the wind out of my sails."

Abbie looked longingly at Keith and squeezed his hand that held her own.

"It's taken all the willpower I could muster to fulfill my academic responsibilities and those at Mistletoe Cottage. The thing is, Keith, even before we got engaged, all I've thought about is you. Pleasing you. Loving you. Building a life together with you. We're not spring chickens, Keith Haliday, and I so want unlimited time, especially in the first year of our marriage, to devote myself entirely to loving you and taking care of you. Frankly, I don't care if I never teach another English class in my life."

A wide smile dawned across Keith's face. "Wow, Mrs. Richardson," he finally said, "that's quite an admission. You'd give up your classroom for little ole me?"

A smile as wide and bright as Keith's flashed across Abbie's face. "I'd give it all up for you, Keith."

The love and admiration these two had for one another pulsed between them, their eyes telegraphing messages too powerful to be spoken.

"How will you make it through this coming spring semester?" Keith inquired, worried that the pressures of wedding planning, house-mothering, and teaching responsibilities might be too much for his fiancée.

"I'm grateful for Don's plan to bring Teencie into the cottage as the new housemother. She'll also be able to fill in for me if I have to be away at times due to planning our big day. Knowing there's a light at the end of the tunnel will be the fuel for my engine. It's hard to keep a good woman down." Abbie giggled at the joke she had made. "My turn," she said, her tone turning more serious.

"Shoot," replied Keith playfully.

"How will your serving as the head of school impact our relationship? While I have a pretty good idea of at least some of the duties and responsibilities of the new office, are there expectations for me as your wife?"

The expression on Abbie's face told Keith that this woman, whom he loved more than life itself, was terrified of disappointing him.

"There will certainly be school activities, dinners, and social events we'll attend together as husband and wife, but there is no job description for the wife of a head of school."

"Doris Fielding has left some pretty big pumps to fill."

Keith laughed at her play on words. "Don't think for a minute," he said, "that I haven't quaked in my boots, wondering if I could ever be half the man Don Fielding has been in this position.

"Though no attribution for this quote has ever been successfully ascertained, these words have soothed my soul and the desperation I've struggled with to be appreciated solely for myself: 'Comparison is the thief of joy.' You be the best Abbie you can be, and I'll be the best Keith. That's all the school and the Board of Trustees can expect. God never asks us to be anyone else but ourselves. Living authentic lives for Him is the goal, not perfection."

Abbie hung on to Keith's every word.

"And when we reach the end of our abilities," Keith concluded, "God will supply us with what we need."

"I can live with that, Mr. Haliday," Abbie said, a flirtatious expression on her face.

At that moment, their waiter reappeared and asked if they would like dessert.

Immediately, Keith replied, "Tiramisu with two spoons." He hoped the coffee-flavored treat would raise Abbie's spirits.

"What do *you* want to do?" she asked once the waiter departed. Finally, one of them addressed the main issue they had avoided.

Long seconds passed as Keith contemplated his reply to her piercing question. Finally, he said, "I think that if I don't accept this position, I'll regret it for the rest of my life." He stared into her soft green eyes before continuing. "Both of us have already lost so much."

She nodded wordlessly, reaching out for his hand.

"I'm not willing to waste any more time in my life," Keith continued. "In Timothy House, I've found a place where I want to invest myself in the people and the programs." He gently squeezed her hand. "With you, my dear Abbie, I feel complete. If you come with me on this journey, I think this could be a marvelous adventure for us."

As Keith uttered these last words, the waiter delivered the dessert, setting two spoons on either side of the plate. "Enjoy," said the young man, leaving as quickly as he had appeared.

Abbie reached for her spoon and, lifting it high, exclaimed, "Here's to new beginnings!"

In the soft candle glow of the restaurant, Keith watched as a look of serenity transformed Abbie's countenance. A sense of God's peace filled his heart, one he'd not experienced in a long time.

God, indeed, had set them on a new path—together.

CHAPTER
32

The new year was now underway. It seemed to Abbie as if a lifetime had passed since her Italian dinner with Keith. His announcement to head Timothy House had caught her off guard. She couldn't have been more surprised if Keith had told her he wanted to run away and join the circus. She was unprepared for how quickly God had turned her heart to line up with Keith's. By the time their dinner ended that evening, though she didn't know where the road would lead, she was on board with the unexpected fork they were traveling.

Tonight, Doris and Don invited Abbie and Keith for coffee and dessert to discuss a path forward as the school transitioned from one leader to another. Keith's selection would not only be a marked departure from what many considered the ideal candidate; it would also be the end of an era when a member of the founder's family served as the head of the school. Even though Don had handpicked Keith for the position, that choice required board approval. How surprised Abbie had been last night when Keith had called to say the group had unanimously approved his nomination. God at work was the only rationale that made sense.

The first people Abbie wanted to call when she hung up with Keith were Drew and Beulah. However, Don wanted to keep the news under wraps until after the student body returned from spring break. As good as Don Fielding had been to both of them, Abbie planned to honor that request.

Abbie squeezed Keith's hand while waiting for Don and Doris to answer the door. He tightened his grip in return and turned to look at her.

"Can you even believe this?" he asked.

"No, not really," Abbie replied, her smile warm and reassuring, "but I know God is with us, and He'll show us the way."

"That's my girl," said Keith, kissing her cheek.

No sooner had he straightened up than the door knob began to turn. Light spilled onto the Manse's porch as Don and Doris Fielding opened the front door.

"Hello, you two," said Doris, her voice cheerful.

"Please come in," Don said, beckoning with his arm.

The younger couple followed the Fieldings into the den of the large stone residence.

As Abbie took her seat, she remembered several special evenings in this room with this husband and wife, who had now become dear friends. She looked forward to hearing Don's ideas about making the transition in leadership as smooth as possible. She knew Keith did, too.

As Doris returned to the kitchen to prepare the dessert tray, Don regaled their guests with news of their recent trip. "We returned from Savannah two days after New Year's." Looking through the open doorway, he watched his wife heading back to the den.

"How was your trip?" asked Abbie. "I've never been to Savannah, but I've always heard what a beautiful place it is. So much character and history."

Doris's voice chimed in as she set the tray down on the coffee table between them. "We had a lovely time." She filled four plates with thick slices of chocolate chess pie, topped with dollops of whipped cream. "Let Don tell you about all we did," she said, as she handed each a dessert before heading back to the kitchen with the empty tray.

As Don gave the couple forks and napkins, he offered a glowing description of their New Year's getaway.

"Did you mention the harbor tour?" Doris asked, her tray now filled with cups of steaming coffee, creamer, and sweetener. After setting it down and taking her place beside her husband, Doris raised her fork as if in a salute. "Bon appétit!"

For the first few seconds after, the Fieldings and their guests savored the delicious treat Doris had made earlier that afternoon.

"Delicious," said Keith, wiping away evidence of whipped cream from the side of his mouth. "You know chocolate is my favorite!"

Doris beamed at the compliment. "Yes," she said slyly, "I do seem to remember hearing that somewhere." She looked conspiratorially at Abbie.

Abbie winked at this dear lady who had become a trusted friend.

As Don and Keith turned to basketball as they ate their pie, Abbie could only eat a few bites before placing the plate on the table. She picked up her coffee and took a few sips to calm herself. Though she agreed wholeheartedly with Keith about this new position, a case of the butterflies had somehow found its way to her stomach. She wondered if anyone noticed her nervousness.

"So, Abbie," Don asked, confirming her suspicions, "what do you think of Keith's new position?"

Abbie looked at Keith to gain courage from the tender look in his deep blue eyes. He seemed to urge her to share her heart when answering the question.

"I was flabbergasted when Keith told me," she said. "The job proposal seemed to come out of left field. Neither of us would have ever sought this out."

"And now?" Don pressed again.

"And now . . ." Abbie considered her words. "And now, I think God has opened the door to a wonderful opportunity for Keith to use his gifts and talents, ones honed through his varied experiences in the business world, in the classroom, and on the court."

"Oh, Abbie," Doris said, chiming in to the conversation. "You're going to be the perfect companion to Keith as he begins this new leg of his career. I told Don you would be," she added as she looked at her husband. "This position as head of school will involve you almost as much it will Keith."

Abbie grinned slightly, not sure how to respond. "You're kind to say so," she said sincerely, looking at Doris, whom she had come to love and admire. "I'll need you to help me and lend advice."

"You know I'll do anything I can to help," was her warm reply.

"Both of us," Abbie continued, "love Timothy House and those in its school family. Though I've enjoyed teaching, I'm thinking about leaving the classroom. It would be nice to focus solely on Keith." Looking around the den of the Manse, she continued, "I'm especially excited about making our house a home."

"Glad you mentioned 'making a home,'" Don said, rising from his chair. He picked up a large brown envelope neither Keith nor Abbie had noticed and handed the packet to Keith.

Seemingly unsure of what Don had given him, Keith sat briefly with the envelope in hand.

"Open it," Don said, a grin on his face.

Keith turned the packet over, undid the clasp, and slid a finger under the sealed flap. Reaching into the mouth of the envelope, he pulled out a thick sheath of papers. The page on top appeared to be some sort of legal document. "What is this?" Keith asked

"This, my friend," replied Don, with a look of pure delight, "is a gift Doris and I want to give you and Abbie."

At this, Keith and Abbie exchanged puzzled glances but said nothing.

Continuing, Don explained, "When Doris and I came to Timothy House all those years ago, we, too, were in the same position as you. At that time, the Manse was the home of Uncle Roger and Aunt Marie. When I came on board as head of school, one perk was the housing accommodation of this masterfully built stone home. Roger and Marie purchased a small house in town and moved into it, allowing us to claim the Manse as our own.

"The monetary gift of a renovation allowance accompanied that accommodation, allowing us to add our touches. Doris and I now want to share that same gift with you. The paperwork in your hands explains how you will access funds for a complete renovation."

Abbie was stunned. Glancing at Keith, she saw the same look of incredulity that was spreading across her own. *Lord*, she thought, *did I hear Don correctly?* The gift from Audry had been dumbfounding, but Abbie could hardly wrap her head around Don's announcement of this additional monetary legacy. *Your ways are definitely not ours*, she thought before focusing once more on Don's words.

"Uncle Roger's financial expertise has allowed the school to operate debt-free all these years. Careful investment of this money has yielded yet more profit. Though you don't have to spend it all, you can access up to seventy-five thousand dollars of this restoration fund before using your own money."

Now seeming to find his words, Keith stammered, "This is much too generous, Don." Glancing at Abbie, he quickly said, "We can't accept this. The school needs this money."

Don leaned forward in his chair as if to make a point. "Keith, you *can* accept the gift," he said, "and you *will*, just as we did all those years ago. Though not all schools can make this type of offer to a new administrator, Timothy House is in the fortunate position to do so. Uncle Roger would be happy to know you and Abbie will make the Manse your home."

As if finally understanding the enormity of what it meant for Don to pass on to his protégé this mantle of approval, Keith nodded slowly.

Don took hold of his wife's hand. "We were blessed to be the recipients of such a financial gift, and it's our joy to pass it along to you. I want your transition into this new position to be as seamless as possible. Lifting much of the financial burden is the least I can do."

Finding his voice, Keith said, "I don't know what to say, but thank you would be a start." A lopsided grin spread slowly across his face. "Abbie and I will spend every penny as wisely as possible."

Too moved to speak, Abbie mouthed her thanks silently as tears threatened to spill from her eyes.

As the four friends rose to say their goodbyes, the words of the ancient prophet Jeremiah whispered in Abbie's heart, "For I know the plans that I have for you . . . to give you a future and a hope."

Lord, Abbie thought as she and Keith followed Don and Doris toward the front door. *What kind of plan is this?*

Relieved she would only have to walk a block to the courthouse, Hayley Collins sprang out of her car and clicked her key fob before sprinting down the sidewalk to catch the green light at the crosswalk. The Washington County Courthouse, large and imposing with its red-brick façade and tall Ionic columns, loomed ahead.

Hayley took the front steps two at a time and pulled the building's main door wide. *I will not be another adult to disappoint this child*, she thought as she took a deep breath to calm the butterflies fluttering in her stomach before entering Judge Paxton Turner's courtroom. The minute Hayley stepped inside, she found Chloe Minton turned around in her seat as if scanning the room. It might as well have been Christmas Day by the smile that electrified the girl's face. Hayley gave her a thumbs-up. The child turned to the man beside her and tugged at his sleeve.

"I'm here, Martin," Hayley said, stepping up to the bar separating visitors from the well, the front area of the courtroom reserved for the judge, attorneys, their clients, and other officers of the court. Martin Gregory, the attorney handling Chloe's abuse case, stood and extended his hand. Hayley shook it firmly. "I'm sorry I'm running late this morning. Had an interview that ran long."

"Not a problem," Martin said as the clock on the courtroom's paneled wall caught his eye. "Glad you made it before the arraignment began. You know how Judge Turner hates interruptions."

"Don't I, though," replied Haley, a slight grin on her face. The Honorable Paxton Turner was not someone Hayley wanted to cross.

Turning her attention to the client seated next to Martin, Hayley crouched at the rail to be at eye level as she spoke to Chloe. "You'll be fine today," she said, reaching out to take the child's hand. "Remember, you don't have to say anything. It's just important that you're here."

Giving the child's hand a tight squeeze, the investigator continued, "I am so proud of you, Chloe. You are a fearless girl."

Chloe's dark eyes beamed like bright marbles in the fluorescent lights of the courtroom. She squeezed Hayley's hand in return. "Thank you, Miss Hayley," she whispered.

"Good girl," replied Hayley, giving Chloe's hand one more squeeze before releasing it. Standing up, she gestured to the row where she would take her place. "Chloe, I'm going to be sitting right there with the Nunleys. See Mr. Don and Mr. Keith? Miss Doris and Miss Abbie?"

Chloe's supporters waved at her. Chief Trent Lockhart and Detective Tony DiMarco sat nearby.

As Hayley turned away from Chloe, she glimpsed the jury box. Although empty today, in the not-too-distant future, a jury of the Hendersons' peers might fill that box should the couple go to trial. The investigator hoped justice would move swiftly. She knew how difficult it was to convict foster parents accused of abusing children left in their care, and yet, she had a strong hunch this case might be the exception.

No sooner had this thought crossed Hayley's mind than she felt a piercing stare directed her way. Turning her head, she caught the eye of Hope Henderson, who was glaring at her as if wanting to kill her with one look. The woman's eyes were cold and unflinching, like looking into the eyes of a poisonous viper. Hayley smiled and nodded to her.

We'll see who has the last laugh, Hayley thought as she turned her attention back to the front of the courtroom.

A door behind the bench opened, and the bailiff entered—a large, well-built man who looked like he ate nails for breakfast. "All rise!" the man exclaimed loudly, confident and commanding. A collective whoosh sounded throughout the mahogany-paneled courtroom as a crowd of forty or so rose; most of those in the gallery sat behind the plaintiff's desk. Only a handful of individuals were behind the defendant's table, where Hope and Kevin Henderson stood with their counsel.

The bailiff continued, "The court is now in session. The Honorable Paxton Turner is presiding."

Judge Paxton Turner looked more like a mountain man robed in black than a legal scholar. He was well over six feet, three inches. A thick head of shoulder-length gray hair that any woman would envy was pulled back in a ponytail. Broad shoulders better suited to an ox's yoke filled out the long robe. The crisp, white collar standing up from the neck of the robe gave Turner the appearance of a Puritan minister about to rain down fire and brimstone on his congregation. The man could have quickly passed for a Renaissance-period artist if clad in a painter's smock.

Paxton Turner was well known for advocating for children in abusive or dysfunctional situations. Hayley had been in this courtroom many times before in her long career with the Tennessee Department of Children's Services. She knew how hard everyone had worked to put Chloe's case together. It was now time to see how those efforts might be rewarded.

Judge Turner clasped his hands before him and began his opening remarks.

As he did, Hayley swallowed hard. *Oh boy*, she thought. *This arraignment will be interesting.*

The proceedings went better than expected. As Hayley had hoped, the judge denied the Hendersons' motion to dismiss the charges before the attorney completed his statement. Judge Turner, it seemed, was in no mood for any shenanigans. Martin Gregory had presented the state's case masterfully. When the closing gavel sounded, Paxton Turner set the stage for the legal battle that would resume in eight months with the Hendersons' trial. Hayley could hardly wait to leave the courtroom and talk to Trent and Tony.

CHAPTER
34

After the meal was over, Keith made another pot of coffee. Several of the men were now on their second or third cup. For the past hour, the Barnabas Brothers and DeSean had sat on the comfortable sofas and recliners in Keith's den. They gathered to talk with the teen about his future once DeSean graduated from high school in two months. Due to his athletic prowess on the basketball court, several attractive offers from area colleges—East Tennessee State University, King University, and Walters State Community College—had come DeSean's way. These same schools also had ROTC programs.

Of all the men assembled, Keith and Lance were the only two who had experience with DeSean's two main interests. Keith had played four years of college basketball. Though recently retired, Lance had enjoyed a storied twenty-nine-year Army career and remained well-connected within military circles. Both men's insights would add more depth to this conversation.

Don leaned forward, looking over at DeSean. "Son," he began, "do you know what you'd like to study? Even if you accept a basketball scholarship, you'll still have to declare a major."

Keith watched with interest as he waited for the teen's response.

"I'm not sure, Mr. Don," was his reply.

Honest, Keith thought.

Seemingly not content to let the answer slide, Don posed another question. "Do you at least know a field of study, like math or science or history, that interests you?"

DeSean's face reddened a bit. Keith had been around the teen long enough to recognize this physical reaction when the teen became flustered or cornered. *Hang in there*, he thought.

"I guess . . ." DeSean said slowly, after some hesitation, "if I had to nail it down to one subject I like best, it would be science. I like knowing how things work."

"Bingo," said Don. "That's a start."

"You've been working hard, DeSean," said Josh, praising the young man. "I'm proud of all you've accomplished.

Rod Eichman spoke next. "Have you considered whether you'd like to attend a two-year or four-year school?"

"Not really," was DeSean's quick reply. "Joining an ROTC program at a four-year school would be my first choice." The boy looked down for a second and then glanced back at the Wright's Creek church pastor. "But school's never been easy for me, and I'm not sure I could cut it academically."

Keith sat forward in his recliner, paying closer attention to DeSean. Though he knew school had been a challenge for DeSean, this was the first time he'd heard the teen put the thought into words. Keith caught Lance's eye.

Lance now entered the conversation. "Another path to your future that you may not have considered is enlistment in the military after you graduate from Timothy House."

DeSean leaned forward slightly as if he were finally hearing something that interested him.

"Though I would be the first to tell you higher education is always beneficial," continued Lance, "I also realize college isn't for everyone. You are an incredibly talented athlete and a fine young man any coach would be proud to have on his team."

DeSean ducked his chin a little, apparently unsure how to accept these words of praise.

"You certainly don't have to decide now, but consider taking the ASVAB next month. Though college may not be a path that interests you now, it may appeal to you later. One benefit of serving your country is that the military helps pay for college. I'm happy to help you prep for the test if you decide to take it."

"Thank you, sir," was the polite reply.

"DeSean," Trent began as all eyes turned to him. "One thing to consider is that it's okay if you don't know what you want to do with the rest of your life." The police chief had picked up on DeSean's uncertainty, and the teen's shoulders relaxed.

Trent continued, "I've had many times when I knew I needed to decide a matter, but for whatever reason, the answer wouldn't come. Waiting can sometimes be the best choice."

Though DeSean didn't speak as he acknowledged Trent's comments with a nod, his eyes spoke volumes. Apparently, the chief had struck a chord.

From what Josh had shared with Keith, DeSean enjoyed being at Timothy House but felt tremendous pressure, either imagined or real, to fit into a specific mold. Looking around the room at the men assembled on this young man's behalf, Keith knew none of them would ever want DeSean to settle for second best, even if it meant deferring his college education or giving up a prestigious sports scholarship.

"Don't move ahead," Josh added, "until you know you've gotten a clear green light. My high school coach always told me to pay attention to any inner hesitation I felt about situations in life. If you let Him, God will hone this inner warning system within you. I've found He helps me when making important decisions."

DeSean sat still, as if soaking in all the wisdom shared by the Barnabas Brothers. He looked at his hands clasped tightly in his lap, then sat a bit straighter. "There haven't been many people in my life that have cared about me and done nice things for me as you have, and I don't want to disappoint any of you."

Don spoke first. "There's not a one of us here that would want you to do anything—enter college, accept a basketball scholarship, enlist in the military—unless you had some sort of peace about your first steps. It isn't about pleasing us—you need to be pleased with your decision.

"Believe me when I say there'll be many times in your life when you won't have all the answers. The way forward will seem foggy or unclear.

You'll swing back and forth between several options. Take a step forward in the direction you believe you're supposed to head, and trust that the Lord will show you the rest of the way. Think about it. Pray about it. Talk with the Smiths and us about it if you want. Son, I believe God will make clear which path to take."

"Thank you, Mr. Don," said DeSean. Seeming to relax against the back of the chair, he continued, "I appreciate your advice."

After glancing at his watch, Keith smiled. "Sorry to break up this gathering, but if we don't end soon, Miss Edna will have my hide. I promised to have DeSean back at her house for his weekend visit by one o'clock. Let's gather around DeSean and ask the Lord for direction."

The six men approached the wing chair where the teen sat, each placing a hand on the boy's shoulder.

"Lord," said Keith, "thank You for creating such a marvelous young man in DeSean Matthews. Thank You also for bringing him into our family here at Timothy House. He needs Your help deciding his future, Lord. Give him Your wisdom and guidance, and help him step out in faith toward the future You've prepared for him. All this we ask in Your most holy name. Amen."

When they raised their heads, Keith knew the mission for the Barnabas Brothers—pray for guidance for DeSean.

Five days later, on a Thursday morning, DeSean showed up at Keith's office thirty minutes before the school day began. Keith could hardly believe his eyes when he saw the teen standing in the doorway. *Didn't even know this kid got up this early*, he thought.

Looking a bit chagrined, DeSean said, "Morning, Coach. Can I talk to you?"

"Certainly," Keith replied. "Why don't you close the door and take a seat?"

DeSean sat in an armchair across the desk from his basketball coach, running his hands over the upholstered arms. "I've decided what I want to do once I graduate, and I wanted to talk to you about it."

"That's great, DeSean," Keith answered. "I'm all ears."

"I want to enlist in the Army." DeSean's statement hung between the two for a few seconds.

"Wow," said Keith. "That's terrific!"

Even before DeSean explained his rationale, Keith could tell that an incredible amount of maturation had occurred within the young man's heart in a short amount of time. It was like the boy had decided to put on his man clothes.

"Yes, sir," the student continued. "I love playing basketball, Coach, and I appreciate getting to play for you this year."

"It's been our honor to have you on the team," the coach said sincerely.

"The scholarship offers are tempting, but when I think about having to play ball and study at the same time, my stomach gets tied up in a knot. Ever since I was a little kid, I've dreamed of serving in the military. I know I'll receive a lot of training. There might be a chance of going to college later. I'm scared that if I don't do this now, I'll regret it."

This last line echoed what Keith had said to Abbie almost three months ago when telling her about Don's offer. Keith had no doubt he would have regretted turning down the job.

"I'm proud of you for standing up for yourself and deciding based on what you want to do, and not on what you think others would want you to," Keith said proudly. "You're an incredibly smart young man. Never tell yourself otherwise. Just because you've had academic struggles doesn't mean you'll always have them. You may be surprised that once you get past basic training and are assigned to a duty station, you'll find a subject area you're passionate about. Learning more about subjects means more when you want to learn the facts rather than being required to. Either way, you'll be a great asset to the Army."

"There's a favor I need to ask," continued the student. "There are now three coaches I'll need to contact about those scholarship offers. Would you help me make those calls?"

Keith's grin widened into a smile that spread from ear to ear. "Meet me in my office at three, and we'll start dialing."

CHAPTER
35

Back at the hotel after an early dinner, Abbie sat in the bathroom of her room in the desk chair Lane had dragged from the sitting area. Now that it was late March, her wedding was only eight weeks away. The two friends had planned a girls' weekend for themselves—complete with spa treatments, dinners out, and plenty of time to visit.

Standing behind her like a stylist, Lane held several bobby pins between her teeth as she ran a brush softly through Abbie's mahogany-colored hair. Various styling gels and sprays and a warm curling iron stood on the counter before them. Lane had a natural talent for hair design—tonight's role play aimed to discover how Abbie might like her hair styled for her wedding.

The two laughed, almost until they cried, as Lane arranged Abbie's hair this way and that. She parted it in different ways, brushed out the long locks after curling them, piled the hair high on Abbie's head, pulled it back in a sedate ponytail at the nape of her neck. Lane even French braided a lock of hair on each side of Abbie's face and tucked it into a chignon.

"Have you decided between the two dresses you told me about?" Lane asked as she pinned back a lock of hair that had fallen around Abbie's face.

"Not yet," said Abbie, watching Lane in the bathroom mirror as she worked her magic. "I'm leaning toward the plain white satin one with capped sleeves and a sweetheart neckline. It's simple, yet elegant."

"Sounds beautiful," Lane said, reaching for a can of hairspray. "Keith will love whatever you select."

Abbie blushed and smiled. "Laney," she began, her voice taking on a more serious tone. "I still can't quite believe I'll be Mrs. Keith Alexander Haliday in two short months."

After patting her friend reassuringly on the shoulder, Lane reached for a teasing comb. "Believe it, my friend."

"Even though I'm thankful for all God has done in this past year to help me put all the hurt and pain behind me, I still struggle with letting go of the anger and woundedness. I've had so many imaginary conversations with Joe—finally getting my day in court to tell him how he cut my heart to shreds with his dishonesty and selfishness. Like a broken record, I replay them over and over in my mind.

"I think Drew's made greater progress on this score," Abbie continued. "I've always thought part of his desire to be a pastor was to share with others God's answers to some of life's hardest questions, ones like he's wrestled with."

Lane listened attentively as she picked up another length of Abbie's hair.

"Beulah recently shared a Bible verse with me that I've read probably a hundred times, but this time, the words reached out from the page and grabbed my heart. It's one of those verses in the love chapter from a recently-released edition of the Bible, the New Living Version. I'd never seen it before."

"First Corinthians 13?" Lane inquired. Her eyes smiled encouragingly as the friends looked at their reflections in the mirror.

Abbie nodded wordlessly, her eyes swimming with tears. Several moments passed before she had her emotions under control. "'Love does not remember the suffering that comes from being hurt by someone,'" she said in a voice barely above a whisper.

"You could easily substitute 'chooses not to' for 'does not' when talking about rehashing all those pain-filled memories." Lane released the length of hair in her hand and walked around to face Abbie.

"That's the conclusion I'm coming to," said Abbie, looking up at her best friend leaning against the bathroom counter. "Another translation of First Corinthians 13:5 says that love 'does not keep an account of a wrong suffered.' I've finally realized that even though I've forgiven Joe or thought I had, I relish ticking off his list of offenses. It's like some perverse pleasure.

"God has helped me see that I'm the prisoner who needs freeing, not Joe. Joe's dead. I, however, am alive. But as long as I nurse those hurts, I might as well be locked away in a castle tower beyond all rescue."

"What is God telling you to do?" Lane asked softly.

Abbie smiled slightly, "The Lord has been reminding me that this passage from First Corinthians—verses four through eight—is not only a word picture of how we are to love others but, most importantly, explains how God loves me."

Pushing a wayward strand of hair behind her ear, Abbie continued. "God, through Jesus, does not keep an account of my wrongs. Since He doesn't, it's a sin for me to keep holding on to Joe's." Giggling out loud, she mused, "You know, as I've tried to wrap my head around this, I now wonder why it's taken me so long to see the futility of my refusal to forgive Joe."

"Like St. Augustine's quote about 'drinking poison and waiting for the other person to die?'"

"Exactly," replied Abbie, her voice full of hope-filled determination. "You remember I told you about Winnie's Target Plan?"

"Aim small; don't miss at all."

"That's the one," said Abbie. "Every time a hurtful thought about Joe runs through my mind, I stop, pray, and ask God to forgive me for it and to replace it with a thought that honors Him. Love is an act of will, and I'm choosing to employ my will squarely in line with what God would have me do." Abbie reached out her hand for Lane's. "Life is too short and precious to do anything less."

Lane squeezed Abbie's hand and said, "Amen!"

Peering around to look into the mirror, Abbie tousled her hair and said brightly, "Now, what about the wedding hairdo?"

Lane laughed and moved back behind Abbie. Reaching to pick up the comb from the counter, Lane ran it gently over the top of Abbie's hair. Looking at her dear friend's reflection, she said, "Many friends have been praying for you. God honors the prayers of His people when they faithfully call out to Him."

Abbie nodded wordlessly, tears filling her eyes. Trying to keep her bottom lip from quivering, she said softly, "But I don't deserve Keith or any of this happiness I've found with him."

Lane stopped what she was doing and looked at Abbie solemnly in the mirror. "*None* of us deserve anything God does for us, if the truth be told. But, as our Heavenly Father, He lavishes good gifts upon us. At this moment, Keith Haliday is the best of those gifts in your life."

"I agree with you on that," said Abbie, her expression brighter. Looking in the mirror, she saw Lane had completed her latest hair design. "This has been so much fun, but I've had enough hairstyling ideas for one day. If it's okay with you, I'd rather visit. There's so much I have to tell you."

"You're breaking my heart, Abbie," Lane said in mock disgust, setting the hairbrush on the bathroom counter. "As long as you've gotten one or two ideas before tomorrow's appointment with the stylist, all my efforts will have been worth it." Grabbing the back of the desk chair, Lane swiveled Abbie around until she was facing the door to the bedroom. Careful not to bump the door frame, Lane rolled Abbie through the doorway and back across the hotel room to the desk.

Stepping out from behind the chair, Lane offered in a mock French accent, "Madame, thank you again for your visit to Maison de Lane." She bowed slightly, holding one arm before her so that it almost swept the ground.

As she stood, Abbie giggled. "You are the best! I mean it," continued Abbie, trying to suppress another laugh. "Thanks so much for spending all that time helping me decide on a hairstyle." Rising from the chair, she hugged her best friend.

"You are so welcome," replied Lane as she headed toward the connecting door between their hotel rooms.

Abbie glanced at the clock on the bedside table. "It's almost ten now. What do you say if we change into our pajamas? I brought treats for us. Popcorn, gingersnaps, and chocolate bars. I've also brought plenty of tea. Our mani-pedis aren't until ten-thirty tomorrow morning, so we'll have a little time to sleep in if our conversation runs long."

Reaching the door that led into her bedroom, Lane turned back toward Abbie. "Oh, I knew there was something I forgot to tell you at dinner."

Abbie listened carefully, eager to hear what her friend had to say.

"Eric wanted me to tell you that he thinks Keith's the finest man he's met, maybe ever."

For a few seconds, Abbie didn't know what to say. Eric and Lane and Abbie and Joe had been best friends. The couple's sons were close. As her relationship with Keith grew, Abbie hoped they would develop a solid friendship with the Wyatts, but she knew that wasn't a given.

"Wow, Lane," said Abbie softly, tears threatening. "Please tell Eric his approval means the world to me. I know it will mean a lot to Keith as well."

Lane placed her hand on the doorknob. "One more thing you need to know," she said, as a wide grin spread across her face. "Eric and Keith made a bet to see how long we'd stay up talking tonight. Not sure of the time they each chose, but Eric told me he's pretty sure he'll win."

Abbie smiled. "What's the prize for winning the bet?"

"The loser has to buy the winner dinner at his favorite restaurant."

With a playful gleam in her eye, Abbie said, "Winner, winner, chicken dinner. See you soon!"

CHAPTER
36

Abbie watched trees whizz past the window as Keith's SUV zipped down the highway. Spring was in full bloom in eastern Tennessee and had adorned the trees in the bright baby green of new growth. It was a beautiful Saturday morning to visit McHenry. Several of Abbie's treasured friends had planned a bridal shower today, and Keith had insisted on driving Abbie to it. Drew had also come, making this day a family affair.

Craning her head to check on her son, Abbie smiled as she discovered him fast asleep in the back seat, his head rolled against the headrest. *This week has been busy for you*, she thought, watching her precious son, now a man. In the middle of packing to leave Tennessee for seminary in Texas, Drew was about to embark on a new life journey.

Facing forward, Abbie pulled down her sun visor and lifted the flap for the vanity mirror. She adjusted it until she could see out the rear window. Behind them were four friends from Robbinsonville whom Abbie had wanted at the shower. She never expected them to make the three-hour drive. Still, after the invitations had arrived, Doris Fielding, Portia Dockery, Evelyn Benson, and Taylor Nunley followed Keith and Abbie to the event in Doris's four-door sedan. How thankful Abbie was that her new friends could be with her today.

Snapping the mirror closed, Abbie folded the visor. Glancing at Keith, she asked, "What will you and Drew do while we're at the party?"

"Well, for starters, Drew said he wanted to take me to a great hamburger joint in town that makes fabulous milkshakes."

"Ah, yes," said Abbie, catching on. "Riley's. You'll love it! Their shakes are so thick the straws stand up by themselves. They also make enormous fried onion rings that are out of this world."

"Stop," said Keith in mock horror. "I won't be able to stand this long ride if you don't." Chancing a look at Abbie, he said, "Don't you worry about me and Drew. We've got all sorts of trouble to get into."

Abbie slapped playfully at his arm. "That's what I'm afraid of."

When she looked back at the road before them, Abbie saw they were already coming into McHenry. *How is that possible?* she thought.

A noise from the back seat let her know Drew was waking up.

"Did you get a good nap?"

"Too good." Drew yawned as he tried to fend off the cobwebs of sleep.

Keith's truck stopped in front of Winnie Jeffers's home. Abbie's friend and former colleague was hosting the shower, and she couldn't wait to see her other McHenry friends.

The ladies from Robbinsonville parked behind Keith. *I can't wait to introduce you all to each other*, she thought, grateful for the gift of sweet friends God had given to her.

Abbie might as well be twenty-one, Winnie thought as she observed Abbie's excitement.

In groups of twos and threes, the guests arrived. The cheerful sounds of laughter and long-awaited reunions filled the front hall of Winnie's house as Abbie and her guests exchanged hugs. As Winnie and Abbie stood together to greet their company, Lane ferried shower gifts into the den, where the guest of honor would soon open them.

As soon as each guest had made her way around the table, filling plates with finger sandwiches, caramel cake, mixed nuts, and large butter mints, Lane directed Abbie's friends into Winnie's den. The vaulted ceiling over the brick fireplace gave the room a certain airiness. Oversized, comfortable chairs and sofas sat around the spacious room in several groupings. A large tapestry-style rug covered wide-plank hardwood floors. Winnie directed Abbie to sit in an overstuffed wing chair near the table laden with gifts.

Abbie's conversations with her friends from McHenry, ones she hadn't seen for a while, picked up where they had ended—a sign of true friendship.

"How is Murphy?" Abbie asked Wilma Jennings as she cut a bite of cake with her fork. "Are you keeping him straight at the law firm?"

"You better believe it," replied Wilma, a mischievous twinkle in her eye.

Looking over at the Kent Academy school secretary, Abbie queried, "Rosie, has this been a good year at school?"

"It has," said Rosie, wiping her mouth before continuing. "But not at all the same without you and Mr. Patterson."

Both Rosie and Abbie caught the eye of Lucille, Arthur Patterson's wife, who beamed at the compliment.

It amazed Winnie how Abbie's friends from Robbinsonville seemed to fit right in, weaving their comments into the tapestry of conversation among this fellowship of women. *Once again*, Winnie thought, *the Lord is taking care of my dear friend.*

Soon, Winnie clinked a spoon against her punch glass. "Ladies," she said, looking at all who had gathered to celebrate the goodness of God in the life of their friend. "How delighted I and your other hostesses are to have you here today. Abbie, all of us have been honored to play a special part in your life. To say we're happy for you and Keith would be the understatement of the century. We hope the gifts you receive today will become treasures, serving as reminders of the new gifts God brings to each of us every day. Not because we deserve them, but because He loves us and wants to lavish that love upon us."

Winnie searched the room until her eyes found Lane looking back at her. When their eyes met, an unspoken message passed between them—the revelation that God was indeed working in Abbie's heart and helping her to lay down her burdens from her past once and for all. Abbie had called Winnie three days earlier and told her about the conversation she and Lane had about forgiveness. Like co-conspirators in some grand scheme, they smiled knowingly at one another.

Soon, the tearing of paper and the metallic sound of scissors opening and closing filled the den. The ladies gathered and watched as Abbie opened each of their gifts. As she removed presents from their wrapping, each perfect in its own way, Abbie could hear oohs and aahs.

"Thanks so much, Rosie," said Abbie, holding up the white ceramic pie plate the Kent Academy secretary had given her. "Keith loves chess pie, and you can bet I'll often cook one in this beautiful dish."

Next, Abbie unwrapped two linen tea towels hand-embroidered with the initial "H." "Oh, Wilma, these are so beautiful. Thank you!" Wilma smiled while watching her gift make its way around the room for all to see.

Lane handed Abbie a small, rectangular package adorned with an elegant satin ribbon. Abbie removed the top of the box, unwrapped the item within, and then drew in a breath of surprise as she discovered an antique pearl-handled, serving spoon.

"Lucille," Abbie exclaimed, "this is so special." The older woman smiled through tear-filled eyes.

Finally, two large packages were left. Lane placed the smaller of the two in front of Abbie's chair.

"Wonder what this could be?" queried Abbie as she excitedly looked for the seam of the paper. A small card was taped to the front of the package beside the bow. Removing it from the box, Abbie withdrew the card and read the message written and signed by her Robbinsonville friends. Doris, Portia, Evelyn, and Taylor watched as Abbie opened the deluxe coffee machine they had purchased. "Thank you, ladies," Abbie said cheerfully. Each of them looked extremely pleased.

Finally, it was time for the hostesses to present their gift. The box was so large, Winnie and Lane had to lift it together. Everyone in the room seemed to lean forward to make sure they could see. As Abbie peeled away the wrapping paper, the photo of a commercial electric mixer appeared.

Looking up, Abbie exclaimed, "You all are much too generous." Once again, sheer delight shone across her face. "This is such a terrific gift. Thank you!" Winnie, Lane, Beulah, Muriel, and Gladys waved at their favorite girl. A collective "You're welcome!" could be heard from them.

Happy chatter filled the air in Winnie's den. However, she didn't want this time to slip away before passing along some particular thoughts to her friend, who had persevered through unthinkable trials. Stepping into the middle of the room, Winnie waited until the noise died down. "Abbie, I want you to stand next to me for a minute."

Immediately, the room grew silent.

Winnie put her arm around Abbie's shoulders, her wiry hair cascading around her face. "Dear Abbie, all of us in this room know how much you have been through in the last few years. Though you may not have believed it could happen, each of us, at least those of us in McHenry, have been praying God would bring you a man who would love and cherish you as the treasure we know you to be. God has answered those prayers in Keith Haliday. Before we leave today, I'd like to bless you and Keith and ask for the Lord's guidance in this new season ahead."

Winnie looked around the room. "Would you please pray with me?" When Winnie's arm tightened around Abbie's shoulders, tears spilled from Abbie's eyes.

"Dearest Lord, we thank You for our wonderful friend, Abbie. Only You know the extent of her and Drew's sorrow and pain. Though we don't understand why, we know You sometimes use suffering in our lives to fashion us more closely into Your likeness. We are grateful You have answered our prayers with Keith Haliday. May each of us gathered here today do all in our power to support and assist this couple as they prepare for their wedding and new life ahead.

"Lord, knit their hearts together as one. Encourage them when they are down. Strengthen them when they are weak. Empower them to make a difference in this dark world for You. May their home be a place where all who enter experience Your presence. Bless Abbie and Keith, and seal their hearts with Your love. Mark their lives with Your peace. In the strong and precious name of Jesus, I pray. Amen."

As Winnie looked at Abbie and her dear friends gathered to celebrate, she knew God's presence would surely lead Abbie and Keith as they moved to higher ground.

Abbie was grateful she had asked Keith to come back to Winnie's instead of riding back with Lane. Within thirty minutes of the last guest's departure, he had cheerfully appeared on Winnie's front porch. It took them several trips to ferry their many new wedding gifts to the back of Keith's SUV. After one more emotion-filled round of hugs and thank-yous given to Winnie and the other hostesses, Keith escorted Abbie to the vehicle.

"Looks like you enjoyed quite the soirée," said Keith as he cranked the engine.

"I'll say," she replied while adjusting her visor to block the mid-afternoon sun. "I feel spoiled." She sank into the seat. "My dear friends have made sure our home will be well-appointed and our kitchen well stocked."

"How thoughtful of them," replied Keith. "I know all in attendance loved getting to see you. I talked to Eric earlier this week, and he told me how so many in McHenry miss you." Keith pulled out from the curb and drove down the street.

Pausing as if to gather her thoughts, Abbie replied, "I have missed my friends, too. Though I love Robbinsonville, so much of my life was lived in this place."

Glancing at the dashboard, Abbie noted the time—four thirty-seven. "What time are we meeting Laney and Eric for dinner?" she asked, turning to Keith.

"Eric took Drew, along with his guys, to a movie during the shower. The show should be over by now. He said to pick them up at seven. Do you have somewhere you'd like to go?"

"I do, Keith, as a matter of fact," Abbie replied slowly, as if unsure of what to say next.

"Your wish is my command," her fiancé replied, a silly grin plastered across his face, the same one he had been wearing constantly in these past weeks.

Abbie took such a long time to respond that Keith finally pulled the car over to the curb.

"Abbie," he said softly. "What's wrong?" Keith turned to look at this woman whom he loved more than life itself, quiet sobs now racking her body. "Sweetheart, please tell me what's the matter," urgency evident in his voice as he reached over to hug her.

For the longest time, Abbie sat protected within Keith's embrace as the emotional storm passed. Finally, she moved away from him and wiped the tears streaming down her face.

"I need to go to the chapel at my old church," Abbie said in a voice hardly above a whisper.

"Oak Hills Community Church?"

The nod of her head was the only answer Abbie could offer.

"We'll head there now," said Keith, tenderness apparent in his tone.

For the next twenty minutes, neither said a word. When Keith pulled into the church's parking lot, he found a space and parked his SUV.

Turning off the ignition, he said softly, "You take all the time you need."

Shaking her head, Abbie offered Keith a weak smile. "Thanks, Keith. I'm sorry about this unexpected stop. I'll explain all this to you later, but for now, I need to talk to the Lord about something I've been wrestling with for a very long time. He's been knocking on my heart about it, but I've been ignoring Him. After we left Winnie's house a little while ago, the sound of His knock turned into a loud pounding. I've learned it's best not to ignore Him."

Pushing back a strand of her hair behind one ear, Abbie continued, "Could you give me an hour?"

"Certainly," said Keith brightly. "I'm happy to call Eric and cancel our dinner reservations if you want me to."

Glancing at her watch, Abbie shook her head. "No, that won't be necessary. I'll be back here by six." Reaching for the handle, she opened her door and stepped out onto the pavement. Once the door closed, Abbie brought a hand to her mouth. Kissing her fingers, she then gently blew a kiss to him.

Keith returned one of his own as he watched Abbie turn and walk into the chapel, a place where he knew she had found healing and refuge before.

Once through the heavy doorway, Abbie made her way to a pew near the front of the chapel. The afternoon sun announced its comforting presence with muted shafts of light that pierced the beveled-glass panes like Heaven's arrows. It was similar to a visit a little over a year ago, when Abbie wrestled with her decision to join the faculty of Timothy House and how to proceed in her relationship with Keith. Now, she had returned to face a dilemma that had haunted her for many years, one that needed to be laid to rest once and for all.

Though Abbie had moved ahead with her life, the ball and chain of the unforgiving spirit she continued to harbor against Joe Richardson still clanked its way into every fragment of her soul. Throughout the years, Abbie had become skilled in putting on the mask that seemed to say to the world that all was right within her, though she knew it was a lie. If she were honest, she had come to savor the perverse pleasure she took in holding on to the pain and suffering Joe had inflicted on her and their son. The worst part was that Abbie had tried to hide this pitiless attitude from God, as if He could not see what was hidden in the darkest corners of her heart.

Thinking about Drew's upcoming departure for seminary, Abbie also knew she had a responsibility before God to set a good example for her only son. Smiling tenderly, Abbie thought about how hard Drew had worked to forgive his father for his emotional abuse and betrayal. Could Abbie do no less?

What was it that Beulah had told her one time about Joe and Abbie's refusal to forgive him? *We're all prodigals, Abbie. Some just wander a little farther off God's front porch than others.*

The line had been reverberating in her heart and mind for weeks now. Looking up at the carved stone cross that hung at the front of the small sanctuary, Abbie knew the hound of Heaven had finally cornered her. *Joe's not the only prodigal*, she thought.

For the longest time, Abbie focused on the cross and the intricate details of the images cut into its marble surface. Just as some unnamed stone mason had left his mark on this testament to his talent, so, too, had the Lord used the wounds caused by Joe's betrayal to shape Abbie into the woman she had come to be. Though she knew not the name of the artist who had created this beautiful cross before her, he had created within her a desire to learn more about this mason and his craft.

Being used by God to show His love to others was Abbie's heart's deepest desire. Just as many would not understand the One who had transformed her heart and mind and rescued her from the pit of despair, she prayed the marks of Jesus's transforming love would be evident in her life, drawing others to want to know more about Him. However, if all they saw was the mask of Abbie Richardson's making, none would ever learn her story of His redeeming power in her life.

More of Beulah's sage wisdom came to mind. *You can hold all the anger and pain tightly in your heart and your hand, much like a toddler does when grasping a toy, or you can unclasp your fingers, open your hand, and offer back to God all your hurt as a sacrifice. Give it to Him so He can put all those pieces together, working them out for good in your life.*

Thinking about the prodigal son, Abbie knew she had been a runaway, too, only one of a different kind. Instead of facing her pain, she had buried it, thinking that because she had secreted it away in a locked room of her own making, it could not hurt her anymore. Nothing could be further from the truth. By Abbie's taking matters into her own hands and refusing the Lord access to that dungeon of pain, she had forced Him into a stalemate.

God is a gentleman, Abbie, Beulah had told her. *He won't force you to open your heart, but His cleansing, life-changing power can't operate deep within you until you do.* With her wedding to Keith only weeks away, Abbie knew it was time to give God the key that would enable Him to free her from this prison of suffering. It was time to let Joe go.

As Abbie bowed her head, the words she had refused to speak aloud for so long began to trickle out from the depths of her soul.

"Oh, Lord, I have been carrying this burden for so long, and I am tired of holding on to it. Even as many years as it's been, I still can't believe what Joe did to Drew and me. Please forgive me for the anger I've held onto for so long. Help me to forgive Joe. There's a root of bitterness that's sprung up from the seeds of that anger, and I can't pull it out of the soil of my heart. Please do that for me."

Abbie wiped away the tears that had begun their silent journey down her cheeks.

"Lord, I've focused all these years on the speck in Joe's eye without, at all, acknowledging the log in my own. I've held myself up as some paragon of virtue, nursing the victim role I was thrust into after Joe's misdeeds were uncovered. Though bearing different consequences, my sin of unforgiveness is no different than his sin of betrayal. *All* sin is abhorrent to You. Forgive me, Lord, for setting myself as some arbiter, choosing the sins of another to gloat over, and failing to take accountability for none of my own.

"I cannot even begin to thank You for the gift You have brought to me in Keith. He deserves so much happiness. Though I love him with all of my heart, our marriage will be too crowded if I drag my ball and chain into it."

Abbie slowly opened her eyes and noticed that both her hands were clenched in tight fists. She had been so lost in pouring out her heart to the Lord that she had lost any awareness of how her body was reacting to the petition. Abbie slowly unfurled the fingers of her hands and held them up to the sunlight shining across her pew. As she did, the words of Frances Havergal's hymn whispered to her soul, "Take my life, and let it be, consecrated, Lord, to thee."

With outstretched hands and head bowed, Abbie finished her prayer. "God, I don't know how to do this." Lifting her hands higher, she continued. "Take from me what's in my hands. My pain. My bitterness. My suffering. My critical spirit. My spiritual snobbery. Please forgive me for holding on to these hard feelings against Joe for far too long. Release me from this prison of my own making.

"Give me the courage to follow You every day. Wash me clean through Your word that lives within my heart and teach me through Your Holy

Spirit how to walk as a redeemed daughter of the King. Equip me with a supernatural ability to love and cherish Keith as You would have me do.

"Thank You, most of all, Lord, for not giving up on me. How puny my efforts are in the light of all You gave for me on Calvary's Tree. I give You permission to use me in whatever way You see fit for as much time as You have planned for me on this earth."

Her "Amen" gently ended the cleansing flood of prayer. Lifting her head, Abbie wiped away the last of her tears. A peace, unlike any she had known, wrapped itself around her like a special robe given to her by her Heavenly Father, reminding her that she was a prodigal no more.

Joy coursed through Abbie as she pushed open the heavy door of the chapel at Oak Hills Community Church. Turning to glance once more at the stone cross, she murmured a thank you to the One who loved her like no other.

Stepping out onto the sidewalk and into the late afternoon sunlight that gently caressed her face, Abbie could see Keith waiting patiently for her in his SUV.

Reaching for the door handle, she glimpsed the time on her watch. Five fifty-seven.

God's time is always perfect, she thought.

CHAPTER
38

Abbie and Drew were working this Saturday morning to pack all his belongings. Cardboard boxes of varying sizes and clumps of crumpled packing paper were scattered around the small apartment. In three days, Drew would leave Tennessee for Texas. His acceptance to Dallas Theological Seminary had arrived less than a month ago, and ever since, the momentum of his life had accelerated. Myriad details had to be attended to, including notifying his landlady, ensuring his older model SUV was roadworthy, and finalizing departure plans with his current employers—Timothy House and Wright's Creek Community Church.

Usually, Abbie would have been at Mistletoe Cottage on a Saturday morning, taking care of the girls who had not gone home for the weekend. Thanks to Teencie Curtis, Abbie could take care of Drew and wedding planning.

At the moment, Abbie stood at the kitchenette sink. Movement outside the window caught her attention. She watched with amusement as two squirrels chased each other, leaping like circus acrobats from branch to branch of the large oak tree behind the garage. The furry creatures moved without a care in the world. Abbie smiled, thinking how Drew's life was somewhat carefree thanks to Audry.

Abbie pulled open a drawer next to the sink and took out several dish towels and hot pads. Thinking about the new kitchen she would soon stock once she and Keith moved into the Manse, she offered a silent prayer of thanksgiving for Audry's financial gift. Abbie had spent a portion of it to buy two sets of china, glassware, flatware, and various odds and ends for her new home. Determined to leave the past in the past, Abbie had given away or sold the household items acquired during her marriage to Joe.

Reaching into a cabinet next to the sink, she pulled out a stack of stoneware dishes and placed it on the kitchen table. After wrapping the plates, she carefully stacked each inside a cardboard box on a nearby chair. She then wadded extra packing paper and wedged it into the space between the dishes. After sealing the box with packing tape, she wrote "Kitchen - Plates" in large block letters with a permanent marker and carried the box to a growing stack near the front door.

The closet door was open, and Abbie heard the sounds of coat hangers clanking together inside it.

"Drew?" Abbie called out.

"Just a minute, Mom," he replied.

Abbie stood in the open doorway. Smiling, she watched Drew, who seemed engaged in a wrestling match with an armful of shirts on hangers. At the moment, the shirts appeared to have the upper hand. A jumbled assortment of belts lay at his feet, reminding Abbie of the earthworms young Drew had dug up from their backyard. Against the far wall of the closet, a pile of jeans and slacks lay neatly folded. One large box, filled with athletic shoes and other footwear, sat near the entrance to the closet.

Drew stumbled backward, almost losing his balance, as all the crooked necks of the hangers suddenly slipped from around the bar. Instinctively, Abbie ran to steady him. In the process, she almost tripped over a small laundry hamper.

Laughing, Abbie said, "I think it's time for lunch. What do you think?" She lifted half of the hanging clothes from her son's arms. Making her way from the closet, Abbie placed the stack of shirts and jackets onto the bed. Drew followed close behind and did the same.

"Whew," Drew said, wiping his sweaty brow. "I thought we were about to take a tumble."

"You're not kidding," Abbie replied as she headed to the kitchenette.

Opening the door to the refrigerator, she pulled out two chilled bottles of water and two sack lunches she'd made earlier. Chocolate chip cookies, waiting in an open container on the table, would serve as dessert.

"Lunch is ready," she called out.

Drew joined his mother and sat to eat. Pulling a peanut butter and jelly sandwich from the brown paper bag, he said, "I'm glad to take a break."

"You looked like you could use one," Abbie said as she emptied the contents of her lunch on the table.

Looking around the small apartment as they ate, Abbie could hardly believe they had accomplished so much in such a short time. "When did you say you wanted to leave?"

Drew finished the bite of kettle chips he was munching on and then took a swig from his water bottle. "Seven o'clock Tuesday morning," he replied before popping the last bite of the sandwich into his mouth. "It'll take me about nine hours to get to Little Rock. I booked a room at the same hotel where I last stayed. If I can get back on the road by seven Wednesday morning, that'll put me in Dallas by noon."

"Sounds like a plan to me," said his mother. Though she wanted to brush away the lock of sandy hair that had fallen across Drew's forehead, Abbie restrained herself. She knew that doing so might come across as mothering, and she was trying to give Drew space. She took a bite of a potato chip and wondered, *Will I ever lose these feelings of wanting to care for and protect my son?*

"Mom . . ." Drew said, letting her name hang between them. He took hold of one of her hands. "I'm going to miss you, and I want you to know that."

Tears stung Abbie's eyes. "I'll miss you, too, Drewby," she murmured, her voice low and thick with emotion.

Tightening his grip on his mother's hand, as if to draw from her strength and courage, he continued, "I don't say it often, but I want you to know how much I love you and what a wonderful mother you've been to me. You're the one person in my life who's never given up on me."

Though he rarely displayed deep emotion, Drew's eyes swam with tears. Fighting back a few of her own, Abbie said, "And I never will."

Smiling brightly, Drew swallowed hard and then continued. "I know. I also want you to know that in my counseling sessions with Pastor Rod, I've been working to turn all the anger and pain I still have concerning

Dad over to God. Though I can't change the circumstances, I can, with God's help, allow Him to use that hurt to accomplish a higher purpose in my life."

Abbie found herself holding her breath as she heard her son verbalize the same struggle she had recently turned over to the Lord. *Oh, Father*, she thought, thinking of the many ways in which God had tenderly ministered to the wounds in both their hearts. *Thank You for the power of forgiveness and its ability to changes lives.*

Drew's next statement warmed Abbie's heart beyond telling. "It's important that you know how happy I am for you and Keith. I'm looking forward to being back in town for your wedding."

"Oh, Drew," said Abbie excitedly, "thank you for that sweet blessing. It's hard to believe the wedding's only twenty-eight days away."

Incredulous, Drew stared at her for a minute. "You've been counting the days?"

"You better believe it!" His mother's smile was electric.

"I've come to love and respect Keith. I realize, though, I have a long way to go in learning to trust another man who would be a father figure to me."

Abbie gripped her son's hand tightly. "There's no rush. Keith is there for you and only wants the best for you."

Drew sat silently as Abbie rubbed her thumb gently over his hand. "Even amid incredibly painful circumstances, God has never abandoned or forsaken us. He's led us through some dark valleys. But now, in ways neither of us could have imagined, He's moving us to higher ground. Never try to outguess God."

"Definitely not," was her son's reply.

A dog barked somewhere out in the yard below, breaking their concentration. Abbie glanced at her watch and saw that over an hour had passed since their lunch break began.

"We'd better get back to work," Abbie chirped, pushing her chair back from the table. Gathering the remains of their lunch, she rose to throw the trash away.

Drew stood and stretched his back. "It shouldn't take me long to finish up in the closet."

"Great," said Abbie, pulling open another drawer. "I'll finish packing your kitchen."

She watched her son walk away from her. Knowing her time with him was down to mere days, she uttered a silent prayer. *Lord, please take care of my boy, and show me how to let him go as he begins this new chapter of his life.*

The peace in Abbie's heart was the assurance that God had already answered this prayer.

CHAPTER
39

Peter's Chapel was abuzz with noise, excitement, and a sense of wonder in the air. Tonight, the entire Timothy House family—administrators, faculty, staff, students, patrons, and board members—packed into the stone sanctuary. Tonight's service would be a first for the school, as Don planned this special ceremony to ask the Lord's blessing on Tim and Taylor Nunley and their recent adoption of Chloe Minton.

Once Keith and Abbie took their seats, Abbie looked around the crowded room. Tim and Taylor sat a few rows ahead, Chloe between them. As if on cue, the child turned around and almost instantly found Abbie in the crowd. Delight flooded Abbie's heart as the precious girl waved happily. Abbie returned the greeting, hoping her smile conveyed all her love for the girl who reminded her so much of herself.

Abbie would also play an essential role in the night's festivities. *What a tremendous debt of gratitude I owe Don Fielding,* she thought, as she watched the head of school in what would be one of his last official roles before his upcoming retirement. Don had even arranged a special meeting with the school's board of trustees for Abbie to establish what she hoped would become an integral part of life at Timothy House and a fitting tribute to the woman whose financial legacy allowed the formation of a scholarship in her name. Abbie prayed that the scholarship would serve as an example for others—that one life *can* make a difference—beginning with tonight's recipients.

Abbie looked at the program in her hand. The title on the front page read "Blessing and Dedication Service for the Adoption of Chloe Isabella Minton," followed by the date—May 5. Looking inside, Abbie read through the program line-up: music to begin the program, Don's opening remarks, Tim and Taylor's testimony, Pastor Eichman's blessing, student recognition, and Don's benediction to close the service. The program didn't mention Abbie's name, as she had requested. Though in years to come, the head of school would announce the scholarship recipients at the annual end-of-the-year awards ceremony, Abbie had asked if she could present the awards during tonight's unique service.

The conversation died down as music rose in the chapel. Celeste Daniels, the choir director, and Heather Phillips opened the program with a piano and violin prelude. Few in the audience knew of Heather's musical abilities, but it was soon apparent that she was a gifted musician. Abbie was amazed at the student's proficiency.

As the strains of the music faded, Don Fielding ascended the platform stairs and put on a pair of reading glasses. "Tonight's special service is a first for Timothy House. Never in the school's sixty-three-year history have we had a story to share as sweet and tender as this one. It's only fitting that we celebrate this milestone event as a family, with all of us gathered together in one place. I'd like to ask Tim and Taylor Nunley to join me on the podium."

As the couple made their way to his side, Don continued, "What we're about to witness tonight is special. Adoption is the sacred process of bringing into a family one who was not originally born into that household. Because of demonstrated promises of love and devotion, the adoptee is grafted into this family's circle and secured there. I've asked Taylor and Tim to share how God led them to this point."

Tim smiled. "God sure has a way of surprising you when you least expect it," he began. "Last summer, totally out of the blue, God answered a prayer for Taylor and me that we thought He'd forgotten about. He opened a door that allowed us to welcome, not only into our home but also into our hearts, a precious little girl we already knew and loved, known as Chloe Minton. We ask that you pray for us as we become a new family unit. We believe, with God's help, it can be done." Looking like he had saved the best news for last, with an expression that looked like Christmas had come early, Tim said, "I am happy to tell you that as of ten o'clock last Thursday morning, Chloe's last name is officially Nunley."

A roar of applause and hoorahs rang out in the stone chapel. As the ovation continued, Tim tenderly placed his hand on Taylor's back. As the noise died down, Taylor stepped closer to the podium.

"Not being able to have children has been one of the great heartaches of our marriage," Taylor began. As she spoke, Taylor's shoulders sagged. Her words trailed off as she lowered her head, her face contorted with emotion. For a few seconds, it seemed as if she would not be able to continue. Finally, she regained her composure and lifted her head. "As most of you know, God's plans are always better than ours. A late-night visit from Don last summer, during Camp 4Ever, totally changed the trajectory of our lives and Chloe's. As Don talked to us that evening, it became clear that God had orchestrated seemingly random events to lead us to where we are tonight. Tim and I covet your prayers as we walk with our precious Chloe in this new life He has given to us."

Once again, warm applause filled the chapel. Hand in hand, the Nunleys backed away as Don's voice quieted those gathered in the stone chapel.

"Next, I'd like to ask Pastor Rod Eichman and Chloe to join me."

Rod walked to where Chloe sat next to Doris Fielding and took the girl's hand. Carefully, he led her up the stairs to where her new parents were waiting.

As Rod unfolded several sheets of paper, the Nunleys and Chloe sat in chairs on the platform.

"Tim, Taylor, and Chloe," he began. "I'm thrilled to be a part of this special evening. I'm especially honored you asked me to voice this blessing as you begin your new life as a family together. Everyone in this room is committed to walking beside you and helping you in any way possible."

After approaching Tim, Rod stood behind him and placed his hand on Tim's head. "Dear Father, we thank You for Tim Nunley and his willingness to follow Your lead, no matter what. As Tim's Heavenly Father, please guide and direct his steps, give him wisdom and guidance, and, most of all, supply him with joy for this journey of parenthood. Bless this new father in Jesus's name. Amen."

Next, Rod stood behind Taylor before gently touching her head. "Dear Lord, we thank You for Taylor Nunley and her willingness to allow

You to help her love another's child as her own. That's the measure by which You love us—freely, unconditionally, and lavishly. Equip Taylor with the wisdom, patience, and energy she will need as a new parent. Supply her with an endless supply of Your love and grace to share with Chloe. Bless this new mother in Jesus's name. Amen."

Last, Rod stood behind Chloe. He whispered something to her before placing his hands on the child's head. "Dear Lord, we thank You for Chloe, Your child of promise to Tim and Taylor. Give her the gifts of wisdom and understanding. Grant her physical health and safety. Fill her heart with Your love and, as You do, knit her heart completely into the hearts of her new parents. May the love this family has for You and each other be a blessing to others in return. We ask all this in Your Son's strong and precious name. Amen."

As he raised his head, he extended his arms. "Ladies and gentlemen, it is my distinct privilege to introduce the Nunley family to you."

As if electrified, the congregation jumped to its feet as thunderous applause broke out and whistles echoed into the rafters of the stone chapel.

Abbie soaked in the magic of this moment. This story's happy ending was one only the Lord Himself could write.

Abbie glanced at Keith, who winked at her. She hoped her news would make the recipients of Audry's generosity extremely happy.

"There is one more part of tonight's service I believe you will find particularly meaningful and encouraging," Don said, locking eyes with Abbie. "I'd like to invite Mrs. Richardson, a member of our English faculty and housemother to our seventh-grade young ladies, to join me."

As Abbie slipped past Keith on her way into the aisle, he whispered, "Audry would be so proud of you." Smiling at these words and knowing their truth, Abbie approached the platform.

"It is my distinct honor," she began, looking out at those seated in the packed pews of Peter's Chapel, "to announce the formation of a new recognition to be awarded annually to a deserving Timothy House student and a faculty member. We have established the Audry MacDonald Promise Award thanks to a generous financial endowment in loving memory of a lady who was a tremendous influence in my life and helped me see the potential I had somehow missed within myself. Rather than qualifying based on grade point average or personal achievement, recipients are selected based on their character and undeveloped potential. This honor carries with it a five-thousand-dollar cash award. I am happy to announce this year's recipients—DeSean Matthews and Tim and Taylor Nunley."

If the excitement level had been high before, it was now off the charts following Abbie's announcement. The congregation was again on its feet, offering hearty applause. Through tear-filled eyes, Abbie watched as the lanky senior and the new parents made their way to the platform. All three looked stunned.

DeSean was the first to receive a Promise Award. As he stepped forward to accept a brass plaque and a sealed envelope from the head of Timothy House, the young man appeared incredulous due to all the attention paid him. Abbie watched the teen's eyes widen and a silly grin make its way slowly across his face as applause rang out once more on his behalf.

Catching Keith's attention across the crowded chapel, Abbie's eyes held his fast as she gave a slight nod of thanks for the life-saving efforts he had made on DeSean's behalf.

Next, the Nunleys walked to where Don was standing. Chloe stood patiently on the platform behind them. After receiving the award from the head of school, the couple made their way over to Abbie. Taylor engulfed the teacher in a tight hug that nearly took Abbie's breath away. Tears of gratitude streamed down the new mother's face.

After waiting patiently until his wife had conveyed her thanks, Tim also offered Abbie a warm embrace, whispering in her ear that God had used her to show them the purpose for their lives.

Abbie watched with delight as the three honorees basked in the glow of the moment, as fellow students and peers alike cheered them on. *Audry would have loved this*, she thought.

As she walked from the platform, Abbie knew with certainty that God had again orchestrated another new beginning.

CHAPTER

40

Keith could hardly believe his eyes at Covenant Kitchen's transformation as he and Abbie arrived. Don and Doris's retirement celebration was in full swing. Charmaine Jenkins, Teencie Curtis, and the other kitchen staff had outdone themselves. Strands of lights hung from the heavy beams that spanned the room, giving the appearance of being in an outdoor European café. The massive room teemed with guests as happy conversations echoed against the high ceiling above. The soft music of a local jazz trio lent a relaxed ambiance to the occasion.

Though the usual dining tables were in place, Charmaine and her talented staff had transformed their rugged features. Long, white tablecloths, overlaid with smaller cloths of varying hues, covered each one. A large arrangement of fresh flowers occupied the center of each table. On either side of the centerpiece, candlelight twinkled along the length of each table in mercury glass votives. High-top tables, decorated similarly, had been placed around the edge of the room. Guests filled every table.

Someone called Keith's name from across the room, capturing his attention. Abbie tugged at his sleeve and gestured toward Eric Wyatt, who was waving from a nearby table. Sitting beside him was Lane. Keith and Abbie worked their way over.

"This is some kind of shindig," said Eric, reaching out his hand in greeting to Keith.

"I'll say," replied Keith, returning the handshake and taking his seat.

Abbie sat beside Lane and gave her a quick hug.

"Can you believe this crowd?" Lane exclaimed. "Charmaine and her staff must have been working for weeks."

"This room looks like a wonderland," Abbie commented.

As Eric shared with Abbie how he had first met Don, Keith caught a glimpse of his boss across the room. A twinge of apprehension ran through him as the enormity of his new role at the school sank in. *Don,* he thought, *how will I do this without you?*

Keeping a close eye on his watch, Keith waited for the moment he, Eric, and other board members would make a special presentation to Don and Doris. Earlier this afternoon, Charmaine met Keith in the dining hall and helped him secure the wrapped gifts for the Fieldings. She suggested Keith not come to get them until close to the presentation. Fifteen minutes later, that time had come.

The two men wound their way to the swinging kitchen door. Beside it stood Charmaine.

With a twinkle in her eye, the kitchen manager said, "You know where they are!"

Eric chatted with Charmaine as Keith disappeared to retrieve the gifts.

It wasn't long before Keith walked back into the dining hall, the door swinging closed behind him. Two large, elaborately wrapped presents in boxes large enough to store a man's suit of clothes filled his arms. Though Don and Doris were the ones receiving the gifts, Keith knew the real treasure lay in the dear friendship he shared with them.

"Thanks again for helping me with this," said Keith, looking at Charmaine.

"My pleasure," was her cheerful reply.

Once the two men reached the stage, Keith was relieved to see a small table near the back of the platform. He unloaded the gifts onto the table. Chuck Hawthorne, the board president, was already onstage, testing the microphone. Turning his attention to Keith, Chuck asked, "Do you think he has any idea?"

"Not a clue," Keith said with a sly smile.

Nodding toward the assembled crowd, Chuck stepped toward the mic. "Let's get this party started!"

The repeated taps on the microphone achieved the intended result. The room grew quiet. Guests who had been standing found their seats. Board members scattered throughout the room gathered on stage.

"I'd like to ask Don and Doris to join us up here," Chuck said.

The Fieldings went to the front. Don, ever the gentleman, held Doris's hand as she climbed the steps and then, once they were both on the platform, placed an arm around his wife's waist, drawing her close to him.

"It's hard to believe this day is finally here," Chuck said. "What a storied career you've had at Timothy House. Folks, please help me thank Don and Doris again for their thirty-three years of selfless service to this school and this community." Thunderous applause filled the cavernous room.

As Keith watched Doris and Don fight back tears, he thought, *How grateful, Lord, I am for the friendship and influence of this man on my life.*

Finally, when the room was exhausted from its show of appreciation, the guests sat.

Turning to Don and Doris, Chuck continued, "We can never adequately say thank you for all you have done for this school and those who've attended it with you at the helm. How grateful we are for the godly impact you've had on the lives of the thousands who have passed through the gates of Timothy House. Just ahead lies a new beginning for you, a season in which you can enjoy time as you wish to spend it, not as you must. We hope these gifts will bring pleasure to you and always remind you of how dearly you are loved by the Timothy House family."

Keith stepped forward from where he'd been standing, holding one of the large gifts in his arms.

"Ladies first," said Chuck, as Keith handed the box to Doris.

She carefully removed the decorative bow and tore away the wrapping paper before removing the box cover and folding back the tissue paper.

Gasping with delight, she pulled out a folded quilt. Portia Dockery grasped one corner of it, allowing Doris to open the handmade coverlet to show the audience the colors and design elements of the stained-glass windows in Peter's Chapel.

"Thank you so much. It's magnificent!" Doris exclaimed loudly. She clasped the quilt to her chest as if it were a soft, warm towel.

Keith handed Don a large, wrapped package, then watched Don remove a long, slender object—a custom-made bamboo fly-fishing rod.

Don's smile said it all as Keith looked into the eyes of this man who had been like a second father. "You're in big trouble, Haliday," Don quipped quietly.

As Keith watched Don pull Doris toward him, he felt fortunate to be one of those whose lives were richer due to the friendships shared with this extraordinary couple.

Now back at the table with Abbie and the Wyatts, Keith enjoyed watching the Fieldings laugh with and hug those who gathered.

All too soon, the party was over, and guests made their way from the dining hall. As the last guests left, Charmaine and her team started the yeoman's task of putting away decorations and dinnerware, the planning of which had taken months to prepare.

Keith and Abbie made their way from Covenant Kitchen to a parking area nearby. After making sure Abbie was safely in her seat, Keith walked around to climb in beside her in his SUV. As he had picked her up earlier at Mistletoe Cottage for the Fieldings' soirée, it was now time to take his princess home.

"So what did you think about the turnout?" asked Abbie excitedly as soon as Keith cranked the ignition.

"I was pleasantly surprised with the crowd." Checking his rearview mirror, he backed slowly out of the parking space. Putting the car in drive, he continued, "I was especially pleased to see how many in this year's student body had come."

"That teens would come to an administrator's retirement celebration speaks volumes about the level of admiration and respect the students have for Don."

Keith nodded as he wound his way through the school's campus.

Abbie continued, her enthusiasm evident about the night's event. "You and Chuck couldn't have selected more perfect gifts for Don and Doris."

"Thanks," replied Keith, thinking that he couldn't wait to talk to Don about his fly-fishing rod, knowing how much his boss loved the sport.

After making one last turn, Mistletoe Cottage loomed in the glow of Keith's headlights. He pulled up in front of the stone building and put the SUV in park.

As she unbuckled her seat belt, Abbie looked over at Keith and asked, "Would you like to come in for a cup of hot chocolate with me and my girls? Teencie walked them back as soon as the banquet ended."

"Thanks, Abbie," said Keith, grateful for the car's darkened interior. "I'm going to beg off tonight. It's been a long day. Can I take a rain check, though?"

Uncertain of why, but recognizing the gentle tug of the Lord's Spirit on his shoulder, Keith felt an overwhelming urge to retreat to the safe confines of Peter's Chapel. It was as if the reality of all the change ahead in his life had hit like a ton of bricks. Accepting the mantle of leadership at Timothy House. Taking a new wife. Beginning a journey as a stepfather to an adult son. Wondering if he could do any of this.

Someday, he thought, *I'll tell Abbie all that's swirling around in my heart. But not today.*

After walking her to the cottage's front door, Keith gave Abbie a tender kiss. "I'll see you tomorrow. Good night, my love," he said quietly.

"Good night," said Abbie. She stood in the door's opening and watched as Keith walked down the stairs and climbed into his SUV.

Keith drove back to Stone's Throw and parked his vehicle in the driveway. He didn't bother to go in and change clothes, instead leaving his sport jacket on the seat of his vehicle. The glow of a rising moon filtered through the trees as Keith headed toward the back of campus and to his sanctuary. By the time he reached the old stone chapel, a few stars shimmered in the night sky. Keith pulled open the heavy door of the building.

Once inside, he needed a moment for his eyes to adjust to the dark interior. Though not brilliant, a beam of moonlight through one of the stained-glass windows shone on a pew near the front. Keith entered the bench and sat down. As he had done so many times before, he sat on the edge of the pew, leaned forward, and rested his arms against the solid, secure surface of the seat in front of him. Bowing his head, Keith sat silently, willing the jumble of emotions and cacophony of thoughts to subside within him. As he slowed his breathing and focused his mind on the Lord, so, too, his spirit seemed to calm.

"Lord," Keith whispered, "I'm terrified. How will I do this? Seeing all those people at the reception and hearing all the compliments and praise heaped on Don makes me afraid I'll never live up to the legacy he's leaving. There's so much I don't know. I don't even have an education degree. My leadership style will be different than Don's. There's *no* way I can fill his shoes."

Keith sat enveloped in the holy silence of the moment. Reaching into his wallet, he pulled out a faded, worn picture taken after the end of his basketball team's game, only hours before his family was killed. He ran his thumb gently over the faces of Genny, Amanda, and David.

Bowed over with grief, he cried aloud, "I miss my family," as his shoulders heaved with emotion. Quiet sobs racked his body. After a time, he wiped away hot tears with the back of his hand. Emotionally spent, he poured out his pent-up sorrow to the Lord. "I love Abbie, and I have no doubt we're supposed to be together. But my heart aches for my first family."

Looking at the picture again, he continued, "Help me, Lord, accept Abbie and Drew just as they are—without comparison to Genny and Amanda and David." For several minutes, Keith stared at the photograph.

Finally, he tucked it carefully into a pocket of his wallet and pulled out another picture, this one newer and less weathered. It was a picture of Abbie and him that a waiter at Giuseppe's had snapped during their first dinner date there last summer. As he had with the other, Keith ran his thumb tenderly across Abbie's face.

What if I can't be the husband Abbie needs me to be? You know how much I love her, Lord. She's been hurt so much, and I couldn't bear it if I caused her any pain. Keith blinked back more tears.

Bowing his head once more, he prayed, "Lord, give me the wisdom, courage, and love to be the friend that Drew needs. Like his mother, he's had to deal with a world of heartache. Please don't ever let me fail him the way Joe did. Maybe someday he'll come to think of me as a dad, but that will have to happen only in Your time and with Your help. Blend us into a strong, new family and bind us together in Your love."

Long minutes passed after the prayer ended.

Oddly enough, admitting the fears in his heart lifted the weight of the burden. Looking up, Keith focused his gaze on the large, hand-carved wooden cross suspended at the front of the chapel. What caught his attention was the intersection of its horizontal and vertical beams. Notes from a sermon he'd heard long ago emerged from his memory. The horizontal beams were described as man's relationship to one's fellow man and the vertical as God's relationship to man. The farther a believer moved on the horizontal axis away from the intersection, the farther away one traveled from God. If one stayed out there on the edge too long, that's when trouble began.

Give me all your worries, Keith, because I care for you, he seemed to hear the Lord say through the words of 1 Peter 5:7.

After focusing for a few more minutes on the joint connecting the cross beams, Keith bowed his head again.

"Thank You, Father, for bringing me back to center, to the center of Your heart, where all fear and doubt are banished. Thank You for understanding my faults and not criticizing me when I lose my way. Please forgive me for wandering away from that point where my frailty ends and Your strength and provision begin. I know I *can't* fulfill any of these roles You've given me, but I believe I *can* with Your help. There are many changes ahead on the road of my life and many curves around which I cannot see. Give me Your eyes to see, Your ears to hear, and Your heart to understand. I'm trusting You, Jesus, to be my Guide and Shepherd and Lord. I ask all this in Your strong and precious name. Amen."

A peace Keith had not experienced in a long while enveloped him as he sat in the now-darkened chapel. He was assured, without a doubt, that God did indeed stand in the road ahead and would provide all Abbie and he needed.

CHAPTER
41

Abbie had come to this sacred place early this morning. Although several close friends had overseen and executed key aspects of her wedding preparations, Abbie had not disclosed this particular task to anyone. As she pulled open the heavy door to Peter's Chapel, rays of sunlight filtered in. Glancing back across the lawn, Abbie caught a glimpse of fog stretching lazily across the surface of Shelter Lake.

Stepping into the cool darkness of the chapel's solid frame, Abbie knew all too well how the Lord had been her shelter and refuge throughout these past difficult years. Oh, how faithful He had been.

A large, flat package, wrapped in brown paper, was propped against the wall just inside the door, just as Don Fielding said it would be. Her co-conspirator had kindly delivered the parcel to the chapel an hour earlier.

Abbie picked up the package and made her way to the front of the chapel. Climbing the steps to the platform, she walked over to a small table, set to one side, that was draped in white cloth that fell in soft folds to the floor. Atop it stood a large brass easel. Taking great care, Abbie gently removed a framed oil painting from its paper shroud and placed it carefully on the decorative stand. Named *Higher Ground*, this was the picture Abbie had seen in the gallery in Craggy Bluff late last year.

She could not have been more surprised than when she opened the gift a few nights before, delighted to discover the picture, her wedding present from Keith. She would always savor the memory of his smile once the painting was unwrapped. He had seemed so pleased with himself.

Since receiving Keith's gift, Abbie had arranged for the painting to be incorporated into the set of the platform and placed to the right of a wooden frame that would serve as the backdrop for the ceremony.

Abbie adjusted the painting once more, making sure it was in its proper place on the table. Before turning to leave, she ran her fingers across the clusters of glass votives, arranged at her request at the base of the easel. Once lit, they would illuminate the canvas.

Making her way down to the floor of the chapel, Abbie turned to look at the painting once more. Smiling to herself, she knew that Keith had no idea she had included his wedding gift in the ceremony. She prayed that its presence would add a special ambiance for her beloved groom.

Timothy House had witnessed many events since its founding in 1942, but the wedding of Abbie Richardson and Keith Haliday in Peter's Chapel was the first held in the school's history. Abbie particularly wanted the ceremony to be simple yet meaningful, with the polished pews of the old stone sanctuary only filled with special friends. It was the last of several memorable occasions on the school's campus in the past few weeks, each marking a turning point in the life of the school. The blessing ceremony for Chloe's adoption. Don and Doris's retirement celebration. And today, she would become the wife of the new head of school and vow to love and support him, stand by his side, and walk with him into this new administrative role.

Later, many would say that the day's music was some of the most beautiful they had heard. As they had three weeks before, Celeste Daniels and Heather Phillips delighted the guests with pre-service selections, both classical and sacred. Stuart Lassiter's talent as a gifted organist added a rich depth to the musical offerings.

The room quickly filled as guests took their seats. Every other pew of the center aisle had a wooden candle stand attached to it with brass fittings. A simple bouquet made from sprigs of ivy tied with white satin ribbon adorned the post of each stand. Atop the slender wooden poles were white candles fitted in tall glass shades, their lights flickering brightly in the darkened room.

As neither Abbie's nor Keith's parents were living, they had decided to dispense with many traditions associated with certain pews and sides of the aisle. However, at Abbie and Keith's request, Don and Doris accepted and sat in the traditional seat of honor at the front right side of the aisle. Tim and Taylor Nunley were seated beside them.

Abbie's only living relatives—her maternal aunt, Caty Nicholson, and her husband, Scott—had traveled across the country from Portland, Oregon, along with their two daughters, Lexie and Jan. Many friends from McHenry had journeyed to be here. New friends made within this last year—Portia Dockery, Evelyn and John Benson, and Summer and Elton Tidwell—were also present.

Keith had been equally delighted to learn that several friends of many years took the time and effort to travel great lengths and share in the joy of this day. One of Keith's best friends, Dan Levings, and his wife, Betse, came from Chattanooga, and Lance Tate and his wife, Claire, arrived from Knoxville. Keith and these two men had been friends since their college days. Keith was also touched to see others present—including Chuck and Barbara Hawthorne, Trent and Mary Lockhart, and Thompson Manning—that represented strong relationships forged in recent years in Robbinsonville. A host of Timothy House staff, including Charmaine Jenkins and Teencie Curtis, sat near the front.

The gothic-style wooden frame Abbie had seen during her early morning visit stood on the platform. Wire mesh filled the inside of the frame. Garlands of greenery were wound through the mesh along the side rails of the arch. Hanging from the top of the arch was a large wreath of eucalyptus, ivy, and blush-colored roses. Two large brass candelabras stood on either side of the frame, the soft glow from their lit candles filling the front of the chapel with a heavenly light. Before this decorated altar screen, Abbie and Keith would soon take their vows.

As Stuart, Celeste, and Heather began the music that marked the start of the wedding service, an air of expectation and excitement filled the room. Guests sat up straighter, and many turned to see if they could glimpse the bride.

The trio began playing the hymn, "For the Beauty of the Earth," and, as they did, Rod Eichman and Keith made their way down the aisle.

Climbing the steps to the platform, they turned and stood before the altar screen.

The music continued as Chloe Nunley practically floated down the aisle in a beautiful white, handmade French-sewn batiste dress, her dark hair glowing in the soft candlelight. Seemingly thrilled to serve as Abbie's bridesmaid, the child walked to her place of honor.

Once Chloe faced the seated guests, an expectant hush fell over the room.

CHAPTER
42

As Abbie entered the back of the chapel on Drew's arm, it was as if she'd waited for this moment all her life. As the pair stood quietly for a moment, listening to the poignant strains of "Ashoken Farewell," any hesitations Abbie had about her new life ahead or misgivings about the failures of circumstances in her past wafted away like smoke from the hundreds of candles that filled this holy room with their gentle glow. A great joy filled Abbie's heart to the point that she felt it would burst, the kind only God Himself could produce.

Her white satin gown glowed soft and creamy in the candlelight, its short train spilling behind her. Pearls and iridescent beads adorning the bodice of her wedding dress glistened. Abbie's hair was swept into a stylish chignon, and a simple white tulle fingertip veil fell from underneath it. Tendrils of her dark hair had been artfully arranged around her face. One hand rested on the arm of her son. In the other, Abbie carried a nosegay of blush-colored roses, the stems wrapped tightly in white satin ribbon. Tucked into the bottom of the arrangement was a lace handkerchief that had belonged to Audry.

Taking her first steps toward the front of the chapel, Abbie saw Keith standing straight and tall in his black tuxedo. Even from this distance, she could spot the love and devotion filling his eyes. Though looking at anyone other than her groom was challenging, Abbie wanted to ensure she remembered those who had gathered with them on this day. As mother and son continued, her heart swelled with gratefulness as Abbie saw many who meant so much. Soon, Drew slowed and helped her climb the platform's steps.

Once on the platform, Abbie's attention was transfixed as Keith's deep, indigo eyes captured hers. It was as if she had waited for him all her life. The gentle touch of Drew's hand on her arm brought Abbie's attention back to the others gathered nearby. Standing between his mother and her groom, Abbie's son could not have been any prouder than her father, Lin Ellis.

"Dearly beloved," Rod Eichman began, "we are gathered here in the presence of God and in the company of these witnesses to join this man and this woman together in holy matrimony."

Following these words of introduction, Rod posed the question, "Who gives this woman to be married to this man?" to which Drew happily answered, "*I* do." Afterward, Drew moved to Keith's side to serve as his stepfather's best man.

As Keith moved to stand next to Abbie, a thrill of excitement ran through her. An electric shock seemed to arc from his hand as he placed her arm on his. For a few seconds, Abbie was only aware of a world containing Keith and herself. Looking up at him, Abbie found the glow of love in his eyes that she knew would last a lifetime.

When a slight movement caught her attention, Abbie glanced to her left and glimpsed Chloe standing next to her.

Rod continued with the service. "Abbie and Keith," he began, "you have come here today so that, through marriage, the Lord can seal the love you have for one another as you make your pledge in the company of God and these witnesses."

Looking intently at the couple standing before him, Rod continued. "Is it your pledge that you both have come here today, freely and without reservation, to join with each other in holy matrimony? If so, please answer, 'I have.'"

Both bride and groom gave their affirmative answer in unison.

"Now, it is time for you to promise yourselves to each other."

At these words, Abbie turned to the girl she loved like a daughter and handed her the nosegay. Solemnly, Chloe carefully took the flowers.

"Please face each other and repeat after me."

As Abbie and Keith turned to face each other, Keith tenderly grasped Abbie's hands.

"Abbie," directed Rod. "We'll begin with you: I, Abbie, take you, Keith . . ."

"I, Abbie, take you, Keith, to be my lawfully wedded husband," spoke Abbie, repeating the age-old vow of fidelity and commitment.

At these words, Keith gently squeezed Abbie's hands.

"To have and to hold from this day forward." Abbie's heart leapt within her as she took in the enormity of what this truly meant—she would never be alone again.

"For better or worse." Her voice quivered with these words. There was not much more either of them could suffer that Abbie or Keith had not already endured.

"For richer or poorer." How grateful Abbie was that she and Keith had the treasure in life that money could not buy—true love, health, the affection and support of family and friends, satisfying work centered on a higher purpose.

"In sickness and in health."

"To love and to cherish." *Oh, how loved and cherished I feel*, thought Abbie.

"Forsaking all others." Though life circumstances and the choices of others had left Abbie and Keith feeling abandoned and adrift, they were now inseparable, united beneath the shield of their love.

"Until we are parted by death. This is my solemn vow."

Tears welled in Abbie's eyes as she promised all of her heart and soul to this adoring man standing in front of her. She felt as if her heart would burst.

After waiting a few moments to allow the gravity of the pledge to be fully appreciated by the couple, Rod turned his attention to the groom. "Keith," he said, "repeat after me."

As Abbie had promised, Keith Haliday vowed to love, support, and cherish this woman whom he loved more than life itself for as many days, weeks, months, and years as the good Lord allowed.

Rod Eichman's calm, melodious voice pierced the trance that seemed to enthrall the happy couple.

"It is now time for the giving and receiving of rings."

He held out his hand as Chloe and Drew placed in it the gold wedding bands Abbie and Keith had selected. Holding them up to the guests assembled, Rod continued, "Each of these rings is in the shape of a circle, which has no beginning and no end. Though timely limits bind this world we mortals live in, take joy in knowing that the love of your Heavenly Father is timeless and will sustain you, not only in this life, but in the life to come."

Focusing his attention on the bride and groom once more, Rod extended his hand to Abbie and said, "Abbie, will you take Keith's ring and place it on his left hand?"

After taking the ring gingerly within her fingers, Abbie turned back to face Keith and slipped the band onto the third finger of his left hand. As she did, she repeated the words of the ring vow, words that were moving and poignant, that spoke light and life into the wounded spaces of her soul that had been shrouded in darkness for far too long.

"I give you this ring, as a symbol of my vow, and with all that I am, and all that I have, I honor you."

Abbie would forever remember the flickering candlelight reflected in the tender gleam in Keith's eyes. As he repeated the same vow that would announce to the world that she was his alone, Abbie hoped Keith saw the sure commitment and deep devotion mirrored in her eyes.

"All that I am." Keith's voice was comforting. Abbie's mind raced over all that the two of them had endured throughout their pasts. How those traumas had reshaped and molded them into the people they had become.

"All that I have." A smile played across Keith's face at this next segment of the oath. This couple had reached rock bottom in their respective lives years before meeting each other. Into this new season, they brought with them wisdom, discernment, humility, and the marvelous freedom that comes when you refuse to take yourself too seriously. Abbie and Keith, on this day, were bringing their hopes and fears, their successes and failures, their longings and dreams, and laying them before the Lord as they gave themselves to each other.

"I honor you." The determined look in her groom's eyes left no doubt in Abbie's mind that this man intended to esteem her as no other ever had. This one key ingredient was what made Keith so precious to her. He honored her. He protected and sheltered her. He put her needs above his own. And, for the first time in her life, Abbie knew she was marrying a man whom she wanted to love and care for in the same way. No holds barred.

Rod Eichman closed the service with one final prayer of blessing. As he finished, Keith stepped closer to his new wife. Gently pulling Abbie's face toward his own, he sealed this sacred moment with a kiss. Opening her eyes, Abbie found Keith's drinking in her own.

Though the certainty of the way forward was not guaranteed, Abbie and Keith had God's assurance that He would lead them safely and surely to where He wanted them to go.

To higher ground.

ACKNOWLEDGMENTS

Writers of fiction usually fall into one of two camps—either the plot drives the creation of the story, or the characters do. It's been twenty-two years since the fall of 2003 when Abbie Richardson, the main character of this trilogy, first stepped onto the front porch of my imagination. Like Abbie, I was a junior high teacher, struggling as she did to balance my work and personal life. Between creating lesson plans and grading papers, I developed the backstory for Timothy House—its curriculum, faculty, and mission—and wrote the beginnings of Book One. Although I never heard voices in my head, Abbie and the various characters of *The Timothy House Chronicles* nonetheless whispered their stories into my heart as I became their scribe.

Abandon Not My Soul was initially self-published in 2012. Subsequently re-released in 2022, the book introduced readers to the searing pain and crippling loss with which Abbie Richardson and Keith Haliday were all too familiar. This first offering in the trilogy also set the stage for what would become a second home for Abbie and Keith—the residential school of Timothy House.

Through a Dark Valley introduced readers to several new characters—DeSean Matthews and C.J. Dykes—and offered greater insight into two of my favorite characters from Book One—Chloe Minton and Teencie Curtis. In Book Two, readers also glimpsed a deepening of the relationship between Abbie and Keith, as well as a future for their careers at Timothy House.

Higher Ground, the last book in this trilogy, brings full circle the lessons of love, forgiveness, and hope learned by various characters in *The Timothy House Chronicles*.

The difficult work of writing is not unlike that of a miner, laboring long, challenging hours beneath the surface of the earth (or within the crucible of a story idea) to dig out and discover the treasure buried within. Writing is a lonely, solitary occupation, but it is also one I find satisfying and thrilling. As a writer who also seeks to honor my Lord through the words of my stories, it is especially meaningful when I experience Him peeking over my shoulder while at the computer, offering guidance for the story and joy for the journey. One writing friend has coined the term "creative download" to explain when this happens. Regardless of the description, I now recognize His holy presence beside me at various times as I write.

Please know how indebted and grateful I am to you, dear reader, for deeming this story and book series worthy of your time and attention. Without our readers, where would writers be? Many of you have shared words of encouragement and praise through emails, letters, phone calls, and reviews. My heart brims with joy in the knowledge that, in some small way, my words have blessed and encouraged your lives.

There are three individuals to whom I am incredibly appreciative for their words and wise counsel that gave me the courage to see this book series through to the end.

First, a heartfelt thank you to my dear friend, Martha Stockstill. For over forty years, your mastery of and prowess in the English language have provided me with knowledge and expertise comparable to the finest Master of Fine Arts degree program anywhere. Your kitchen table was often the classroom where you helped me saw and sand the rough-hewn timbers of story construction for *Abandon Not My Soul*. Your eagle-eyed edit of *Through a Dark Valley* ensured its integrity, and your faithful prayers led to the completion of *Higher Ground*, bringing this trilogy to a successful close. My heart overflows with gratitude.

Second, I will always be eternally grateful for an early editor, Diana S., who, at the time, was working for iUniverse publishing house. When *Abandon Not My Soul* was in the editing phase of its self-publishing process, Diana's thorough developmental edit forced me to come face to face with my many shortcomings as a self-taught writer. Wanting my little story to be the best it could be, I followed this editor's able lead. Diana pushed me to create a thread, a ribbon as it were, that would tie the entire three-book series together. Thank you, Diana, for advising me to aim small and not miss at all.

Finally, I am deeply appreciative of the solid guidance and time-tested wisdom shared by Sarah Peachey, my editor at Sunbury Press. How fortunate I was to have her alongside me as an editor for both *Through a Dark Valley* and *Higher Ground*. Sarah's manuscript margin notes always contained helpful information and often an unexpected kudo or two. Well aware that I came to writing through the back door, constantly educating myself about the finer points of the craft, Sarah welcomed my questions enthusiastically, offering direction on days when I had run out of creativity and extending to me patience and kindness when my lack of professional know-how was apparent. Most of all, Sarah, thank you for seeing through to the heart of the writer I aspire to be.

How blessed I have been throughout the past twenty years to be a part of the Hallowed Hearts Bible study group. A special thank you goes to my sweet friends of that fellowship whose prayers have sustained me.

My sincerest thanks go to my publisher, Lawrence Knorr, for your belief in the worth of this story and the value of this book series. Since 2020, when I first came on board as an author with Sunbury Press, you have become a trusted friend and literary guide. How grateful I am for all you have done for me. Heartfelt appreciation goes to my editor, Sarah Peachey, and Book Designer, Crystal Devine, for your endeavors to make this book shine. How thankful I am for the fine efforts of the greater Sunbury Press team in bringing *Higher Ground* to life.

As always, my love and deepest gratitude go to my better half, Mark. If not for you, the words of these three stories would have never seen the light of day. As you know, many facets of our love story are woven into the pages of this trilogy. God's preparing our own higher ground, and I can't wait to share it with you.

A special thank you goes to my extended family for always cheering me on.

Most of all, my heart abounds with thankfulness to my Lord, from whom all blessings flow.

MAKE A DIFFERENCE

Higher Ground welled up from deep within my heart, and although many of these characters and settings may resemble real people and places, they are fictional, mere figments of my imagination. However, the plot lines involving DeSean Matthews and Chloe Minton illustrate the grim reality of unfortunate circumstances that far too many children face. If this story has touched your heart and you would like to make a positive difference in a child's life, here are four schools and/or organizations I can heartily recommend, through which your sincere desire to help another can become a life-changing reality.

French Camp Academy
1 Fine Place
French Camp, Mississippi 39745
(662) 547-6482
https://frenchcamp.org

Sunnybrook Cares
Sunnybrook Children's Home
222 Sunnybrook Road
Ridgeland, Mississippi 39157
(601) 856-6555
https://sunnybrookms.org

Wears Valley Ranch
100 One Fine Place
Sevierville, Tennessee 37862
(865) 429-5437
https://wvr.org

Black Mountain Home for Children, Youth & Families
80 Lake Eden Road
Black Mountain, North Carolina 28711
(828) 686-3451
https://www.blackmountainhome.org

ABOUT THE AUTHOR

The writings of Sherye S. Green reflect her journey of faith and explore the heart's inner landscapes. An author, singer, and speaker, she has long been intrigued by the power of words to influence and shape thought and action. A former Miss Mississippi, Sherye has enjoyed two careers—one in business, the other in education. She is the award-winning author of two inspirational novels, *Abandon Not My Soul* and *Through a Dark Valley*, the devotional collection *Tending the*  *Garden of My Heart: Reflections on Cultivating a Life of Faith*, the World War II survivor memoir *Surviving Hitler, Evading Stalin: One Woman's Remarkable Escape from Nazi Germany*, the suicide survivor memoir *Mission Vigilant: A Mother's Crusade to Stem the Tide of Veteran Suicide*, and the true-crime account *Beyond the Green Widow: Consequences of the Piney Woods Creek Murders of 1921*. She is the 2021 Mississippi Author of the Year for nonfiction, an honor she shares with Mildred Schindler Janzen. Sherye and her husband make their home in Mississippi.

For more information, please visit:
www.sheryesimmonsgreen.com

Follow her on Facebook at
Sherye Simmons Green

Follow her on Instagram at
sheryegreen

If this story has moved you and you would recommend it to others, please consider writing a review for *Higher Ground* on Amazon.com.